MOMENT OF TRUTH

Evelyn put her satchel on the end of the bed. "Honestly, telling me to shoplift at Neiman-Marcus."

"You look as if you took my advice," said Luke.

"I didn't steal one thing."

"If you say so."

She made a face. Then she removed her gloves and hat and threw them down on the bed. She turned toward him as if she'd just remembered something of monumental importance. "I answered your questions about the horse and the sheriff, now get out of my room."

She went to the door and grasped the knob. But he was beside her in several easy strides and slammed his hand over the top of the door to prevent it from opening. "Not yet."

Eve looked up at him, her expression none too pleased. She stood beneath his arm, the top of her head almost brushing against the sleeve of his duster. "I beg your pardon? We had a deal."

"Right." His arm lowered, and he clicked the lock into place. "I'll get to my end of it in a minute."

HEARTS

"... a marvelous historical romance ... a stupendously smashing story."

—*Affaire de Coeur*

"*Hearts* is a superb historical romance ... tidbits of history are cleverly woven into the plot. Truvy and Jake are a dynamic duo and the support cast adds to the authenticity of the fabulous fourth and final book of ... [the] series."

—*Midwest Book Review*

"A very charming read."

—*The Philadelphia Inquirer*

HONEY

"Stef Ann Holm's *Honey* is a wonderfully rich, heartwarming, deeply romantic novel destined to go straight to the heart. Holm's many fans will be enthralled, and her legions of new readers will feel they have just unwrapped a very special gift. This is romance at its best."

—Amanda Quick

"Few authors paint as warm and wonderful a portrait of small-town America as Stef Ann Holm. The multi-textured plot and three-dimensional characters combined with that Americana feel create a bit of home-spun perfection."

—Kathe Robin, *Romantic Times*

"With plenty of emotion and laughter, Ms. Holm effortlessly draws her audience into the vibrant realm of the early twentieth century."

—*Rendezvous*

HOOKED

"Stef Ann Holm dishes up a slice of Americana that is not only love and laughter at its best, but a darned good emotional read."

—*Calico Trails*

"Guaranteed to bring you hours of enjoyment, laughter, and love. Few writers bring small-town America to life the way Stef Ann Holm does. . . . She breathes life into engaging characters and creates a town where people seem like your neighbors: you'd move in, if you could."

—*Romantic Times*

"This is one book with a title that lives up to its name, as readers will be *Hooked*!"

—*BookBrowser Reviews*

HARMONY

"Stef Ann Holm has no equal when it comes to wit, style, and authenticity. For warmth, charm, story, and unforgettable characters, *Harmony* is a perfect run."

—Maggie Osborne, author of *Band of Gold*

"The most warmhearted, heart-stirring romance of the season."

—*Romantic Times*

"Ms. Holm is one of the best at writing emotionally intense historical romance that leaves nary a dry reader's eye anywhere."

—Amazon.com

Books by Stef Ann Holm

Published by POCKET BOOKS

STEF ANN HOLM

The Runaway Heiress

SONNET BOOKS

New York London Toronto Sydney Singapore

This book is a work of fiction. Names, characters, places and
incidents are products of the author's imagination or are used
fictitiously. Any resemblance to actual events or locales or persons,
living or dead, is entirely coincidental.

An *Original* Publication of POCKET BOOKS

 A Sonnet Book published by
POCKET BOOKS, a division of Simon & Schuster, Inc.
1230 Avenue of the Americas, New York, NY 10020

Copyright © 2002 by Stef Ann Holm

ISBN: 0-671-77549-9

First Sonnet Books printing February 2002

10 9 8 7 6 5 4 3 2 1

SONNET BOOKS and colophon are trademarks of
Simon & Schuster, Inc.

For information regarding special discounts for bulk purchases,
please contact Simon & Schuster Special Sales at 1-800-456-6798
or business@simonandschuster.com

Front cover illustration by Lisa Litwack;
photo credit: Greg Weiner

Printed in the U.S.A.

Acknowledgment

I'm indebted to Robin Lee Hatcher whose
knowledge of software and the Internet
are limitless.
Her generosity in sharing both her time to educate me,
as well as lending me books from her personal library,
contributed to the writing of this novel.
I'm most grateful.

The Runaway Heiress

1

June 1911
Beaumont, Texas

Evelyn Thurgood-Baron felt the compulsion to do something wild. Something wickedly bad. Something utterly vulgar, she thought with a smile. Unfortunately, as the heiress to the richest fortune in Texas—Baron Oil, she'd rarely acted on these moments.

But the invigorating feeling of triumph far outweighed the risk of discovery when she'd stolen her father's silver liquor flask from the top drawer of his study desk. She'd liberally topped it off with his bourbon, a liquor she intended to heartily sample. Taking that flask yesterday was one tiny show of defiance, even though he wouldn't miss the container until tomorrow. And tomorrow she'd be back home from Beaumont.

If she was caught with the flask things would get messy. Her mother would have an apoplectic fit, put her lace hankie beneath her nose, and call for her father to handle the situation. Her father would rant and rave, intimidate her, then send her off to her bedroom for the rest of the evening.

What Evelyn wouldn't do for . . . freedom. But leaving wasn't an easy thing to do. She wasn't like other women.

At a young age, she realized that being born a Baron was a curse. While other girls were able to swim in the swimming holes in Oiler where she grew up, and still lived, she had to stay indoors and read. Since she was the only daughter of Seymour Baron II and Hortensia Thurgood, she missed out on school picnics and was only able to participate in plays if the rehearsals were at her home; she was unable to ride a bicycle, much less do so while wearing trousers. And she was definitely not allowed to attend sleep-over parties. All because her father feared she'd be kidnapped and held for ransom. As Evelyn grew older, and while she knew deep down her father loved her, she came to understand that his fear wasn't exactly for *her*, but rather the possibility of losing a large amount of his money to a criminal.

At the age of fourteen, she rebelled for the first time. She smoked her father's pipe behind the house and read a copy of *The Police Gazette* left in the auto-garage by their chauffeur. When Thompson found her, he didn't scold. In fact, he lit up a cigarette and talked with her about what she was going to do for her birthday that year. She'd told him the same thing she always did: have all her parents' friends in attendance at their sprawling home—very few school friends were of the caliber her family considered respectable—and sit and look pretty. Politely smile, laugh at subtle conversation, and be gay and merry even if she didn't feel like it.

When she was eighteen, she was—thankfully— sent away. The first time she could truly be responsible for herself even in a small way was at Miss Hunnewell's Boarding School in Sabine on the Gulf of Mexico. She had loved the school because of its location near the ocean, but she soon found out the other girls had been brought up just like her. To be china dolls without individual thoughts in their heads aside from landing an equally rich husband and making homes for themselves where they could call on one another, sit and drink tea. Discuss the weather and what fashions would be in vogue for next season.

Pinkie Jenkins was the only girl in her class Evelyn warmed up to right away. Like her, Pinkie was a rebel without enough nerve to fully and completely revolt against her parents. For two years, they were thick as thieves, getting into harmless mischief. Miss Hunnewell hadn't known half the things they did, but there were the obvious pranks that still hadn't been solved. Like when she and Pinkie snuck out of the dormitory to throw yards of water-closet paper on the bare trees in the winter, or when they switched the French instruction recording on the Edison phonograph to a recording of "Give My Regards to Broadway."

In the spring of 1905, on a double-dare from Pinkie, Evelyn recited a ribald soliloquy in drama class and had promptly been expelled from Miss Hunnewell's Boarding School. The severe, and swift, punishment had devastated Evelyn. She'd finally had a friend who understood how she felt and she'd never see her again. But Evelyn had no one to blame but herself.

The incident had served to tame her for a time. Once back in Oiler, Texas, she conformed. She molded. She became a flawless hostess. The ideal Miss Baron. Prim. Proper. Perfect.

Evelyn referred to the next six years as The Dark Years. Little or no hope of seeing the grander world once again. There had never really been trust between herself and her parents, and she had proved them right. So she had to start over to prove them wrong. Show them she could be the daughter they wanted, even though each day was harder to bear.

Over time, her father had offers for her hand in marriage, but none of the candidates were "good enough" for a merger. While Seymour Baron II was a man of means, he hadn't always been that way. He was of the working class; self-made. Her father's business associates were brash and raucous, most coming into their wealth as wildcats without manners who'd been lucky enough to strike it rich. Their sons were no better and were attracted to her stockholder shares, not to her. By twenty-two, she'd abandoned girlish dreams of falling in love and becoming someone's wife.

Filthy oil money had destroyed any chance of her finding romance.

While Evelyn, now at the maidenly age of twenty-six, waited for the supposedly right proposal to come in for her, she had regained her parents' trust enough to travel to Beaumont, Texas for a meeting with the

Ladies Society of Texas, an extremely well-to-do and dignified organization her mother had once presided over. The group was hosting a conference to discuss fund-raising ideas for all the Texas chapters. Not Evelyn's first choice as a destination, but Beaumont— only an hour away from Oiler—was still *out of Oiler*.

So here she was in the opulent Imperial Hotel. With a forbidden flask of bourbon tucked in her garter, awaiting a chance to be . . . wickedly bad.

The hotel was located blocks away from the demi-monde houses and the Crosby Bar famous for its dice, poker and faro tables. Although the Ladies Society of Texas had specifically made reservations at the Imperial to escape the riffraff from Crockett Street and Highland Avenue, Evelyn could still hear the spirited music from her room.

Behind her, the hour tolled nine o'clock.

The members of the Society had retired for the night a while ago, and Evelyn sat at the window looking down at people who, even after sunset, stood in line for banks, the express office, cafés and an establishment called the Dime Box. The Society Sister who'd been assigned to her fell asleep as soon as she'd pulled the coverlet over the curl papers in her mousy brown hair. From the iron-rail bed they were to share, Agatha Bridlesworth's snores came slow and steady.

Laughter and voices drifted to Evelyn, adding to her restlessness. On the other side of the window was a city known for being risqué and rough. She'd hardly seen anything of its decadence.

Daddy damned Beaumont as a dirty haven for the most notorious red-light district in the western hemisphere. Although that never stopped his daily visits to the Beaumont Oil Exchange and Board of Trade to check on stock prices. Earlier today, as Evelyn and the entourage of well set-up ladies traveled in a fine conveyance from the Calder Avenue depot, Evelyn had never seen a more lurid and fantastic place.

The large hotel room was stifling from the summer night humidity. Agatha claimed she couldn't sleep with the window open. A nasal condition aggravated by the sour odor of petroleum and mill smoke, not to mention the noisy machinery, disturbed her so the window had to be shut tight. Evelyn needed air—no matter what it smelled like—or she was going to faint dead away.

She also wanted to sneak some of that bourbon and now that Agatha was sleeping . . . well, that did give her the opportunity.

Evelyn laid her hand over her rich twilight blue taffeta dress and snowy petticoats underneath that covered her thigh. A telltale outline met her fingers. The silver flask was still safely stuck in the elastic of her garter.

Gazing over her shoulder, Evelyn checked on her chaperon. Still out in slumberland. So she crept the thick folds of fabric up her leg and put a hand on the flask. She took another look at Agatha, then slipped the liquor flask free. Evelyn unscrewed the cap and sniffed the contents. A swirl of fiery liquid heat filled her nose. Arching her brows, she brought the flask to her mouth and sampled a taste.

Her eyes instantly watered and her windpipe seemed to close off in a choke. This was certainly not

like the parlor sherry her mother served. In a fast
expulsion of air she tried to be quiet; she blinked back
the swimming tears filling her vision. When the sensation passed, she tried another sip. This one burned
just as badly. But by the fourth and fifth little sips, she
couldn't even tell the difference between the bourbon
and the parlor sherry.

Screwing the top back on the flask, Evelyn buried
her face in the crook of her arm and smothered a hiccup. Recovered, she stood taller and sighed.

She was definitely hotter now. So much so, she felt
as if she would swoon. There could be no objection if
she went down to the lobby to sit for a while in one of
the appointed wing chairs. It wasn't as if she were
going anywhere. Given the unreasonably early hour,
she would be perfectly safe. And perfectly respectable.

She quietly walked to the door. Turning the polished knob slowly, she opened the door, gave Agatha
a glance to make sure the woman had not moved a
single curl paper on her head, and exited the room.

Once in the long hallway, Evelyn smoothed the
turn-back lace cuffs on her flowing blue dress and felt
the twist in her hair to make sure the curls were
pinned in place; then she regally walked down the
stairs, releasing a hiccup that snuck up on her.

The lobby walls were bright from the blazing chandelier, as were the cozily placed chintz lounge chairs
and crushed velvet divans. A large floral arrangement
stood in the center of the room on a round marble-
topped table. The registration counter was a short distance away.

The entry doors to the hotel were blessedly open,

bringing into the large foyer a light breeze that carried the only good fragrance in Beaumont: blooming flowers growing in the boardwalk boxes outside. She could tell exactly which varieties. Carnations, lilies, delphiniums and roses.

Evelyn easily smiled at the night clerk, never realizing until now that he appeared like such a nice young man. She forced herself to walk steady and stately, and continued to a corner of the room where she sat. The room had started to tilt a little to the right in a strange manner. She was awfully hot and even perspiring. She didn't dare dab her hairline with her hankie; the gesture would have been vulgar for a lady. Now in the chair, she kept her knees pressed together, ankles demurely crossed, and watched people coming and going. Soon, she felt a lot cooler.

Barely in the chair five minutes, Evelyn observed a woman stroll into the lobby with her hand on her escort's arm. The blushing pink crepe of her extravagant evening dress swagged over her tiny behind and swished in a most provocative manner. She would have had to practice to walk like that.

"Ah, um, Miss Rosita," the clerk nervously addressed. "I'm afraid you can't be in here. I've been given strict orders from the manager—"

"She's with me," the suave gentleman beside her replied.

"I'm sorry, Mr. Castillo, but rules are rules. The Imperial does not allow performers to loiter in its lobby."

"We aren't going to loiter. We're going to my room."

"S-Sir, that is out of the q-question." For a man wearing an understarched ribbon tie, he was holding his ground, even though his cheeks had turned a bright red.

The woman squeezed her escort's arm, her lace gloved fingers cutting into the fine fabric of his coat. "Let's go back to the Dime Box, Cas. We can watch the talent exhibition. Then we'll go to . . ."

Even while leaning forward, Evelyn wasn't able to make out the last words because they were whispered in his ear, Rosita's lips moving slowly. But Evelyn was quite certain they were wicked.

She sat up taller, poised at the end of her chair. She took a better look at Miss Rosita. Her black glossy curls teased her bare shoulders. Shocking to most. Intriguing to Evelyn. She glanced down at her own dress. Very dignified. Buttoned up to her throat.

"Besides, Cas," Miss Rosita added in a tone that rose above her whisper, "I've got to sing in an hour, and I don't want to be rushed when we . . ." Yet again, her voice lowered to a degree where she couldn't be heard.

But Evelyn knew what Miss Rosita was talking about.

Sex.

Of course, Evelyn had never experienced such intimacies. And she could never raise such an indelicate subject in mixed company. At least not on purpose. The whole notion of sex was a flickering thought in her mind. Like the flame of a candle, the idea of being kissed, touched and embraced wavered back and forth. Sometimes it was a stronger notion; sometimes weaker. Sometimes it was snuffed out altogether. Sometimes it blazed. There were times she feared she might die without experiencing a kiss. The time she saw one of the rig workers without his shirt on had made her stomach feel funny. Looking at his exposed browned skin with corded muscles thick at his neck and shoulders, the breadth of his chest wide and strong, she had to admit—she'd smoldered a bit.

"All right," Mr. Castillo conceded, "we'll go. But—" he looked pointedly at the clerk—"don't expect me to give you my business again."

The clerk gulped, muttered an apology and feigned interest in his bookkeeping.

Miss Rosita and Mr. Castillo turned and headed toward the door. Evelyn's gaze followed the flamboyant couple. Miss Rosita glanced in her direction, smiled in a confident manner as if she hadn't just been treated poorly, then leveled her chin and said, "Cas, let's get some champagne. I feel like dancing tonight."

As the couple departed, Evelyn felt a pang of longing. She would have liked to go dancing . . . perhaps indulge in a splash of champagne now that she'd gotten used to the bourbon.

Evelyn craned her head to follow the couple as they walked down the street. Without conscious effort, she rose and went outside in front of the hotel . . . just to see them better before they disappeared.

Miss Rosita and Mr. Castillo walked into the Dime Box.

A curious name for an establishment. More precisely, an opera house. Evelyn had never been in one before. Well, that wasn't true. She'd never been in a *disreputable* one before. The Texas Symphony Opera Hall could never be termed unsavory.

She stepped off the boardwalk—just to hear the music better. Smiling at the melody pouring from the Dime Box's upstairs windows, she moved closer. She walked in front of the milliner's shop. Closer. The clock repair store. She continued moving forward, moving farther and farther from the Imperial Hotel.

The next thing Evelyn grew aware of was lively music from a pit band. Gaiety surrounded her. She'd entered a forbidden opera house. The place sent her pulse spinning. With an intake of breath, she stood there, amazed.

Smoke hung thickly in the room, swirling over the heads of some gentlemen dressed as dandies and others who had apparently come in directly from the field covered with mud and oil. Drilling equipment and photographs of gushers were mounted to nearly every available inch of wall space.

Evelyn remained in the back, taking in the tall ceiling with its dangling gilded cages suspended high over the stage. They were large enough to hold more than songbirds; it was highly unlikely that they had ever held anything with feathers—unless you counted women wearing the feathers. And there were plenty of them walking through the crowded room.

There was a long bar with two barkeepers who kept shouting, "Belly up to the bar, folks!" The smell of liquor hovered in the air, a mixture of sweet and pungent aromas. Bold innuendos passed between men and women. Whispers and giggles filled the air.

She knew she should, but Evelyn couldn't bring herself to leave. Not just yet.

A man in a coat and tails took the stage and the band quit its playing to offer him a drum roll. Once the crowd gave him their attention, he hollered, "Ladies and gentlemen, it's time for our talent exhibition. Tonight we'll hear some grand singing."

Cheers and enthusiastic applause rose.

"The winner will be awarded ten dollars. Please welcome our first singer, Miss Suzanne Maverick."

Miss Suzanne looked like a maverick. She was dressed in brown and white cowhide from head to toe, with a pile of yellow hair curled and pinned six inches high. She began to sing, a slow song about herding cattle. Big mistake. She was booed off the stage before she reached the chorus of "Home on the Range."

Evelyn remained in the secluded corner at the back of the hall as several more female singers went to the stage. One woman was introduced wearing a spangled red dress. She sang something more to Evelyn's liking—"Under the Bamboo Tree." She knew every word and caught herself softly singing along as the crowd stamped its feet to the beat.

"*I love-a-you and love-a-you true. And if you-a love-a-me. One live as two, two live—*"

"Why don't you sing next?"

Evelyn quit singing and whirled around, to come face-to-face with Miss Rosita. For a split second, she feared she'd been recognized as being the Baron heiress. But that wasn't possible. Only one portrait of her had ever been painted, and that had been on her sixteenth birthday. Photographs were taken with strict rules so her likeness would never turn up printed in the newspaper. The few places she'd traveled had been under the watchful eyes of her parents. Aside from the secluded walls of Miss Hunnewell's Boarding School, she'd never been allowed to venture out of their sight or that of the appropriate chaperon.

Until now.

"Oh!" Evelyn exclaimed. "Well . . . no, I couldn't possibly go up there and sing."

"I don't see why not. You sing beautifully."

Her mother would have been pleased to hear that. Five years of voice lessons had been money well spent. "No, really. I have to be going."

"I saw you at the Imperial."

"Yes, and I should go back right now."

"That's a shame." Miss Rosita took a glass of champagne from a waitress wearing nothing but a scrap of shimmering material as a skirt and hardly more than a corset as a blouse. "Because you have the talent to win."

Evelyn had never been told anything like that. She'd been raised to believe she was better than everyone because of her station in life. Better because the Barons had money and most others did not. Everything about her revolved around her family's name and had nothing to do with her as an individual person. This was one of the few times in her life someone was telling her she had something to offer and that she was good enough to succeed on her own merits.

Perhaps it was the effects of the bourbon or the music flowing through her veins. But suddenly she *did* want to sing.

"All right," Evelyn said with resolve, "I'll do it."

Before she could change her mind, she'd worked her way through the tight circle of tables and was telling the band to play her favorite tune. Then she stood on that stage with a roomful of people waiting for her to do something wonderful.

And wonderful is what she gave them.

"There's a yellow rose of Texas I'm goin' for to see. No other soldier knows her, nobody only me. She cried so when I left her, it was like to broke my heart. And if I ever find her, we never more will part." As the cheers and whistles filled the smoky room, she broke into the chorus. *"But the yellow rose of Texas beats the belles of Tennessee!"*

Evelyn lifted her skirt and lawn petticoats to dance snappy steps; a roar of approval practically blew the rafters from the roof.

Lost in the music and the dance, she smiled and let all her inhibitions go. While ending on a lovely high note, she looked out into the audience, and much to her utter horror, saw Agatha Bridlesworth, Mrs. Clementine Harlow, and the Society president, Mrs. Sarah Prune, who had sucked in her nostrils so tightly, she appeared to have an invisible clothespin on her nose.

Evelyn's legs felt as heavy as weights. She froze, the smile on her lips practically cracking away from the ice being shot at her from those three ladies.

When Evelyn stopped moving, the band's notes grated and slowly petered out. People mumbled and looked at each other. The trio of women marched down the center of the room, skirting tables laden with cards and bottles of liquor.

Once at the foot of the stage, they looked up at her with such disdain, Evelyn could feel it straight down to her toes. Which reminded her that her legs were exposed.

But before she could drop her skirt, the flask slid out from her garter and dropped to the stage with a dull plunk.

Not only did Evelyn lose her associate membership with the Ladies Society of Texas, she gained a fiancé by the name of Guy Winter Hadley.

She wished her father would have closeted her away for life instead of foisting her off on William Hadley's son for a loveless merger with the Texhoma Oil Company. She'd seen a parlor photograph of Guy, whose thin black mustache seemed as if it had been drawn over his equally thin upper lip.

"This is a disgrace of monumental proportions, Evelyn, and it isn't to be borne!" her father shouted. "I say, it is *not* to be borne. You'll marry Hadley, and that's my final word on it."

Evelyn sat in the drawing room of their Oiler mansion, while her father paced in front of the cold hearth, a glass of bourbon in his hand. Normally he sported a top hat, cane, gloves, ascot tie and a large gold watch fob because he was always dashing in and out of some important meeting. This evening, he wore a silk smoking jacket cinched around his prosperous belly. His handlebar mustache was so waxed, it didn't get wet when he drank his bourbon.

On the divan to his right, her mother looked at Evelyn with disappointment in her clear blue eyes. In contrast to her father's brashness, her mother carried herself as if she constantly had a book on top of her head. Evelyn didn't think she'd ever seen Mother with her chin down.

"Evelyn dearest," her mother declared with a deep frown on her forehead, "this really is not acceptable. I'm so ashamed and embarrassed. I shall never be able to show my face to the League again. Honestly, singing in public, and with your skirts lifted, no less. Deplorable. Utterly and unequivocally scandalous. And with liquor on your person. *Evelyn.*" Her name was spoken as if she were a bug to be squished. "I don't know where you picked up such behavior."

"I'm sorry."

"Sorry isn't good enough," her father yelled. "My daughter had a booze flask—*stolen* from my desk drawer—in her garter on display for every rake in the Dime Box Opera House!" He shot back the rest of his bourbon. "Why can't you behave like a proper young lady?"

She had no answer.

For the next long minutes, Evelyn was given such a dressing-down, she felt stripped naked. If only her parents could be more open-minded. They had sheltered her so, that given the opportunity, she had to test her wings. She couldn't help it.

She wanted to soar. She wanted to see and do the things her parents, and now her husband, would never allow. There were so many possibilities outside of Oiler. And she tried to imagine them all. Inside her room were dozens of road maps with places marked that she wanted to see. She'd spent hours poring over them planning trips. Trips that she would never take.

Why, she'd heard that the sunset over the Pacific Ocean was like watching a great big ball of fire disappear below the horizon; it rivaled the sunsets in Texas, only there you could smell the lemons and oranges that grew year round when you watched the day come to an end. The sun always shined. And she'd read in one of her father's periodicals that a projection machine had been invented by Thomas Edison to show moving picture shows. To actually see a thing like that would be—

Her father's voice broke the short silence. "You'll marry Hadley by the end of the month."

"But Daddy—"

"You *will* do as I say. You're a Baron and you'd better remember to conduct yourself as such while you live under my roof. Which won't be for much longer."

He threw up his hands. "Blast it. We trusted you, but you misused our trust. We cannot have another incident like this. You'll sully the family name and we have to be careful to stay out of the newspapers. You're lucky the press didn't get a picture of you and print it across the front page of the newspaper for all to see." Shaking his head, he said with a slight degree of woeful regret, "I'm sorry, Evelyn. But you did this to yourself."

2

L uke Devereaux spotted his wanted poster just as a solidly built U.S. marshal walked past him with a shotgun in his right hand and a handcuffed prisoner in his left. He escorted the man toward the jailhouse, but not before glancing hard—and a little too long—at Luke.

The poster pasted to the exterior wall of the Beaumont Post Office was the first one Luke had seen since he'd left Louisiana. He was barely able to read the print with the marshal only a few feet away. But Luke caught the most noteworthy item on the paper. He was worth four thousand. Dead or alive.

Despite the fact he'd grown a rough beard, thick bristle of mustache, and wore a black hat low on his forehead, Luke could recognize himself in the artist's sketch.

He slipped into the shade at the corner of a building and considered his next move. He had to get on the train without being identified. But doing that wouldn't be easy. The marshal wasn't a backwater blind-eye. He seemed sharp and assessing. A real smart guy; the tin-starred official would come directly back after locking up his charge. Luke had to act quickly. There was a warrant for his arrest on double murder charges in New Orleans. He'd be a fine catch to end some lawman's day.

Stepping off the boardwalk, Luke walked through mud, gumbo and oil in the streets. This side of Texas was a hellhole.

Keeping the crown of his hat tilted over his forehead, and the strap of his travel bag slung high over his back, he made his way to the train depot. He wore an unbuttoned lightweight duster that almost touched the ground, and a concealed Colt .38 Super tucked into a holster belted around his waist. The faded denim of his pants showed the wear of hard travel. When he lifted his hand to his jaw, his black facial hair felt thick and uneven. He needed a bath and a shave. But neither were a luxury he could indulge right now.

As he walked with even strides, he stuck to the busy street as if he belonged. He had to blend in. Be a faceless man among many. But that was hard to do. He was extraordinarily tall. A family trait from his father's side. Luke's three brothers were all over six feet. The Devereaux boys were wide in the shoulders, narrow in the waists, and long on legs. Not only did they bear a striking resemblance to one another, they all had followed in their dad's career footsteps. Each of them had joined police departments in New Orleans. Jayce and Phillipe were junior lieutenants in the Fourteenth Precinct, while Chandler was a sergeant in the Twenty-third. Luke had been, up until ten days ago, a lieutenant on the Sixty-sixth Precinct's payroll. He was still trying to sort out how he'd ended up in Texas—a wanted man on the run.

The sound of motorcars and wagons filled the street with noise, while tremors in the distance signaled the workings of derricks as they plunged into the earth searching for black gold. The musty smell of water came to him, as did the horns from barges. The Neches River had been relatively easy to cross. He'd ridden in the rear of a parcel wagon, unnoticed by the driver. A mile outside of town, he'd slipped out and come the rest of the way on foot.

Now he had to get on a train to take him to Silver City, New Mexico, a journey that he hoped would lead him to his former partner, Henry Boyd.

Henry quite possibly had the information that Luke needed to clear his name. Because Boyd was a key figure in things that had gone wrong in New Orleans for the department. The headlines of the *Daily Picayune* declared the Sixty-sixth Precinct so corrupt, it smelled like a heap of stinking garbage.

But it hadn't always been that way. As the city grew prosperous, so did opportunities. Money flowed into the Bayou Quarter, and with it came a criminal element wanting to cash in. Sinister ties cut across a portion of Jackson Square and to the riverfront. Glittering lights from theaters and saloons, dance halls and high-priced restaurants and hotels were lures for the illicit. At all hours, the narrow streets were clogged with horse-drawn buggies and smoky, motor-driven automobiles.

No city permit could be secured, no building could start and no business could open unless the right person received his payoff. Luke had known about the practice but hadn't figured on how deeply the corruption had run into his department.

Like a steady drizzle of rain that eventually erodes a road, each payoff was another raindrop carving away at the department's credibility. In recent months, Luke had begun to question the behavior and motives of his longtime partner who had started to secrete himself off on "business for Sockeye." Captain James "Sockeye" Mullet—overseer of all the graft and bribery.

Keeping law and order had become a game of chase and hide. The old police commissioner was responsible for the decay, but it went way beyond him. As prostitution infused itself, as did unregulated gambling, pimps and gaming house owners sought protection from prosecution by paying off the police department. The police, in turn, plotted with politicians at city hall. The gaming house owners who refused to pay were promptly raided and put out of business.

Almost two weeks ago, a legitimate raid had been set to occur under the new police commissioner's authority. Big Pat Ellroy, a former captain in the army, vowed to clean up the city in short order when the old commissioner was convicted on racketeering charges. Big Pat moved fast and furious; Luke and his brothers felt hope that things were going to turn around. The purpose of Big Pat's first raid wasn't to collect money—it was to collect violators and prosecute them

fairly. Luke had eagerly looked forward to putting the
Pontchartrain Club out of business.

Only things didn't play out like they were supposed to.

Two sergeants from their precinct had been gunned
down in the raid that night, and Luke was immediately identified as the shooter by Detective Paul Regale
and Sockeye Mullet. Confirming their story, without so
much as a flinch, had been Lieutenant Henry Boyd—
fellow officer and witness to the "crime."

Paul Regale and Sockeye were questioned and
accused Luke Devereaux of being on the take and
hushing two officers who knew too much about his
dirty tactics. Boyd also gave a statement for the events
at the Pontchartrain, and his account matched Paul's
and Sockeye's to the letter. Henry Boyd then suddenly
disappeared when falsified evidence against Luke
began to surface—a gun that he supposedly owned
and used in the shooting. Even though Luke had
adamantly denied everything, his brother Jayce heard
through a trusted source that he was going to be
arrested without being questioned.

Luke hadn't stayed around to find out for sure.

Questions of why Henry would do this to him
plagued Luke; and it was the fact that he didn't have a
chance in hell of getting answers if he stayed in New
Orleans, that he set out to find Boyd.

Having spent years working alongside Henry,
Luke knew a lot about the man. Henry had family in
Silver City and Luke was counting on confronting
him there. It was a long shot, but it was the only thing
he had to go on.

The Calder Avenue depot came into sight. The green two-story building hummed with activity as porters and the baggage carts moved across the platform. The San Antonio and Aransas Pass railroad waited on the tracks, its stack spewing smoke. A string of coach, sleeping, and utility cars were attached to the Lone Star Limited engine, which Luke knew was headed for El Paso. Passengers were beginning to board. All he had to do was buy a ticket. Should be simple if he watched his back. He strode forward, keeping his chin down.

Luke walked toward the ticket counter, but he abruptly changed his direction as the marshal walked toward him with a light grip on his Smith & Wesson. He seemed to have come out of nowhere, and Luke cursed himself for not recognizing the fact that a criminal always needed to be on the move, and a depot was a high road out of town.

The marshal didn't see him, but it would only be a matter of minutes before he did a thorough sweep of the platform.

Luke damned the situation as he wove his way through a grove of juniper trees. At the street, he came upon a man in a butler's uniform arguing with a flatbed driver. On the back of the vehicle were two trunks.

"Listen, mister, I've explained myself to you three times, but for the benefit of the wax in your ears, I'll do so again," the butler enunciated slowly to the slouching driver who frowned down at him. "The luggage has to go back to the Imperial Hotel. Mrs. Smythe cannot depart on the train as scheduled. Her pug dog has taken ill. She won't travel without Mister Wrinkles. I've been sent here to have her trunks returned to the hotel."

"I heard you the other three times, bub." The lazy flatbed driver spit a line of tobacco, barely missing the butler's toes. He jerked backward. "And I'm still telling you—I've got four fares to pick up and there won't be enough room for their suitcases if you don't get hoity-toity Smythe's trunks off the back of my truck."

"Sir, you don't seem to understand. Mrs. Smythe is a very important figure in society. She's the head collector for the Atlanta Museum of Art." The butler boldly lifted his chin and tried to clarify. "Cézanne, Manet, Degas. All men of great importance, and it's her duty to collect them."

"Collects men, huh?"

"I dare say, no! They are artists. Painters."

"I don't care if she collects painters or plumbers." The driver lost all patience. He reached his arm through the window of the cab, stepped on the running board, then hopped up onto the flatbed. With two keen shoves, the trunks were down on the damp ground. "Problem solved." Then he fired up the engine, resumed his seat behind the wheel and drove away.

The butler removed his bowler and looked at the two heavy pieces of luggage.

Luke glanced through the fringed cedar breaks behind him to the platform and saw the marshal talking with the conductor. He felt as if he had no options but for the one crazy idea that came to him in a split second. He turned to the butler, who scratched the back of his head.

"What a pickle," the suited man muttered to himself. "Mrs. Smythe is going to have a conniption fit."

Closing the distance between them, Luke offered, "I can help you with the lady's ticket, mister. I'll pay you ten bucks for it and you've got one less problem. No line to wait in and you make a profit into the bargain."

The butler looked up at him, puzzled. "I beg your pardon? Who are you?"

"Somebody who needs a ticket and doesn't have time to stand in line to get one. I'll help you and you help me." He reached into his pocket for his billfold at the same time two deputies approached the depot from the south. From where he stood, they couldn't see him, but he knew they'd been called out to comb the area. Quickly, Luke presented a bill and said, "Ten and a deal?"

"No."

"Twenty?"

"Sir, you don't understand. I have to rebook Mrs. Smythe's boudoir compartment for Monday and that requires a transfer of funds."

Staring over the butler's narrow shoulder, Luke watched the deputies split up. One went to the east, the other went to the west. *Damn.*

"A sleeping car is considered extra fare and while twenty is generous, I'll have to inform Mrs. Smythe that she has to pay me further and—"

"Fifty."

A slight flicker of hesitation. "Done."

Luke pulled out the correct amount and was handed a ticket for the outbound Limited that left in approximately twenty-five minutes. He had to work quickly.

The butler frowned at the two pieces of luggage. "I don't know how I'm going to get these trunks back to the hotel. This town has no time for anyone. One must grease palms with oil or nothing gets done. If I leave them here, they'll most likely be stolen by the time I return."

"They should be okay here until you can find somebody to help you." Taking each truck by its leather handle, Luke dragged them into the junipers; they semi-disappeared beneath the branches of Indian paintbrush.

"Thank—"

Luke didn't wait around for gratitude. He jogged across the street, his mind focused on his new plan. Deep in thought, he butted arms with a woman urgently dashing past him. Jarred, his gaze connected with hers. He had an instant to realize her eyes were a deep blue.

As they stepped away from each other, he noticed only two other things about her. She was petite in stature, and wore a black-and-white lady's maid uniform.

Neither of them offered an apology. The meeting happened too quickly and they were yards apart before words formed on his lips.

During the next fifteen minutes, Luke made a short visit to the general merchandise store that carried both women's and men's articles. He purchased the necessary items. After that, he found himself in the gents' lavatory behind the Boss Waterloo Saloon.

Luke gazed at his reflection in the mirror. Sleepless hours on the road had darkened his features to a swarthy degree. The shape of his brows seemed sharper; the gray of his eyes deeper. His forehead had tanned below the brim of his hat, and the corners of his eyes bore creases where the sun had not yet touched the skin a bronzed tint. He'd never considered himself the kind of handsome that women wanted in a husband. His jaw was too chiseled, his nose not quite straight. His black hair fell to the collar of his shirt, and he ran his hand through it wishing he could have scrubbed soap into his scalp. All he could do now was comb his hair back from his forehead and go about changing his appearance.

The buzz of an electrical light hummed above his head. The silver looking glass was cloudy and spotted with water droplets and the smear of fingerprints, but he could see his features well enough as he lathered his cheeks and the rough underside of his neck. With precise strokes, he shaved then used a clean section of the roller towel to wipe off his face.

He reached into one of the packages he'd brought into the gents' room with him. It contained a lady's black wig piled up with curls. He paused, stared at the feminine hunk of hair, and felt a churn of discomfort slap him in his gut. If there was any other way. . . . But the presence of one marshal and two deputies gave him no choice.

Minutes later, a very tall, and a very ugly, woman stared back at him.

There was no way he was putting on the bowed

shoes with delicate heels and walking in them. But covering his legs to the tops of his scuffed boots was a plain gray frock. He was able to purchase one that came unhemmed. He hoped nobody would notice. He didn't intend to wear it for very long. Beneath the lace and gathers, he still had on his own clothes as well as his holster and gun.

He bought a single-handle purse that contained his billfold, pocketknife, and a box of bullets. Thrown in were the makings for some smokes and a finger-bottle of whiskey.

Placing his other possessions into his travel bag, he took one last look at himself. *Sweet Judas.* Maybe he shouldn't have used three pairs of his socks to stuff the bodice. He pushed and pulled at them to make the lumps more even. He only made it look worse.

He was thirty-four and dressing like a fifty-year-old woman. A real frightful fifty-year-old woman.

Self-consciously, Luke strode to the depot. Nobody seemed to notice, or care, he wasn't a woman blessed with good looks.

Nearing the station, he caught sight of the marshal with his arms folded over his chest. As he looked over the passengers, he began walking.

Heading straight for Luke.

3

"Yes, hello," the lady's maid said clearly, and in a tone she hoped sounded steady. But inside, the blood seemed to rush in her veins and pulse at a deafening rate in her ears.

The ticket agent looked at her with expectation and little patience given the fact there was a line behind her. "How can I help you, miss?"

"Yes," she repeated, keeping her posture as straight and stiff as her corset. "The lady's maid hired to travel with Mrs. Smythe has been sent out to another position and I've been assigned as her replacement."

Biting the inside of her cheek for nearly having stammered through her words, she tightly clutched onto her black pocketbook. She held her breath, her lungs aching. When the agent didn't readily move, she quickly added, "I believe her ticket is waiting for her. I'll be picking it up."

He looked through a stand-up file with letter separators. It felt as if it took him a good ten minutes before he produced an envelope with a typed name on its front. "Ah, yes. Here it is. Smythe." Raising his head, he gazed at her with a green pallor to his skin that came from the tinted visor he wore. It made his nose seem twice its size as he stared at her.

Let him look. He'd never know who she really was.

The moment Evelyn decided to assume the identity of a lady's maid, she knew there would be complications. Yesterday, it had been her own maid, Flora, who'd told her about a friend who'd been hired to ride in a Pullman car as a lady's maid for Mrs. Smythe. All the way to El Paso. The pay was fifty dollars, but the money was no incentive for Evelyn as she'd listened to the arrangements that would take place today. As Flora had talked, Evelyn had one thing on her mind: getting on this train and fleeing Oiler. She had to get out of her forced marriage. And not being available for the ceremony was the only way.

While her parents slept, Evelyn had packed what she could fit into a valise. To execute her escape, she'd needed help. She'd woken Flora and told her what she was going to do. Flora argued it was too dangerous for Evelyn to travel alone, but in the end Evelyn won her over.

Reluctantly, Flora gave her instructions on how to pick up the ticket at the depot while Evelyn handed Flora one hundred dollars to pay her friend as compensation for no longer accompanying Mrs. Smythe. Nobody would think to look for Evelyn Thurgood-Baron as a lady's maid. Flora's loyalty could be counted on. She gave Evelyn one of her uniforms and made sure the way was clear just before sunrise.

With everything in place, Evelyn had saddled two horses. Flora was riding along so she could bring Evelyn's horse back home without discovery in Beaumont. Once in Beaumont, there had been a moment when Flora changed her mind and begged Evelyn to come back to the mansion with her and make peace with her parents and discuss alternatives to marrying Guy Hadley. But having gone as far as she had, Evelyn was determined and stood her ground; so Flora rode back to Oiler by herself with a final promise to keep Evelyn's whereabouts a secret.

Evelyn had waited several hours for the Lone Star Limited to pull into Beaumont. She would have been at the depot thirty minutes earlier if she hadn't been recognized by Miss Rosita from the Dime Box. Miss Rosita had insisted they go to the opera house so Evelyn could receive her ten dollar prize money she'd been unable to collect while being marched out by the Ladies Society of Texas. Once there, she was congratulated by the owner, barkeepers and several of the saloon girls.

By the time Evelyn broke free, she had less than ten minutes to make it to the station.

Now that she was here, she felt as if she'd faint from the heat and her excitement while the ticket agent slowly extended his arm. "All right, miss." He handed her the ticket, and she had to refrain from melting with relief. Gazing at its lovely print informing her she was to reside in Car 4, Boudoir 4B, she was nearly overwhelmed.

"Enjoy your trip to El Paso," he stated formally before calling, "Next in line."

"Oh, yes, sir. I most certainly will. Thank you."

With that, she turned on her heel and went for the stairs leading to the No. 4 Pullman sleeping car. Gripping the handle of her English Garden petit point valise tightly in her hand, she couldn't contain a smile of sheer elation.

She'd done it. She was free.

Luke's white-gloved hand grasped the door handle to compartment 4B. He'd made it onto the train. He was damn pleased with himself for pulling off such a ruse. The lawman hadn't given him even a cursory glance as they'd passed on the street minutes ago.

Now that he was aboard, he was through with being Smythe. *She* was going to be sick for the entire journey, and she wasn't leaving her compartment. Luke couldn't wait to get out of the dress and wig, pour himself a drink, then light a smoke and relax as the miles rolled past.

He turned the latch and swung the door inward with a smile. But the slight curve on his lips caught in a snag when he saw the lady's maid sitting on the narrow bed smoothing her black stockings—her shapely legs still in them, her dress hiked above her knees.

As she looked up in surprise, she quickly tossed her skirts down and bolted off the mattress.

"Mrs. Smythe, madam, I'm sorry, I—"

"What—" Luke clenched his jaw, cleared his throat and raised his tone about three octaves. When he spoke, he sounded like his privates were being squeezed between a pair of bookends. "What are you doing in my compartment?"

"I-I'm . . ." She looked directly at him, then averted her gaze from his face. Staring at the stainless sink that had been pulled out of the wall closet, she replied, "I'm the maid the agency sent."

He was so thrown off guard, he momentarily couldn't think to reply. What agency? What was going on? The butler had failed to mention Smythe wasn't the only occupant in the compartment.

"Who the hel—" He immediately rephrased in a softer voice, cutting off the curse. "Who the help is, isn't a concern of mine . . . *dear.*" Think. Think. Think. The holster strapped at his hip and the wig suffocating his head scrambled his thinking. And the maid's unexpected presence mucked up his plan.

His disguise wasn't meant for close inspection. The slight woman before him stood just over an arm's width away, the farthest distance the parlor car allowed. If she backed up any farther, she'd be on her backside flat on the bed. He gave her a fast glance.

At that moment, Luke recognized her. He'd bumped into her on the street. Blue eyes. More than blue eyes now. A pretty mouth and honey-colored hair to go with them. Her beauty seemed fragile, just as her mood. He had to get rid of her.

"I don't require any assistance on this trip and I canceled my maid." He forced a stance of feminine authority, going as far as holding his shoulders back. He didn't look down to see if he was lopsided in the bodice. "Apparently you didn't get the message. Now that you know, you can get out of here."

The maid didn't move.

"You can go," he repeated. "I don't need your services."

All he saw was the top of her lace cap as she continued to bow her head. Narrowing his gaze on her slender shoulders, he detected a slight quiver. No. Not now. He didn't want to deal with a crying female.

As Luke lifted his hand to rub his jaw, he paused before he touched his skin, remembering the rice powder. He had to change the way he was talking to her or else she'd get suspicious.

"Dear, I'm sorry I spoke so harshly." He tried to be tactful without making her cry. "I'm sure you're very qualified, but I don't need you."

The door was hit with a knock.

Both he and the maid jumped and stared at the mahogany panels. He didn't take the time to wonder what she was so skittish about. All that zeroed in on his mind was: *If the marshal is on the other side of the door, what am I going to do about it?*

He fought the inclination to lift his skirt and pull out his Colt. If it wasn't the marshal, he had to keep up the pretext of being Smythe and not blow his cover. Slowly, he unclasped his purse and fingered the pocketknife. He kept his gloved thumb over the lock that could spring the blade free in an instant.

A second knock sounded.

"Mrs. Smythe, ma'am." A man's voice penetrated through the wood. "It's the porter, ma'am. We've found your luggage behind the depot and brought it to you."

Dammit all to hell. That butler was supposed to haul those trunks back to the Imperial Hotel. What had happened? Luke had no choice but to open the door.

He stepped aside as a young man of color wearing a white suit coat entered. "Afternoon, ma'am." He touched the bill of his patent black cap; a white smile brightened his face. "A definite bit of good luck for you today." He brought first one trunk, then the second, into the compartment.

"Um, yes," Luke managed, wondering what the man was talking about. He didn't have to wonder long.

"Very curious to find them in the brush, ma'am," the porter declared, "but they've been recovered thanks to the watchful eyes of Beaumont's deputies. They were searching the area."

"Who were they looking for?"

Both Luke and the porter turned to look at the lady's maid. Her eyes were bright and shiny with anxiousness.

The porter replied, "Well, miss, I didn't get that far, but you're right, it was a 'who' indeed. I heard tell, the deputies are searching for a dangerous criminal." Facing Luke, he added informatively, "Didn't find the scoundrel, but they found your trunks, ma'am."

"Oh, goody." Luke forced an airy appreciation. "Thanks, kid."

The porter gave him a sideways glance, then returned with measured words, "My pleasure, ma'am, to give you the good news." He stood just inside the open door, that smile pasted to his face, and his arms behind his back. "If I may be of any service at any time, ma'am, my name is Nate." He pointed to the brass name plate pinned to the breast of his coat jacket. Then resumed his waiting position.

Luke dug into his purse for his billfold. He couldn't take it out with people watching, so he turned his back, slipped open the wallet and came out with a bill. Presenting himself to Nate, he handed him the tip. "Thank you, uh, Nate, dear."

He nodded. "Yes, ma'am. Thank you indeed."

Then he left.

Luke had momentarily forgotten about the lady's maid and now turned to her. She appeared as if she was going to fall onto the bed with a sigh of relief. Everything about her relaxed when the door closed.

He took in her appearance on closer examination. The crow black dress and starched white apron didn't compliment her skin; but he figured a woman didn't take a position with the colors of her uniform in mind. Her hair was thick and shined as the afternoon sun came through the window in a slight beam of muted light. Her complexion was flawless. Her figure was quite nice.

Her mannerisms left him undecided.

She refused to look at him. He couldn't blame her. He'd seen his reflection.

"Now, ah, miss, it's time for you to go."

Her chin shot up, and she set it in a firm angle. This, he thought, was the first show of feistiness in her. "I can't."

"Why not?"

"Because—"

But her "because" became a moot point. Because— the train bolted forward. She was thrown against his

side with the sudden action. His automatic reaction
had him slipping his arm around her to steady her on
her feet. In doing so, he placed her flush against his
false bodice. He could feel her stiffen beneath his
embrace. He quickly nudged her away from him. The
car began to rock. She reached out and held onto the
edge of the square sink counter.

A whistle sounded, as did the clang of a bell.

The train began to pick up speed.

Luke felt every cord in his muscles tighten with
strain. They were stuck together until the next stop
where one of them was going to have to get off the
train. And it wasn't going to be him.

A grinding silence rubbed through the room as if
the air would explode. He couldn't think about how
they'd manage to share the small space without her
figuring out he was a man.

Forgetting to be delicate, he sank onto the day
bench with its tufted cushion and silk pillows. His
legs sprawled in front of him, and he yanked his skirt
down to cover his shoes. Forcing himself to sit straight
and proper, he had no choice but to play his part.
"What's your name anyway?" She made no reply, and
he added, "Dear? Your name?"

She hesitated, and he could almost see her mind
working in the depths of her blue eyes.

Then easily, she replied, "Eve. Eve Pierce."

Mrs. Smythe was the most mannish woman Evelyn
had ever seen. She was practically a giant with grossly
exaggerated proportions.

And that face!

Her rice powder had been put on way too thick—probably to hide a skin disfigurement such as pox scars, and her rouge was tinted far too deeply over her cheeks, making it look like she had two apples painted on her face.

The overall shape of her face could be pleasantly squared if she didn't wear her ringlet curls so close to her ears. She had no talent for using a curl iron—even on her wig, which was obvious, as there were pieces that hung inches above or below others.

In her favor, she had nice eyes and lips. Her mouth was wide and soft-looking without any false lip color, while her eyes were a bluish charcoal gray that, in this case, did go nicely with her black hair. Most often, women who had such dark eyes came across looking too dour.

Sadly, however, even Mrs. Smythe's better qualities couldn't be considered assets. She was not an attractive woman by any means.

Be that as it may, as the train swayed and rolled forward, Evelyn could hardly contain herself. She'd actually followed through with her outrageous escape. And it had worked. She was leaving Oiler behind.

She'd finally be able to visit the places on her maps. Everything was perfect. Except for one thing . . .

For a duration, she was truly employed as a lady's maid.

Evelyn looked at Mrs. Smythe, whose large gloved hands rested on her knees. Quite improper. While never being employed in any kind of service, Evelyn reasoned she could do this job. After all, she'd given orders to help all her life. Knowing that, she chastised herself for the mistake she'd already made: being caught on her employer's bed adjusting the knit in her stockings. The help must be staunch and seasoned, helpful and friendly, at all times. Never do things that could be remotely construed as being of a personal nature.

Putting herself into a no-nonsense mode, Evelyn said with renewed conviction, "Well, madam, I'll be unpacking your trunks for you now."

As she moved into action, Evelyn noted her valise rested on the bed. Another violation, but Mrs. Smythe didn't seem to notice. With a guilty heat suffusing her cheeks, Evelyn lifted her valise and hung it up on a wall hook.

Mrs. Smythe made no comment about her trunks. She sat there and stared, trancelike, out at the terrain rolling in a blur past the window. She seemed moody. More than irritable.

There was no way to judge her age, but perhaps she was going through what one of Mother's medical books called the "The Change of Life." An entire chapter outlined symptoms with references to headaches, biliousness, sour stomach, piles, itching of the private parts, and pains in the back and loins.

From the way Mrs. Smythe was poised, every bone in her body must be feeling brittle. She was on edge, both on the seat and by the rough position of her broad shoulders.

Evelyn tentatively broached the subject of unpacking once more. "Would that be all right, madam?" She knew that when her monthly came and she wasn't feeling like herself, it was nice to have things in order.

Since Mrs. Smythe didn't answer, Evelyn went to the trunks and tried the latch on the first one. It was locked. "Madam, I need your key."

Mrs. Smythe gazed at her. Each time the woman had pointedly looked at Evelyn, she had to hold herself as still as she could manage and not grimace.

"Key?"

"Yes, madam." Oh dear. Mrs. Smythe's powder was uneven at her upper lip from where she'd rubbed it with her forefinger. It took every ounce of drummed-in decorum and willpower not to stare. "I'd imagine your key is in your pocketbook. I can look for you—"

"No!" With a sharp jerk, Mrs. Smythe held her purse away and hooked its handle through her arm.

Evelyn rose and stood back. She'd never acted like this toward any of her family's help. Good intentions shouldn't be met with gruff barks. Indeed, the more she thought about it, Mrs. Smythe clearly was a crabapple on a tree growing barren.

"I . . . I'm sorry." Evelyn was at a near loss.

"Eve Pierce," Mrs. Smythe said, pointedly glaring at her as if she were in grave pain. The tone of her voice had even deepened, like her insides were twisting into one big knot. "I'd like to be alone for a while. Go do something. Leave."

It took Evelyn a moment to adjust to the sound of her fake name. While Grandfather Jimmy had called her Eve, nobody had called her Eve since he'd passed on. When Mrs. Smythe asked her what her name was, she'd decided to use a first name she could answer to or else she might not reply when spoken to. Yesterday afternoon, her father's new Pierce-Arrow had arrived, so she'd taken a part of its illustrious name and added that to her nickname.

Eve Pierce.

"All right, madam." Evelyn ran her moist hands down Flora's cotton apron. It certainly wasn't pleasant being snapped at. "What time should I come back?"

Mrs. Smythe was quite biting when she remarked, "You needn't."

4

L uke drew the strap of the purse down his arm, opened the clasp, and took out the finger-bottle of bourbon. He drank the entire amount in three precise tilts of his chin. The liquor went down his throat with a slow burn, but with the hot pleasure he'd needed more than anything at this moment.

He leaned his back on the bench, legs out in front of him, his denim pants showing below the hem of his stupid gray dress. This was insane. *He* was insane. It wasn't going to work. He couldn't pull off being Smythe. Not with another person in a boudoir compartment barely big enough for one woman, much less two. *Much less with one of them really being a man.*

Eve Pierce, with her refined features and poise, wasn't what he assumed a lady's maid would be like. Were maids supposed to be that confident? Did they just take over? Ask for trunk keys? Try and rifle through purses?

What would she have said if she discovered what

he kept in there? Hell, he knew. She would have become agitated. Maybe call out for Nate and have every porter onboard running to find out what the problem was. A pocketknife and billfold weren't reason enough to be hollering for help; but the box of bullets was unusual for a woman to carry. As was a man's billfold.

Luke rose, went to the sink, and stared at himself.

The reflection made him shudder. His rice powder was uneven where he'd rubbed his upper lip and jaw. The artificial paleness of his skin, especially at his brows, made his eyes seem bloodshot; which they probably were, but putting white next to red made him look all the worse. It was a damn wonder Eve Pierce didn't point a finger at him and laugh.

Bracing his arms on either side of the sink, he wondered what he was going to do about her.

Right now, he simply didn't know.

He looked over his shoulder at the pair of trunks he didn't have a key for. He bent and examined the locks on each. They were the same. He used the tip of his knife blade as a pick.

Once each lock snapped open, Luke lifted the lids and took inventory. Lots of satin stuff. Stockings. Shirtwaists. Large underwear. Hair doodads. Skirts. Dresses. He held up a green frock with lots of lace on the sleeves and neck. Wouldn't fit him in the length, but the width looked as if it could wrap around him. Twice. He tossed it aside. There were corsets and shoes. What felt to be pictures on canvases wrapped in heavy brown paper; he didn't pull the strings on the packages. He wasn't concerned about Smythe's personal effects. Not even her jewelry, which was in a neat velvet box.

Luke stood. Everything inside the trunks was useless to him.

He leaned over the bed and looked out the window. Just a bunch of grassland with thickets of junipers. The territory was plain to him. Not like New Orleans with its oak trees draped in moss. The bright colors of flowers and deep greenery. Texas was a far cry from the Vieux Carré, and he'd give anything to be back there. With his brothers. And his mother, whom he'd last seen a couple of weeks ago. She'd had him, his brothers and their wives, over to her house for lawn games and a barbeque supper. The Pontchartrain Club shootings had left her shaken; she'd been the first one to his Garden District townhouse to make sure he was all right. In days afterward, she'd spoken to department officials and assured them her son was not a murderer.

The thought of her worrying and not knowing where he'd gone gave Luke solemn pause. Only Jayce knew where he was headed.

It was better that way for everyone concerned.

Evelyn struggled to maintain her balance in the rocking accordion-like appendage connecting cars three and four. There was nobody else in the small passage because the sign above her stated no passengers were allowed to stand on the platform. She'd only paused for a minute while walking from one car to the next to the back of the train.

Each Pullman on the San Antonio and Aransas Pass

was elaborate in its decorations. This was only the third time she had been on a train. Her most memorable experience on a train had been the two-hour trip to boarding school and the return trip, after being expelled and sent home.

She passed through the drawing room car that was decorated with gold-leaf framed mirrors, extravagant upholstery and rugs. The wood was mahogany and highly polished. Velvet carpets had been installed on the floor of the smoking car, while silk draperies and white silk curtains hung on its windows. Revolving chairs were plush. The walls were embellished with marquetry, and for decoration, potted plants were carefully arranged around the chairs. The odor of smoke hung in the tight space.

Delicious smells drifted to her as she crossed through the enclosed vestibule. She'd reached the dining car and found that she was ravenous. She had her Dime Box ten dollars on her, tucked into her corset for safekeeping. Did one just sit down and order? Or was there a necessity of showing one's ticket?

Smelling that food made her mouth water.

She held back at the front of the car to look at the scene. To savor its appearance. The people inside. Everything looked as if it could be picked up and put in an actual dining room. Above the windows were stained-glass motifs depicting various scenes. Square tables next to the windows were covered with crisp white linens. The cutlery seemed to be silver. Even vases of fresh flowers centered on the tabletops. Menus were in the patrons' hands. Amazing. They had their choice of food. Evelyn thought the entire concept was ingenious.

Nate, the porter, came toward her from the rear of the car, a towel folded over his arm. "Miss," he addressed, his voice more informal than it had been with Mrs. Smythe. "What are you doing back here? Does Mrs. Smythe need anything?"

"I was just wondering what was on the menu."

He grabbed one from a designated slot in the wall and handed it to her. "If she wants to order, you tell Tom. He's in dining tonight."

"Oh . . . well, I'd hoped to get a little something to eat, then ask my employer if she wants anything."

"You go on then and show Tom your ticket."

"I don't have it on me."

Nate shook his head. "Then you'd best get on out of the car, miss. You're in the way and I'm in an awful hurry for filling in."

She didn't understand what "filling in" meant, nor the fact that her being in the dining car could get them into trouble. She moved back and stood on the platform reading what the menu had to offer. As she looked over the items, her stomach growled.

Oysters. Sugar-cured ham. Chicken salad. Eggs. Beefsteak with potatoes. Mutton chops. French coffee.

Maybe they'd make an exception if she promised to show them her ticket after she ate and returned to her room to get it.

She went to open the door of the dining car once more to see about ordering dinner; but Nate appeared on the other side coming toward her with a glare and holding onto a round platter with a silver dome. Food. She could smell the ham with potatoes.

"Now, miss. I done told you, no ticket, no dinner. You go on now."

"But I was hoping to have whatever it is that you're holding," she said, feeling as if her insides were gnawing against her ribs.

"Quit joshing with Nate, miss." He scowled down at her, taking in her uniform. One she'd forgotten she was wearing. "I don't have time for your tomfoolery. The Big E wants his dinner and I'm in charge of getting it to him."

"The Big E?"

"Engineer," he replied with some shortness. "Now, you know you shouldn't be out here looking to snap on cinders."

"Snap on cinders?"

"The skipper find you out here and you'll be in for it."

"The skipper?"

"Conductor!" Narrowing his dark brown eyes at her, he said with a snort, "Is this the first time you been on a train, miss?"

"Well, in a way . . . yes."

"Then you get back on into your room with your employer and you see to it she made comfortable. You tell her dinner be served until eight. If she don't want none, after eight, you can get yourself a samwich."

"Samwich?"

"Pieces of bread with samwich meat, miss." He shook his hatted head. "Don't you know nothing?"

"I know lots of things."

"Me, too. That's why I'm moving on to get this to

the Big E before it's cold." He scooted past her to the fore-car door. "Now, you best listen to Nate on this one or you'll find yourself looking for another job next stop. Get on back to Mrs. Smythe. Although I don't blame you for wanting to be out of there. She is a strange one, if you'll excuse me saying so."

"You're excused," Evelyn replied, wondering if help really did talk like this out of their employer's hearing. "I thought the same thing myself."

Nate held onto a chuckle, then was gone.

Not wanting to test the wrath of the skipper if he came across her, Evelyn followed Nate out of the car and walked back to compartment 4B with an emptiness in her stomach longing to be filled. She was terribly hungry. What time was it? Eight o'clock seemed so far off since she hadn't eaten any lunch.

Once at the door, she stared at it to rethink what she had to do. She had to renew her efforts at being efficient. Take charge. Put Mrs. Smythe at ease that she was being well-cared for.

With a firm nod of her head, Evelyn knocked on the door and let herself inside. "Mrs. Smythe, I know we didn't get off to the right st—"

Mrs. Smythe knelt on the bed and was fanning smoke through the open window. With a twitch and wrinkle of her nose, Evelyn sniffed the compartment. Tobacco smoke hung in the air.

"There was a fire in here," Mrs. Smythe explained, her large frame bent as she tried to rid the room of the odor by waving her hat at the glass opening in the window.

"A fire, Mrs. Smythe?"

"Yes, something got on fire."

Evelyn approached. "Something, Mrs. Smythe?"

"Yes. Something burned up."

Taking a quick examination of the room, Evelyn saw nothing that had been charred.

Mrs. Smythe stopped moving her arm and turned to Evelyn with a frown flattening her brows. Just when she thought she'd grown used to Mrs. Smythe's appearance, she had to force herself not to grimace.

"Nothing burned," Evelyn said. "You were smoking a cigarette."

In a painfully high-pitched tone, she made a showy fluff and flutter of her neckline collar before pursing her lips in a prudish manner. "Ah no, dear. You're mistaken."

Evelyn had to prove to Mrs. Smythe she could be dependable. And trustworthy. She laid a hand on the woman's arm, trying not to notice the hard feel of muscle beneath her palm. The change of life must do things to a woman's body Evelyn hadn't realized.

At the sympathetic contact, Mrs. Smythe practically jumped out of her dress.

"It's all right," Evelyn assured in a confidential whisper. "I won't tell anyone." Oddly, the fact that Mrs. Smythe indulged in a habit such as smoking tobacco, made her almost feel lucky to have stumbled on this strange relationship forming between them.

Evelyn had tried bourbon and now she wanted to do something else that her father would heartily disapprove of.

"I won't tell because . . ." She licked her lips. "Would you mind rolling me one?"

Mrs. Smythe looked at her through a critical squint. Then she sat on the edge of the bed. "I'll be damned."

Once more the woman's phraseology left Evelyn puzzled, and curious. Clearly Mrs. Smythe was from humble beginnings. A lady of her caliber would have never sworn. Evelyn had rarely, if ever, even made a slip inside her head.

Although Daddy slipped up a lot with colorful language and Mother was forever correcting him. Her parents were like crude oil and perfume—they didn't mix. Their marriage had been based on a monetary foundation. Mother's old family money and grace; Daddy's new oil wells and stocks.

"Are you sure, *dear?*" Mrs. Smythe asked with a lowering of her chin. "You don't look like the kind of woman who would smoke."

Evelyn almost said: *I'd like to be.* But she refrained.

"Of course I smoke," she airily replied. "Don't all women in vogue smoke?"

Mrs. Smythe rubbed her jaw. "I wouldn't know about all women." Evelyn didn't let her gaze linger at the spot of skin that was revealed.

Agilely rolling a cigarette, Mrs. Smythe passed her a tightly rolled cylinder of tobacco and even offered to light it for her.

"Why thank you, madam." Evelyn brought it to her mouth and as soon as the end was burning, she inhaled as if she were seasoned. With a hand on her hip, she took in a deep draw, held it—and nearly passed out from the instantaneous suffocation that invaded her lungs.

It was all she could do not to cough up her stomach, empty as the contents were. She sputtered and coughed and choked and reached out blindly for her purse where she had a handkerchief to cry into. Her eyes stung and watered; tears streamed down her cheeks.

How could her father and those men in his office consume these things without immediate death by asphyxiation?

She cried into her tatted hankie as Mrs. Smythe briskly patted her on the back. "There, dear. Let it all out. I told you—you didn't look the type."

"I-I," she gasped, "guess you're r-right."

And with that admission, suddenly every trying thing about the day came crashing in around her. Doubt swirled like fall leaves being pulled off a tree in a storm. What had she gotten herself into? She was away from home. Alone and on her own. She couldn't order dinner right, she couldn't smoke, she couldn't be a good lady's maid. Perhaps she was ill-equipped to take care of herself, much less Mrs. Smythe.

At the depot, she'd been so excited to be out on her own. To be on her way to see and do things she'd only imagined. To make her own choices and decide her own fate. There was a part of her now that was scared.

But it was too late. She couldn't turn back. If she did, she'd have to admit to her father that he was right about her: She could do nothing but sully the family name. She was nothing but a commodity to be acquired by Guy Hadley.

If she went home, she'd be trapped in a marriage of convenience not convenient for her.

While Mrs. Smythe continued her gruff ministrations with pats to her back, Evelyn wiped her eyes and pulled herself together.

On a sniffle into her handkerchief, she told herself she'd rather be a little afraid, sharing a train compartment with a lady whose character was questionable, than facing the consequences at home.

5

~~~ ❧ ~~~

Through the tears of her coughing spell, Eve's eyes had changed color from vibrant blue to a softer hue. Luke let her cry out the cigarette smoke until she calmed down, but he didn't relax.

It was her handkerchief that threw him. Namely, the initials sewn on one of the corners. There was a discrepancy. But he wouldn't ask. He didn't need to know about it. Hell, he didn't *want* to know.

According to his map, they should be coming into Nacogdoches in about two hours for a fueling stop. There, it would be *adios* to Eve Pierce. He was convincing her to head back to Beaumont. And he could be damn persuasive when push came to shove.

"Would you like some dinner, Mrs. Smythe?" Back in order, Eve let out a deep breath and gave him a pretty smile that he should have ignored, but couldn't. Each time he looked at her, he stared too long. It shouldn't matter, but he wondered how old she was. He'd guess twenty-four or -five; for a woman past her prime marriageable age, she was still attractive.

Her facial bones were delicate and her wealth of golden hair shined like strands of spun silk. He tried to imagine how long her hair was when it was free of pins. Her mouth was full and a deep rose. Against his will, he wondered how many men had kissed her.

"You can go to the dining car," Eve said, the strength returning to her voice, "and order practically anything you'd like. I was there and the smells are luscious."

Luke wasn't sitting in a dining car. Not even if they were serving imported whiskey and the finest cut of beefsteak. "No, I'm staying here."

Disappointment softened the set of Eve's shoulders. She pressed a hand over her stomach and swallowed with a sigh. He was pretty sure if the rail noise from the train didn't echo through the compartment, he could have heard her hunger pangs. He had a tin of crackers, some jerky, and a few other things to eat in his travel bag.

He said, "But if you want to go, feel free."

"It's usually customary for an employee to follow her employer's lead. If you aren't eating, then I shouldn't."

Luke thought things over in a matter of seconds, then said, "Order me whatever you're hungry for. Get two plates."

Without pause, she agreed. "I'll need your ticket. We have to show our tickets for food."

He handed her Smythe's ticket.

"Wonderful!" she exclaimed. "I'm in the mood for

beef and potatoes. And a slice of apple pie. If they don't have pie, I'll get us some cake."

She turned toward the door and quickly departed.

Within fifteen minutes, she was back juggling a tray. He held the door open for her as she brought in two plates of food. Gravy pot roast, potatoes, relish, bread and a slice of crumb-topped apple pie shoved onto the edges.

She presented the meal to him. "All the trimmings."

Now that he smelled the food, a tin of crackers wasn't going to satisfy him.

"Good thinking, Miss Pierce," he said, closing the door. "I was more hungry than I thought. Let's dig in."

"Dig in?"

It was bad enough he had to sit across from her in a dress; worse yet to constantly foul up what should have been Mrs. Smythe's cultured dialogue.

In one word, he explained his meaning. "Eat."

Standing in the center of the compartment, Eve looked around for a place to set the plate. He realized there was no table to sit at. The bench seat took up the lower corner. The upper was taken by the sink counter that collapsed inside a false wall to give the room more space when it wasn't being used. Neither made a good eating area. That left the floor. Or the bed.

Since his legs were caught up in fabric, maneuvering himself onto a carpet wasn't something he wanted to do. "Right there." He motioned to the bed, sat, and took the tray from her.

She followed him and picked up her utensils.

At first, they ate in silence.

Holding herself with perfect posture, Eve brushed a crumb of bread from her fingers. "I have to say, madam, that this is a strange circumstance. I'm not a seasoned lady's maid, but I think this is unusual. Us sharing a meal on the bed like this."

"What difference do the rules make?" Luke returned, not really understanding her problem. It didn't matter. Nobody was in the room. They were hungry. Who cared. "We can make our own."

Eve gazed at him, thoughtfulness in the depths of her eyes. "You really are a very nice woman." While selecting a wedge of potato, she went on with an observation that had Luke fighting not to laugh. "I'd bet that if you curled your hair differently and perhaps reapplied your powder in another manner that wasn't so thick, you could be almost pretty."

After that piece of advice, she put her hand over her mouth and quit. "Oh, I'm so terribly sorry, madam! It isn't my place to say such a thing. I feel awful. Forgive me!"

Luke couldn't immediately reply. But her thinking that he could be a pretty lady if he rethought his appearance had him feeling the first hint of humor in his heart since he'd left Louisiana. He didn't realize until now how badly he needed something to draw him away from the dark path his life had taken in the past couple of weeks. If only for a matter of short minutes.

"I don't know why I do this," she said. "Sometimes I just talk without thinking. My mother is constantly harping on me that it's a horrible trait and not befitting a woman of my station." She paused, glanced at him and added, "My low station as a lady's maid."

Luke commented as a man who was able to do and say what he wanted, when he wanted. "I think a woman in any station ought to be able to speak her mind."

Eve's surprised expression told him he'd crossed a line somewhere. Either she was in strong disagreement with him, or she was shocked. "Are you in favor of the women's movement? Are you a suffragette?"

"Not personally. But I know a lot of women who are." And that was true.

He'd arrested quite a few suffragettes for disturbing the peace. He couldn't say he had a disdain for them, because he did agree with a lot of what they were trying to gain in a man's world. But there were some real aggressive women troublemakers. They could make him crazy. Once, he'd had to put out a corset fire set on the steps of the local courthouse. He hauled in a group of women for being public nuisances; they had all been in their underwear while protesting a Bourbon Street bar not allowing them to play in a high stakes poker game. Then there was the time a militant march took over the lobby of the Grande Bleu restaurant; they demanded the establishment hire a woman as the chef. He could understand their gripes, but the manner in which they got their points across gave the police department grief.

But to have that kind of grief once more instead of—

"That's so interesting, madam." Eve ate the last bite of bread. "I never would have guessed you for an associate of the liberators. I'd always thought women of that sort were more flamboyant."

"Yeah, well—" Luke primped his wig and adjusted the collar of his frock, "—appearances can be deceiving."

Her hand stilled, and she seemed to have sudden difficulty swallowing. "Yes," she managed in a choke. "That does happen. Sometimes."

Evelyn caught one of the dining service waiters in the hall of their car and had him take their dinner plates and tray. While he balanced the service, Mrs. Smythe spoke from behind her in the doorway.

"Excuse me—yoo-hoo, young man?" Mrs. Smythe trilled. "Do you know when exactly we'll be getting into Nacogdoches?"

"We passed Nacogdoches ten minutes ago."

"What the hell?"

With a start, Evelyn turned around. "Mrs. Smythe?"

Mrs. Smythe gripped the window curtain in her fist and tugged the draperies open as far as they would go. All Evelyn could see was the interior reflection of the room. It was dark outside.

Jerking her head around, Mrs. Smythe remarked tightly, "I thought we were fueling in Nacogdoches."

"No, ma'am. We're running straight through to Dallas."

"*Dammit.*"

Evelyn heard the muttered oath as she closed the door. She pressed her back to it, uncertain what to make of the scathing tone. Mrs. Smythe perplexed her.

One minute a lady, the next coarse and unrefined. She'd never been in the company of another woman like her.

Evelyn broached the subject with caution. "Was there anything in particular you needed in Nacogdoches?"

"No," she barked. "It was more for you."

"Me?" Evelyn blinked with bafflement, and a thread of panic jumped to life in her. Had Mrs. Smythe somehow figured out she was on this train under false pretenses?

"It doesn't matter now," she vented. "We won't hit Dallas until sunrise so we might as well get some shut-eye while we can."

Mrs. Smythe locked the door, checking the bolt twice.

Evelyn's mind faltered. She knew what a lady's maid was supposed to do next, but she was hesitant to do it. Mrs. Smythe's behavior was anything but normal.

Pulling her shoulders back with resolve, Evelyn said, "I'll assist you in undressing for bed."

"No!"

Evelyn stood back, aghast. Well, Mrs. Smythe was certainly a very touchy woman. One minute chatty about suffragettes, and the next, as sour as a glass of unsweetened lemonade. But then Evelyn remembered the symptoms of the change of life and attributed the alteration in personality to her suspected medical condition. "I'm sorry. I don't have to if you don't want me to."

A probing query came into the woman's eyes, and

for the shortest of moments, Evelyn thought she saw something more. A piece of emotion that didn't match the feminine hair and powder. As if they were merely cosmetic props to hide the real person. She couldn't put her finger on it. She couldn't even understand why such a feeling of bewilderment would well inside her. But there really was something different. Something revealed. She couldn't pinpoint what it was, but it made her aware of just how sheltered she'd been.

"I'm not myself these days," Mrs. Smythe said, confirming Evelyn's conclusion of ill health. "I'd like you to unpack my trunks for me now."

Slowly nodding, Evelyn lowered to the carpet and lifted the lids. Glad for a task to take her away from Mrs. Smythe's gaze, she folded the petticoats and chemises and put them into the bureau drawers. She placed them the way she preferred hers to be organized, and she made sure the stockings were in sets and rolled to a soft tightness. When she reached the three dresses, something seemed out of the ordinary, yet she made no immediate connection with anything.

As she was lifting out a pair of satin pumps, paper caught on her knuckle and she felt a rip. Horrified, she looked inside the trunk to see she'd torn a package of Mrs. Smythe's. "I'm so sorry, madam. It was an accident."

"What was it?" Mrs. Smythe looked over her shoulder at the tiny parlor paintings by Charles Leyster.

Evelyn easily recognized the style from the large painting of *The Blue Lady* her father hung in his study by one and the same. Leyster's use of watercolor was unsurpassed.

"Your paintings." Evelyn gently picked them up and tried to rewrap them with the edges of the paper. "May I say, they're exquisite, Mrs. Smythe. A real treasure to have. Leyster is to be admired and complimented on his talent."

"Oh, yes. He's a wonderful, wonderful artist." She clapped her hands in the same way Mother's parlor ladies did when she sang a solo for them with piano accompaniment—with the tips of her fingers from one hand tapping the palm of her other in slight little motions. "Just wonderful! Oh my, yes. I adore him."

In an orderly fashion, Evelyn had everything stored in its place. She rose to her feet with nothing left to do but ready herself for bed.

"Well . . . I suppose I'll . . ." The words trailed.

Mrs. Smythe's examination of her made her feel awkward. Her stomach grew unsettled, and it wasn't from the dinner or nerves. After several long seconds, Evelyn could bear the deep gray eyes on her face no longer, and she asked in a high-pitched rush, "Is there something wrong, madam?"

"No."

"All right . . . then." Slowly, she reached for her valise and excused herself to the lavatory. Once inside the tiny space, she sat on the commode seat that was flipped down and rested her face in her hands. This trip was turning into a disaster. Mrs. Smythe was an odd one. And she was stuck with her.

She wouldn't exactly say she was afraid of the woman. She was more confused by her. Nothing had prepared her for dealing with this type of situation. She'd done everything she could to be gracious and pleasant. But Mrs. Smythe had a shortness about her that was unpredictable.

She had to think about what to do. Just how far was El Paso anyway? She'd forgotten to ask the ticket man. Oh—her ticket should show the times. Congratulating herself on her ingenuity, Evelyn read the departure and arrival times on her ticket. They should be in El Paso by Tuesday, 1:48 A.M.

She really had no choice but to accept things until then.

Evelyn stayed in the lavatory as long as respectable, then came out wearing her nightie and robe, as well as felt slippers.

Mrs. Smythe was laying down on her back on the bed. Fully clothed.

Evelyn stopped in her tracks. She covered her bodice with her hand, holding her petit point valise close to her chest. "Aren't you going to change?"

"Insomnia." With an overly dramatic wave of her hand, she explained, "It hits me hard when I travel. I have to get up and walk in the middle of the night. I never wear my nightgown."

In a strange way, that made sense. "Oh."

"Yes, insomnia," Mrs. Smythe repeated. "That's why I sleep in my clothes."

"My Grandfather Jimmy was an insomniac." Evelyn ran her fingertip into her dress collar. She brought out a necklace with a diamond and gold locket. She opened the clasp and revealed a photograph of a dapper-looking man. "This is him." She extended the locket as far as she could on the chain, and Mrs. Smythe gave the portrait a glance. "This is my Grandfather Jimmy. He's gone now, but he was quite smart. For his insomnia, he read what he called 'insufferable' poetry to put him to sleep. It always did the trick."

Mrs. Smythe's harsh features grew surprisingly soft. "I'll take that under advisement."

Evelyn closed the locket and let the chain slip down her gown-front once more.

Reaching over, Mrs. Smythe switched the ceiling light off and the room was cast in a muted darkness; the small boudoir sink light remained on, giving a pale haze to the walls. Above Mrs. Smythe's bed, a berth extended out in a parallel manner. It seemed to have come from nowhere. A ladder went from the top edge to the floor.

"I pulled out the bed for you," Mrs. Smythe said. "You're such a small thing, you probably couldn't manage the cord."

Evelyn didn't know what or where the cord was.

Before going up, she took her hair down and ran her brush through it less than half the time she normally did. She returned her brush and comb set to her valise, then stretching on tiptoes, she took the valise and set it on her bed. Carefully placing her foot on the bottom rung, she gave Mrs. Smythe a polite smile. "Good night, then, madam."

"Good night."

Making sure her nightgown wouldn't get caught in her feet and trip her, she slowly climbed the ladder with her hem high at her knees. Once she was in her bed, she laid on her back and hugged her valise to her side.

While the day had been long and eventful, she was

unable to fall asleep. She should have been exhausted, but her mind went in various directions as she thought of what was ahead for her. What she had left behind.

Eventually, the motion of the car as it clacked and rumbled over the rails soothed her to drowsiness. But just as she was about to doze off into sleep, she sat upright.

It finally came to her what was wrong with those trunks.

The satin pump shoes. They weren't Mrs. Smythe's size. Nor were the dresses. They were both too small.

Her heartbeat rose to a frantic level as she eased back into the linens and covered them up to her chin.

Just *who* was Mrs. Smythe?

6

ast night, Luke had noted the fine quality of
Eve's picture locket. A certain sparkling shine
came from diamonds and real gold; the jewelry
wasn't an item he would have expected a lady's maid
to own.

He'd noticed something else about Eve, too. Her
legs as she slowly took the rungs of the ladder. She
had the kind of shapely calves, smooth knees and nice
thighs to get a man's imagination going.

When she'd come out dressed in a nightgown and
robe, he hadn't been prepared for the sight of her in
flowing white. The frilly stuff looked expensive and
soft to touch, as well as not being affordable on her
salary.

Things about her weren't stacking up. The fine
linen hankie. The way she moved. Talked. Her
demeanor. Her clothes.

And this morning he'd gotten a few answers as to
why not.

It had only been a matter of seconds that she'd been gone to find him some strong coffee. In her absence, he'd snooped inside her valise. There was another handkerchief with the initials *E.B.* Not a match yet again, given she'd stated her last name as starting with a "P." She had a mirror cast out of silver to match the silver hair set. An engraved compact for powder was solid gold. The satin underwear did set off a warning light. So did a rich-textured blouse, an embroidered skirt and a dress made out of what his mother referred to as silk crepe.

And really odd were all the road maps with the pen markings on them. Maps of Texas, Arizona, New Mexico, Utah. California. The one for California had a heart drawn on the cover in red ink. Yeah, *odd.*

But by far, the most damning evidence was in her purse. He didn't count all the money, but in a quick fan of bills, he guessed she had to have over a grand.

He didn't know who or what she was, but he highly suspected she'd ripped off some unsuspecting woman and was on the lam with her goods.

He didn't need this: another person being hunted by the law. If they caught Eve, he didn't want to be anywhere near her.

Pushing down an oath, Luke checked the time on his wristwatch. Dallas would be coming up soon. He had to shave.

His reflection in the mirror showed the signs of a heavy beard that no amount of powder could hide. He was lucky to get twelve hours being Smythe without sprouting facial hair on the woman.

Luke twisted the water faucet and lathered his face.

Methodically and precisely, he ran a razor over his skin and was wiping off the soap from his neck as the door latch jiggled. He'd locked it as soon as Eve left.

As he hung up the towel, her voice came through to him.

"Mrs. Smythe? Oh, Mrs. Smythe?"

Taking a fast check of his appearance, he didn't readily answer her.

She knocked again.

"Mrs. Smythe. Oh, dear me. Mrs. Smythe?"

A series of frantic knocks followed, and he narrowed his eyes on the door as she became impatient. "Mrs. Smythe. You need to open the door. Right now."

Evelyn should have taken her valise with her. What had she been thinking? That was the trouble—she hadn't been thinking. She never had to be responsible for a large sum of money; everything she purchased was put on her father's credit accounts.

Without credit at her disposal, her escape money was tucked inside her purse. She'd given herself an advance from her father's safe after spending half the night trying to get the combination right. She'd tried every number sequence she knew of that had importance to him and finally hit upon the right combination at two o'clock in the morning. While taking the stacks of bills, she'd had a guilty conscience. But hadn't her father always said that everything that was his was going to be hers one day?

"Open the door, please," Evelyn called once more.

Mrs. Smythe wasn't answering, and as each second ticked off, the more Evelyn's pulse raced.

She'd woken up this morning after a fretful night, and Mrs. Smythe was still in bed with the coverlet over her head. Muttering from beneath the bed linens, the giant woman had said she needed coffee right away.

Evelyn had quickly dressed with one thought on her mind: To tell a railroad official there might very well be an imposter in her compartment.

But as soon as she reached the dining car, she realized she couldn't say anything. Her plan not only doomed Mrs. Smythe—or whoever she was—but it also doomed her. She ran the risk of bringing her own real identity to light.

Facing that quandary, she'd raced back to 4B without the coffee and with an intense purpose fueling her steps. All she could do was collect her valise, then disembark in Dallas before the brakes were even firmly engaged.

Evelyn knocked on the door until her knuckles hurt. The longer it went unanswered, the more she feared the worst had happened. Mrs. Smythe had found her money and made off with it.

Her breath came in tight gasps, and she nearly fell into the room as the door suddenly opened. Mrs. Smythe stepped aside and Evelyn came forward.

"Oh thank heavens," she gushed as she saw her valise still on her bed where she'd left it. "I was knocking and knocking. What took you so long to answer the door?"

Mrs. Smythe stood back, and as stoic as a minister on Sunday, said, "I was occupied."

Staring at the woman, Evelyn noticed a trace of shave lather on the underside of her chin. *Dreaded facial hair?* Or was there another reason for the soap to be there? Her mind couldn't register the significance. She was sick with indecision, and she had to catch her breath or she'd grow dizzy.

Not wanting to faint, she inched toward the bed and came within reach of her valise. Once there, she latched onto the handle with a death grip. The valise safely in her keeping, she sat on Mrs. Smythe's unmade bed. She didn't care if it wasn't hers to sit on.

One burning thought was imprinting itself in her brain.

"Uh, Mrs. Smythe," Evelyn began in a tone she forced to be light. "It was extraordinary to view your Leyster paintings last night. I've never seen one up close before but I've heard about them—the colors are quite unique. Have you owned them long?"

"I just bought them." Mrs. Smythe tugged on her hairpiece revealing more than she should at her ear. *Were those sideburns?*

Tamping down her fears, in her best conversational tone, Evelyn said, "Mr. Leyster gave a show in Beaumont a week ago. I read about it in the newspaper at the maid agency. We all wished we could have met him. Was he as nice as his photograph in the *Beaumont Herald* made him out to be?"

"Charming man. Wonderful artist."

Evelyn had to force her bosom from rising and falling as sheer anxiety rioted through her. She had difficulty staying seated to the spot and not flying out the door screaming.

A stammer filtered itself in her reply. "I-It's nice to know a newspaper wasn't s-stretching the truth about him." There was an unevenness to her words that contradicted every sense wildly spinning out of control within her.

Clearing her throat, Evelyn continued, "Well, then." She rose and forced a calmer air about her that she'd practiced in Miss Hunnewell's school when she and Pinkie arranged a meeting to get out of political science class. "I'll go see if the coffee is ready now. When I was in the dining car earlier, the server told me they were still brewing pots."

Holding fast to her valise, she scooted toward the door with such a friendly smile plastered on her mouth her cheeks ached.

She had to escape.

Heaven help her, she had to tell somebody who she was in the same compartment with. She'd figured it out. Mrs. Smythe was a criminal. A *dangerous* art thief! None other than the evil scoundrel Nate had said the authorities were looking for in Beaumont.

The Leyster paintings. Mrs. Smythe couldn't possibly have talked with Charles Leyster. The artist had died six months ago in a tragic motorcar accident. That's why nothing added up. A trunk with clothing that didn't come close to fitting The Imposter's large frame. Inaccuracies in information. The heavy powder. The hairpiece. Everything pointed to deception. For all Evelyn knew, the woman could be armed and had no qualms about shooting.

But how could Evelyn inform the authorities without getting involved with the police herself?

She'd . . . she'd write a note! She'd write a note and give it to Nate, and have him hand the list of incriminating evidence directly over to the skipper. Amid all that chaos, she'd be slipping off the train.

"Wait!" came Mrs. Smythe's call.

Evelyn swallowed hard. "Yes?"

"I like cream in mine, dear."

Laughing slightly hysterically, she nodded without looking at The Imposter. "Certainly, madam."

Then she hurried out of the room with her valise and without a backward glance.

Still wearing ladies' clothing, Luke held onto his travel bag; he'd left the compartment minutes after Eve. He abandoned Smythe's trunk, leaving a note on it that said "Return to the Imperial Hotel in Beaumont, Texas," and moved forward with calculated steps.

He was jumping off the train before they pulled into Dallas.

After the way Eve reacted to him this morning, he couldn't risk her talking to some railroad official. She'd had that wild and skittish look in her eyes—like the first time he saw her in the compartment. Not only could she be dragging the law behind her, she was up to something that gave him a bad feeling.

Although it would have been faster to reach New Mexico by train, he had no choice but to continue on by a different method of transportation.

Walking headlong through each car, he kept his focus forward and his eyes on the vestibule doors as they came. They were made up of a small enclosed platform with a thick leather appendage he couldn't break through without jimmying the locking devices. There was only one place he could get off fast.

The open-platform observation lounge.

In this case, it was furnished on the Pullman No. 10. He'd already checked it when he came aboard the train. There was a green leather ceiling hood that could be opened or closed, and a four-foot-high railing of wrought iron that didn't cut into the passengers' view when they sat. A gate was on either side of the platform so that when the train was stationary, travelers could disembark from that area as well as the accordion enclosures between the rest of the cars.

As he crossed through the No. 10, he felt the motion of the train begin to slow down slightly. People started to gather their belongings from the observation car that not only had a viewing area, but tall glass windows. Seats were crushed velvet and were reserved for extra-fare ticket holders. Richly suited men and highbrow women pressed into the aisle, organizing hat boxes, packages, and business cases, making it difficult for Luke to get through.

Once he reached the end, he turned the latch on the door and exited the car. Relief flooded his body when he saw that nobody stood on the platform. For what he planned on doing, he didn't need any witnesses.

Even though the Lone Star Limited was losing its steam coasting into Dallas, the train still careened at a fairly good speed. He figured they were five minutes from stopping. Wind whipped the wig's black curls into his face, and he shoved them out of his eyes. The brim on his flower hat flapped and irritated him while he looked over the railing at the gravel and railroad ties beneath him. They passed in a blur of gray and oiled brown.

Holding onto the metal gate at the side of the car, he gazed at the ground speeding beneath him. He took in several sharp breaths. This was his only chance.

Evelyn shoved the note at Nate in the No. 3 car and exclaimed, "Read that right now!"

Then she ran all the way to the back end of the train.

The rocking pushed her into the side of the doorway. She fought to keep her footing secure. With the wind blowing underneath the leather hood, her heartbeat sped like the engine. She would wait here, partially inside the doorway.

She made a quick survey of the observation car's interior.

That man in the last seat, standing with a work case.

She knew him! She knew the gray suit and coat. The black as coal felt derby and the silver-capped lion's head walking stick. It was Mr. Vanderhoff, one of Daddy's closest business associates. He'd recognize her immediately. He'd been to their house countless times.

She moved to turn away, but she put herself in motion too late. She met his eyes for only an instant.

"Evelyn?"

The call of her name made her stomach turn over.

Gazing pointedly at her face, he came toward her.

Whirling out of the corridor, she stumbled through the open door.

The voice followed her. "I say there—Evelyn Baron, is that you?"

Once on the platform, the maid's cap flew off her head in the wind and she saw she wasn't alone.

Mrs. Smythe!

She'd flipped the safety lock from the outside and was swinging the door open with her skirts pulled up.

Gracious, she was going to jump!

Evelyn's valise handle was hooked loosely through the crook of her arm, and she kept her hand in a vise-like hold on the railing. From the velocity of the train, she feared she'd fly right off the end of the car.

Right along with The Imposter.

"Evelyn, what are you doing?" A firm hand slammed over her elbow.

She tilted her head at Mr. Vanderhoff. "Let go of me!" She gave an irritated tug on her sleeve where he held her, but she couldn't break free.

Sharp and assessing, his eyes practically sliced right through her. "What the dickens are you doing dressed in that maid's costume?"

She couldn't answer. A shiver clutched her. She grew quite cold even though the wind gave off heat like a flatiron; the oddly chilling sensation penetrated through her clothes. She envisioned being dragged back to Oiler. In complete disgrace in her parents' eyes. Facing her father. Guy Hadley. Marriage. Doom. A life shackled to the Texhoma Oil Company.

Thoughts of her dismal future erupted before her in a veil of darkness that closed her throat. She felt as if she were suffocating.

No! She wasn't going home!

"Let go of me!" she repeated. Her voice was icy and exact. She dragged in a deep breath and braced herself to use every ounce of strength she had to pull away.

Only she didn't have to pull. She was *being* pulled. In the opposite direction. To Mrs. Smythe. The woman had grabbed her by the wrist. The contact was startling. It felt like an electric shock reverberating through her.

The next thing she knew, she was flying through a hot current of air and letting out a scream so hideous it scared her worse than the fall which was going to crush every bone in her body.

7

Evelyn landed on top of Mrs. Smythe, who took the brunt of the impact as they landed on a patch of tall dry grass. Their legs were tangled in a twist of skirts, and the top of Evelyn's head got tucked beneath Mrs. Smythe's chin. Evelyn's left hand rested on something lumpy.

The buzz of insects filled her ears. The vibration from the train as it gripped the thick iron rails shook the ground beneath them. Slowly, the tremor faded until there was no trace of it.

Dazed, Evelyn tried to move. Everything inside her felt brittle and battered. Shifting slightly, she winced. She didn't think she'd broken or sprained anything. A miracle.

"We're alive," she whispered in amazement. Then confused anger set in as she thought of what had just happened. "You—you pulled me off the train with you. You made me jump."

Mrs. Smythe didn't answer.

With effort, Evelyn pushed herself up through the throbbing scrapes to her elbows, seeing nothing but blond curls. "You could have killed us both. We could be lying here dead." She brushed aside a curl from her eyes and stared at a face that was not—

Evelyn heard her voice, stiff and unnatural, through an expression she'd heard her father say on many occasions: "Holy cow!"

Mrs. Smythe was no lady!

The person she was sandwiched up to was a—*man*. Gone was the hat. The wig. She now picked up on the eye color being deeper than she thought, and absolutely more intense as *he* gazed at her with a wince of pain on his mouth. That mouth! The one she'd thought looked soft. A harsh rip at the dress's high-collar neckline revealed a heavily corded neck. Definitely not a feminine attribute. And now that she was looking hard, she saw the telltale Adam's apple as he worked through a tightness in his jaw to swallow. Then he made a deep grunting sound.

Her fingers curled. As her left hand closed, she inadvertently squeezed the lump beneath her palm. It was soft and mushy. Was it—a bosom? As if she'd been burned by her curl iron, she jerked her hand away.

Frantic to break out of their entanglement, she tried to get her legs off of his so she could stand up and put some distance between them.

"Not so fast." The first words he'd spoken as a man, and they were resonant and deep without the slightest bit of "trill" to them.

Riotous fear soared inside her. If he was loose-screwed enough to jump off a train, he'd have no qualms about snuffing out her life. "Uh, don't worry. I-I won't tell anyone about your fetish to dress like a woman."

His brows slanted in a sharp frown. "I don't have any damn fetish. But I've got *you* draped over me like a blanket and I'm still asking myself—why?"

His tone worried her. She tried to wriggle free. His wide hands clamped onto her shoulders and held her still. The wild beat of her heart knocked against her ribs.

The corner of his mouth curled, and not with amusement. "In a moment I will never understand, I saved you from that man. So you'd better tell me who in the hell he was."

"Th-That man?" she stammered. Why would he care about Mr. Vanderhoff?

Mrs. Smythe—whoever—put slight pressure into the tender curve where her neck muscles blended into her narrow shoulders. He was hurting her but he obviously didn't care because when he glared, he meant business.

"What kind of rap sheet do you have? Bunko? Fanning? Pennyweighter? Safe blower? Was that your accomplice grabbing onto you?"

She forgot about the throb in her shoulders and the pressure of his hands. "My accomplice? I'm no thief— you are."

He denied it in a half-laugh. "I'm not a hoister."

She had no inkling as to what a hoister was, but she knew one sure thing and she spoke it.

"The Leyster paintings." She gulped after the accusation, daring herself to say something further and risk having her life snuffed out in seconds. He'd insulted her intelligence. "You think I'm a nitwit, but you're the nitwit. Charles Leyster died six months ago. You said you met him. Well, you'd had to have dug him up in order to have a conversation. And even then it would have been one-sided."

Realizing she'd really tempted fate, she gave an abrupt jerk to her shoulders to extricate herself, but his hands wouldn't budge. He had her in an unbreakable grip.

She wasn't going to let him end her blaze of freedom before she'd even enjoyed it.

Thinking fast, she slid her knee up and aimed for the area between his legs. The unconventional etiquette instructor—not formally hired for the job—who'd taught her the move had been their cook. A bossy old woman who always said a lady had to be prepared for any situation.

The length of hardness nestled where his privates were practically cracked her kneecap when she pressed into it as damaging as she could. Shocked by the definition of maleness, she quickly thought: The cook had never told her men were built like a rod of steel. But whatever the case, the end result was satisfying.

"*Arrrggghhhh!*" came the man's groan.

Hah! Unmitigated success.

He gritted his even white teeth, and instantly, his hold slackened. She scrambled out from his clutches and rose to her feet. Staggering backward, she looked down at him with guilty triumph. She'd never purposefully harmed anyone before.

She had to get her valise and get away before he recovered. She took in the immediate area around them. Small rocks. Dry brush. Reddish soil. Tall brown grasses. Stunted junipers. But no pretty petit point, English Garden pattern valise with all her belongings.

Doing her best to ignore the growing terror coursing in her blood, she told herself to be calm. It was here. Somewhere. She just couldn't see it.

Scouring the area, she assessed everything. She batted at branches and looked behind rocks large enough to conceal a lady's valise. Nothing turned up. How could it not be here? She'd had the handle looped through her arm when Mrs. Smythe had pulled her with him. She was sure of it. But she didn't remember what happened next.

Her eyes slammed closed, and she pressed her fingertips to her forehead. She could sift through the details and make sense out of them. Remember. Step by step. She'd felt the wind surround her. Then the current rise beneath her feet. Then the solid thunk of Mrs. Smythe's—rather, *his*—chest cushioning her when they fell. But what came before it?

Think back, Evelyn.

Arguing with Mr. Vanderhoff. Momentary indecision. But her mind's eye image of her and Guy Hadley sharing a wedding portrait had soured her stomach as if she'd eaten a rotten apple. That had spurred her into action. There had been that forceful pull on her elbow by Mr. Vanderhoff as he attempted to restrain her. In a half second, she was free of him and flying out the gate of the observation car. With the criminal. But without her valise.

Oh dear heaven. Oh dear. Oh my. Oh no.

Mr. Vanderhoff had her valise. It had to have slid off her arm when she broke free of him. The handle had probably gone right into his hand. Everything was gone. Clothing, personal items, and her . . . a sob wrenched itself from her throat . . . her money.

The realization sunk in, and Evelyn sat on a rock and put her hand over her eyes to shield them from the blinding Texas sun. Without money, she was going nowhere. How could she have ever cursed its existence in her life? She'd just lost $1,456.39 neatly tucked away in her leather purse, which was in her valise.

A shudder made the breath she exhaled grow choppy. She was past the point of crying. She thought about it, though. The only thing that stopped her from falling apart was something more dismal than her missing money. It was the fact that Mr. Vanderhoff had recognized her on the train.

She wondered if the train had screeched to a stop somewhere not far from here or it had continued on the short distance to Dallas. The Lone Star Limited could be backing up right now to come collect her, or it had arrived in the depot and a lawman and an anxiously baying bloodhound was sniffing her out. Although, all that she heard was dead calm quietly mixed with the sound of dread in her ears.

Mr. Vanderhoff would give her father the evidence of her being on that train—her valise. Her father would find out she'd been on her way to El Paso and send that gumshoe of his, Cecil Woodworth, after her. No doubt about it, with her clothing as proof, the

money in her purse, and her initials on her handkerchief, she—*Oh great!*

Her maps. Her precious road maps. Now that she
could actually use them, they were gone.

She propped her elbows on her knees and hunched
forward. A pebble in her shoe cut into her heel and she
lifted her skirt and kicked off her step-in Cuban-
heeled shoe. She had a hole in her stocking at her big
toe.

A shadow passed over her.

"Nice foot." The tall, broad-shouldered man had
risen and stood in front of her with his ridiculous gray
dress all in a twist at the arm seams and distorted
waist. The garment was ripped in several places. The
rice powder on his face had smeared and was taken
over by reddish dust on his right cheek. "Nice toes."

She could no longer maintain any decorum at all.
"Be quiet. Just be quiet." He didn't know half the trouble she was in. He didn't know— "Wait, what do you
think you're doing?" she asked in a rush.

His hands had lifted to the neckline of his tired
dress, and he was pulling apart the bodice with a
swift tug. Pearl buttons flew in different directions.
He lowered the shoulders and quite a few pairs of
socks fell to the ground. *The false bosom.* Revealed
was his wide chest covered by a black cotton shirt,
soft and closely woven, with a neck placket—the top
two buttons were unfastened. With a jerk, the dress
came down to his waist.

Gray fabric slid off his hips, and she feared he was
wearing a set of pantalets. She didn't want to see what
she'd smacked with her knee. With a squeak, she

turned away, only to be pulled back by his biting laughter.

"What's the matter, honey?" His dark eyes bore down on her. "Never seen a gun before?"

Darting her eyes to the vicinity of his privates, she saw a revolver encased in a long holster. He adjusted the gun belt to where the weapon rested firmly against his taut thigh instead of between his legs. It was then she noticed he filled out a pair of denim trousers with hardly a spare inch of fabric.

"You may have gotten the gun with your knee, but you still got a piece of me." In a warning voice, he added, "Don't ever do that again."

With a firm jerk, he tore a wedge of fabric from the dress and used it to brush off the grime and paint on his face. In spite of his ragtag appearance, beneath it, she sensed, was a polished veneer. No doubt, he was a virile man. She'd been blinded by the disguise—one she acknowledged now as being thin, at best.

As he rubbed the dirt from his collar, she noticed his hands without lady's gloves for the first time. The skin on top of his wrists was seasoned by sun and perhaps the leather of reins.

"Your name obviously isn't Mrs. Smythe."

Without looking at her, he commented, "Right."

"What is it?"

"Just 'mister' to you."

"Of course you won't give me an honest answer. You're someone notorious, and we both know it. You just want me to—" She cut herself short as a thought burst into her mind. An art thief, yes, but perhaps something much, much more heinous. "Oh my goodness— What did you do with the real Mrs. Smythe?"

"Nothing."

"I-I don't believe you." Fright worked its way back up her spine. She couldn't make any sudden moves. Don't give him any reason to suspect she was ready to dash away in an instant. Evelyn pushed herself onto her feet, stepped back into her shoe, and grew poised to run. "You have Mrs. Smythe's valuable paintings. You have her trunk. You have her identity. You could have harmed her or done worse." She gulped. "You . . . you killed her for the paintings." The muscles in her legs quivered, burned.

"I could have."

Double holy cow!

"But I didn't. I don't heist art. Smythe is an art collector. Frankly, I thought those paintings were ugly."

"That's your opinion, but I know the value of a Leyster. They're worth a small fortune. And you had them."

"Well, they're not worth a damn to me and they're on their way back to the real Mrs. Smythe. I left a note on the trunk to return them to Beaumont."

"You left a note, too?"

His eyes narrowed. "What do you mean 'too'?"

"Nothing. No, I didn't leave a note."

His mouth clamped and his expression turned sardonic. "Why is it, I don't believe you? Maybe because of your valise."

A pull of hope tugged at her. Perhaps she'd miscalculated. "You have my valise? Where is it?"

"I don't know, and I don't care." He began to walk, and his next words trailed behind him. "No great loss—the fancy stuff wasn't yours anyway. I saw what you had in there."

Aghast, she called out, "You looked through my things?"

Evelyn propelled herself after him. He walked faster than she with no extra effort. She'd swear his legs were twice the length of hers. One of his steps made her take two hops to catch up.

"Just trying to figure out who you are." His voice was low and smooth. "You're sure as hell no lady's maid. Even I can tell that and I've never had one."

"If you looked through my things, then you saw—"

"Your foo-fee handkerchief with your initials on it—E.B.?"

She was going to say "underwear," but the detail on the handkerchief was worse than him seeing the pink roses on her chemise. And she only had herself to blame. She'd all but waved it in front of his face when she had that coughing spell from the cigarette. Details. She'd been careless.

He slanted a quick glance at her face. "That's odd. You said your name was Eve Pierce. With a P."

Evelyn grappled for a plausible explanation to steer him away from the truth. "I sent a wire to the seamstress that said I wanted 'E.P.' They must have spilled something on the paper and blurred the ink. The P ran into a B."

A deep chuckle broke into the cry of a mockingbird roosting in a nearby evergreen. "Save it for somebody stupid. I'm not your guy. This is where we say goodbye, *dear*. I go my way and you go whatever way isn't my way."

Evelyn's mouth dropped open. He was leaving her, heading away from the railroad tracks and not staying parallel to them. Disoriented, she didn't know which direction led to Dallas. She didn't want to be anywhere near him either, but she also didn't want to mistakenly walk back to Beaumont. Then again—

That's right!

A thought leaped to life in her.

"Wait!" she shouted at his back as she ran to catch up. "Wait a minute. You're not going anywhere without me. You owe me one thousand four hundred and fifty-six dollars and thirty-nine cents, and I want it back right now."

That stopped Luke cold. He looked down at the petite woman with a wealth of golden curls and the smudge of dirt on her pointed chin. For being so slight, she looked ready to take him on.

"It's your fault I don't have any money. If you hadn't pulled me off the train with you, I'd still be there with over one thousand dollars in my purse."

"If I hadn't pulled you off—hell, I should have left you on it. I was insane to think you *needed* my help."

"Well, I didn't. I had everything under control. I was planning on getting off in Dallas. Respectably. Like a regular passenger. Down the exit steps of the observation car since it was the last car on the track and I could then—" She chewed the end of the thought, literally, by a catch to the lower lip with her teeth. He saw a quick glimpse of white. "In any case, it doesn't matter. Nate's read my note by now—"

Luke's gut clamped down. "Hold on. You said you didn't write a note."

"I lied."

"No surprise. So what was in the note?"

"I told Nate to report you to the train officials. That you were an imposter. Not Mrs. Smythe, but a woman who was taking her place."

"Dammit, that was not good," he ground out between clenched teeth. The creases in his palms tingled; his hand hovered over the top of his holster, his thumb brushing the handle of the Colt .38 Super. He wouldn't shoot her, but this was the first time he'd ever been tempted to draw on an unarmed person—just because he felt like the world would be a happier place without them. "So." He nodded. "So, you wanted Nate to get Smythe, huh?" Sarcasm seeped into his words, and he raked his hand through his hair.

"What did you expect me to do? I'm an honest citizen and there was an act of thievery I knew about and it was my duty to tell what I knew. But it doesn't matter. Because I never saw Nate after I gave him the note, but I saw Mr. Vanderhoff—"

"Who's Mr. Vanderhoff?" Luke rubbed deeply at his temple, trying to keep the pain from shooting up into his brain.

"One of my—that is to say . . ." The lip was bit once more, then a soft reply followed, "Just that man who was trying to stop me. A person my father is acquainted with and who will no doubt tell him where he saw me and I'll be looked for and—"

Tossing his travel bag at his feet with disgust, Luke stated in a flat tone, "Excellent."

The blood in his neck vein must have been visibly

pulsing because the bravado she'd been displaying dissipated to a trickle. "W-Why does it matter so much to you about Mr. Vanderhoff?"

In frustration, he kicked a rock with the tip of his boot. The brown missile ricocheted off the trunk of a thorny scrub. "It matters because if what you say is true, you'll have every sheriff in the state coming after you because you're a runaway, mixed-up woman with a daddy who wants her back."

The flutter to her lashes wasn't from something in her eyes. She was on the verge of crying. But he simply didn't care right now.

"Who are you—*really?*" He looked briefly at her; in speculation he said, "The cook's daughter? The chauffeur's daughter? Daddy and you work out a plan to steal from m'lady—the one with the 'E.B.' initials?" The long, deep breath he took didn't help the tight knots in his aching back tendons begging for release. When they'd hit the ground, he'd felt the impact right to his bones. "All that stuff in your valise wasn't yours and you know it."

She was silent for a long while, as if contemplating lying further. So it sort of surprised him when she confessed, "You're right. I am the chauffeur's daughter and . . . yes, those were my mistress's things." A gleam of determination relit in her eyes. "*But*, the money was mine. I swear to you on my Grandma Katherine's grave, I will be—*am*—entitled to it."

A second silence engulfed them. He tried weighing the whole structure of events from the minute he'd seen her. Nothing had ever added up about her. Half of it still didn't. But the fact was, Luke didn't really care whose money she'd had in her valise. He had to move on. Quickly. Henry could be getting antsy in one place, and Luke might miss him in Silver City—if he was there at all. Talking in circles with Eve was wasting time.

"Okay," he said. "You convinced me." He bent down and picked up his travel bag. "I won't see you around."

"Just a moment, that still doesn't change the fact that my money is missing. Without it, I can't get anywhere."

He pointed at her legs. "Those are free. Start walking"—he aimed in the direction of the sunrise while he was headed for the sunset—"that way."

Without another comment, Luke set off again. A cobalt blue sky stretched high overhead, while brush scattered out before him. In the immediate distance, the trees grew thicker. He knew this side of Dallas had a countryside park at the edge of town. Oak Lawn Park or something. Those trees must mean there was water ahead. Some kind of moderate population. He was going to get a horse and head north on the flatland.

An armadillo waddled ahead of them and disappeared with a scatter of pebbles. Eve's arms marched to and fro to keep up the pace. He really hadn't thought he'd seen the last of her. Yet.

He lacked the humor just then to think up something offensive to say. "Thought we said good-bye back there."

"*You* did." She pulled the strings of her maid's apron and threw it onto the ground. All that remained of her uniform was the black dress. "But I—"

"You're done speaking. I believe you're already associated with my gun. Don't make me use it on you."

"You wouldn't. You've had plenty of chances."

When he made no reply, she didn't counter with another remark. Nothing further was exchanged between them and the time was taken by closing the distance between countryside and town.

The grove of maple and oak trees thickened, and the outlines of country houses appeared. From what Luke could see, they were laid out in a grid for people to walk. There were no shops or businesses. Just homes and a school. There was a small lake where rowboats were paddled and an outdoor stage in a park. The dirt beneath his feet changed to pavement.

Nearing an intersection, Luke realized his companion was no longer beside him. Turning, he watched as Eve caught up with an effort. She'd lagged behind, her face red. Wiping her brow with the cuff of her dress, she looked in need of water.

The rumble of motorized transportation vibrated beneath him. Embedded in the cobblestones were rail lines. A street railway system. The trolley appeared with a clang of its bell. The car was painted red with brass trim, and advertisement boards for Neiman-Marcus covered the sides and rear. At the open window was a notice stating the fare was a nickel. The sign on the header above the driver's glass booth read: Hord's Cliff. Luke had no idea where that was but the trolley was headed toward Dallas. Good enough for him.

He fingered a coin from the depth of his pocket and

waited at the corner. Eve came up to him, licking her dry lips. "Thank goodness."

"Yeah, that's what I thought. A ride into the city."

The trolley bell rang and the brakes locked. Luke took the three short steps onto the car and dropped a nickel into the fare box.

Behind him, he heard Eve tell the driver, "He's taking care of my fare."

"Is she with you, mister?" the driver shot back as Luke sat in an open seat.

Stretching out his legs, he replied, "Does she have to be?"

Eve's cheeks brightened. "Oh! Honestly. Never mind. I'm not with him at all. Pardon me, please, driver. If you will, just a moment."

She turned away and subtly slipped a hand down the front of her bodice. In a few seconds, she came up with a bill. She got her change and walked to a front row seat.

The trolley rolled forward, and before long, they were in the midst of city traffic. At the second stop, Eve pulled the cord and stepped down. From the curb, she said in a low voice to Luke, "Never underestimate a woman with emergency money in her corset."

Luke leaned his arm out and directed her to the sign with a point of his finger. "Neiman-Marcus. You can lift a few things in the lady's department."

The glare she gave him could have doused a three-alarm fire.

When the trolley moved into motion, she called out, "You were much nicer as a woman!"

8

————— ❧ —————

While Evelyn Thurgood-Baron was slightly down on her luck, she didn't let that ruin her first visit to a large city. She marveled at the modern wonders of Dallas. The Henderson Building, Guild Building, the Dallas News Building, and E.M. Powell's at 400 Main Street.

At Neiman-Marcus, she'd bought a simple toile dress in Delft blue with a draped black satin belt. Its straight sleeves were three-quarter and touched with lace cuffs. A drape and tuck flounce of toile wrapped around the backside. Unable to resist the subtle elegance of a Madame Colombin, rue de la Tour d'Auvergne chapeaux for young matrons, she purchased that as well. Her heart sang with delight when she found a folding pocket toothbrush. In spite of all the hard walking she'd done, her snappy high-toe, two-strap shoes were in good shape, as were her undergarments. She did have to buy a pair of visiting gloves, purse, and a club satchel from the half-off table. A hairbrush and one ten-cent box of crimped hairpins.

She took her items into the ladies' washroom lounge, freshened up and changed into her new ensemble with renewed excitement over her trip to California. And—with the resolve to put that oafish, dress-wearing criminal out of her mind forever.

After leaving the department store, she'd eaten a juicy hamburger and drank a Coca-Cola at the Metropolitan Bar and Buffet. Paying her bill with what was left from her Dime Box fund, she then looked at the photographs in the corner windows of Church's Photography. She saw the courthouse rising up three stories with a two-story clock tower. From there, she wandered over to Tuttle's Standard Oil filling station. Located blocks away from the bustling and congested intersections, the painted white brick building had a simple, and single, curb pump. Inside, they sold pre-filled cans of kerosene and other cooking fuels. They offered automobile repairs, lubrications, tire replacements and tire servicing. She picked up a road map of Texas and asked directions to the nearest stage line.

Now, as she sat on a hard wooden bench in the Red Crown stage line station waiting for the 3:05 P.M. to Sweetwater, she reflected back on a day that had begun with a series of disasters, but was ending quite nicely. Thanks to her enterprising venture.

And her locket.

Evelyn had negotiated a resaonable price for her necklace at a pawn store on Akard and Pacific. The locket was quality gold with bright diamonds. Her father had given it to her after he hit a new gusher with big results. She had never felt any deep and sentimental attachment to the necklace, but she highly valued the portrait of her Grandfather Jimmy she'd kept inside. The photograph was now in her satchel, and she was once again on the move.

After expenses—including a one-way coach ticket to Sweetwater, she had thirty-six dollars and twenty-two cents left. And the funny thing was, she didn't feel destitute. She felt quite good about her accomplishments.

Being resourceful could actually prove to be a challenge. Look at how well things had worked out in Dallas.

The Red Crown wasn't nearly as large of an outfit as the Wells-Fargo, but it operated a Six-Pass Rockaway pulled by four horses that were being harnessed right now. The coach suited Evelyn just fine after all that walking. Being able to sit and have the comfort of a conveyance made for six, only shared by four, sounded delightful.

When she'd stood in the ticket line, she'd been behind two men and a woman going to Sweetwater, too. Gazing across the room, Evelyn noted the trio sat by the window, not a one of them engaged in conversation. They all wore black and perhaps were on their way to a funeral.

She hoped this leg of her trip would prove uneventful. She'd already had a fair amount of trouble on the Lone Star Limited, not counting the obvious: Mr. Vanderhoff recognizing her. But she just couldn't worry about his appearance on that train. She'd suffered a far worse shock when "Mrs. Smythe" had defrocked her—*him*self. Then he had the nerve to think she was a thief! And the chauffeur's daughter.

She was more saddened by his misconception than anything else. In a way, she was more Thompson's daughter than she was her father's. It was he who discussed daily issues in the newspaper, and who let her watch him spit and polish a hubcap. He'd shown her how to make a blade of grass screech when you held it between your thumbs just right and blew on it. Thompson had taught her the trivialities of life. And with all of that, her knowledge still wasn't vast.

She'd been utterly heartbroken when her father had dismissed him two years ago for no good reason. But she knew. Deep down, she knew why. Her father resented Thompson . . . and their relationship, in which he could gain her attention and respect.

"Sweetwater!" came the porter's cry and Evelyn was glad to get up and move. Her feet had fallen asleep. The four of them boarded, both women facing front as was protocol, while the two men sat across from Evelyn and the woman who had been introduced as Marcella Graves. The gentlemen were her husband, Filbert, and her husband's brother, Gregory.

The coach got under way, and with the monotonous rocking motion, Evelyn drifted off to a half-sleep—that place where a person is conscious of what is going on around them, but they dream. Her dreams were nothing but fuzzy visions of an ugly woman in a gray dress and the two of them jumping off a train. They flew and flew through the air but never landed on the ground.

The tufted plum leather sides of the Rockaway's interior were not well padded, nor soundly built. The squab was hard and uncomfortable. A broken arm handle above her head knocked at the crown of her large-brimmed hat whenever the carriage wheels bounced off a hole in the rutted road. It was that *whack* of the leather strap tail that pulled her out of her light sleep. She woke feeling worse than when she'd dozed off.

After discreetly yawning behind her gloved hand, she attempted a smile at the other passengers. But they made no kind of facial, nor vocal, response. Their faces remained stoic while their hands stretched out tensely on their knees. All three of them. Like they had to keep themselves from pouncing on one another. The gentlemen's green eyes were frosty, and the woman's were nervously darting from man to man.

Evelyn scooted farther into her corner of the coach, wishing she'd had a book to read to distract her. Instead, she lifted the edge of the shade on the half-open glass window.

The landscape was marked by broad expanses of plains and broken prairies that grew few trees. She wondered what she would find in Sweetwater. She'd been informed it was a small cattle town.

On that thought, she went to reach for her club satchel at her feet to get the map and see if she could figure out the mileage they'd traveled. Just as she leaned forward, Mr. Filbert Graves erupted with, "How long have you been having an affair with my wife, you bastard?"

Startled, Evelyn quickly straightened. She took in a

quick breath of utter astonishment. She stared at Gregory Graves's now ashen face, tensely awaiting his answer while the woman in black taffeta beside her said nothing.

Gregory said at last, "Your marriage with Marcella has been over for months."

"You bastard!" Then at his wife, "You whore."

Evelyn pressed her knees together, and clasped her hands tightly in her lap. Oh dear. With rapid motion, she looked first at Filbert, quickly at Marcella, then darted back to Gregory. Then out the window—as if deeply engrossed in the desert flora. But of course it was obvious she'd heard them; yet how did one put themselves out of further hearing distance in the space of a coach?

"Filbert, you're a complete fool," Gregory said, "only you've been too absorbed in your position as the chief iron and pipe purchaser to see it. All you care about is gaining favoritism with the workers."

"How dare you," Filbert countered in an ominous tone of voice. "Our father left Graves and Graves Waterworks to the both of us, and if it weren't for me, you'd be out on the streets with nothing."

"Perhaps." Gregory's calm demeanor boasted a true confidence as he added, "I'd say it's better to be indoors if the company you keep is to your liking. *And pleasure.*"

With that, Evelyn shot her gaze at the woman, as did Filbert. As did Gregory.

"Tell him, Marcella," Gregory insisted.

"Yes, tell me, *my dove.* I need to hear it from your lips." Filbert's rakish hat had been lifted away from his forehead and a shock of thick blond hair fell at his brow—a brow that was lifted in a dangerous arch. "How long have you been sleeping with my brother?"

Marcella showed the first signs of true fright. She licked her rose-tinted lips, fought to keep her delicate chin level, and replied, "I don't think this is the proper time to discuss this."

"You obviously don't care what's *proper.* So tell me. Why?"

"I was lonely . . . Filbert, I didn't mean for this to happen." Inhaling, she confessed, "But I love your brother, and he loves me."

"Damn you!" he bellowed. "Damn you *both* straight to hell!"

Eyes wide, Evelyn pressed her shoulder as firmly into the corner as she could. She didn't want to be near them by even an extra half inch.

"Don't damn her, Filbert," Gregory stated. "She's a lady and should be treated as such."

"Treated as such?" The bluster in Filbert's huff could have blown out the candles on a birthday cake. "By taking you into her bed?"

"Actually, I took Marcella into *your* bed those times you were in Dallas on business."

The hot color on Filbert's face deepened to the red of Cook's tomato bisque. He slowly turned so he could face his brother directly, and then shoved his hand into his broadcloth coat. A small but menacing derringer came out of a pocket in his suit lining and was aimed at Gregory.

Evelyn's gasp was muffled in the fabric of her glove as she covered her mouth in terror. She couldn't take her eyes off the barrel as Filbert cocked the gleaming hammer with precision. The noise the click made seemed to sound ten decibels higher than the highest note on the stately pipe organ in Oiler's only Episcopal church. Filbert meant business.

Marcella reached out. "Filbert! For the love of God, put that away. You don't mean to use it."

"Don't I?" Filbert's eyes shined with evil intent.

Everything inside Evelyn tensed. She quickly wondered if she had the ability to jump off of the Rockaway like she had the train. But how could she? There was nobody to yank her out. She'd have to jump on her own and be at the mercy of—

"Please, Filbert," Marcella implored. *"Don't do it."*

"Don't waste your time, Marcella," Gregory said, not looking the slightest bit worried. "He wouldn't do it. All his life he's had no backbone. Why do you think you came to me? You needed a man and I—"

"Don't say that!" Marcella cried as she lunged toward her husband when he put his finger over the trigger.

Evelyn covered her head with her arms.

Bam!

The shot reverberated through the interior of the coach and Evelyn braced herself for the worst. Tensing every muscle in her body, she held her breath. But she didn't feel a bullet pierce her flesh. She hadn't accidentally been hit. The only sounds in the coach were those of the horses' shod foot-claps over the earth, and that of her irregular breathing echoing through her ears.

Cautiously lowering her arms, she couldn't tell if

Gregory was dead or not. Chaos abounded. Gregory's black-clad body was upright in the corner as he struggled with his brother over possession of the gun. Their hands were interlocked, the derringer still in Filbert's grasp. Evelyn had no place to duck. No place to hide. Marcella was pleading to the both of them and trying to break them apart. Another shot exploded from the gun.

Within seconds, Evelyn felt the speed of the coach drastically slow down. The driver must have heard the shot, and he was coming to apprehend both men and put a stop to their reckless behavior. In the meantime, she wasn't going to sit around like a lame duck and wait for the next round.

While the Rockaway was still rolling, Evelyn reached her arm out the window and fumbled for the door handle. Finding it, she clicked it downward, and flung the door open. She went to her feet and spilled out of the coach in a frantic twist of skirt and petticoats, barely landing upright from the motion of coach and ground underneath her feet at the same time.

She ran to catch up with the red and gold painted coach that had stopped in its tracks without the aid of the brake lever. Looking up at the box to the seasoned man in fringed rawhide sitting atop the bench seat, she put a hand over her wildly beating heart.

"They were shooting!" she called to the driver. "One of them has a gun! Filbert Graves! He's inside and—"

Without acknowledging her, the driver leaned to his right, then fell over and onto the floor of the high deck.

"Oh my goodness!" Evelyn reached for the handle behind the front boot on the driver's box. She planted one foot on the bracing, and using the handle to help her, she pulled herself up to the driver's level.

"Mister!" she cried to him, gently putting a hand on his shoulder. Glazed eyes met her worried inquiry.

She saw traces of blood on the buckskin covering the outer side of his ribs. She didn't know a thing about assessing the severity of gunshot wounds. She'd never known anyone who'd been the victim of one. "Get ahold of my Winchester under the bench, then take cover," he muttered. "We're being ambushed."

"Um, no, mister," she uttered in an unsteady tone. "That's not what happened."

"No?"

"There was an argument in the coach between two of the gentlemen passengers, and a gun belonging to one of them discharged." She hastily added, "By mistake." Which was partially true. There had been no intention to take out the driver . . . only one's brother.

The driver's strong arm lifted, and he grabbed hold of the cuff on her sleeve. She followed the motion of his hand where he touched her. A smear of blood marred the light-colored trimming. His eyes were a cloudless blue. "No ambush?"

"No."

"You mean to tell me I got shot by somebody I was hauling?"

"Two men were fighting over a gun and it went off. That must be how the bullet came through the roof of the coach and hit you."

"If that don't beat all. Then definitely get me my Winchester so I can blow their heads off."

"That's not a good idea. No. I don't think that will do at all. You need help." Fear made her babble.

"I don't need any help." He struggled to sit up, but slumped back over. "Sum-bitch, that hurts."

Worried, Evelyn gingerly patted his arm. "You need help—"

"What's happened?" Marcella asked, swaying Evelyn's attention to the woman who stood below. Her hair was out of place, and her laydown collar was crooked. "Is our driver all right?"

"No he's not, thanks to your husband or your lover."

"Don't get impertinent with me, young lady."

Young lady. The form of address grated. Evelyn doubted she was younger than Marcella Graves. If anything, she was older by two years. The prudish manner offended her in light of what had transpired. Their driver had been shot and if he didn't get medical attention . . .

The Graves gentlemen—if they could be called that—appeared, the derringer they'd fought over nowhere in sight. Both of them looked as if they'd been dragged behind the coach instead of sitting inside it. Each bore numerous battle scars. Cut lips, a gash in a brow, nicks on an ear. Their coats and shirts were ruffled and torn as if they'd engaged in more than a fight over the gun. Filbert held onto his shoulder, wincing in deep pain that strained his features. Gregory didn't fare much better. He favored his right leg.

Filbert Graves's voice had a penetrating edge to it. "Why have we stopped?"

Gregory put in his own request for information. "You up there, tell us what the hold-up is."

Evelyn wanted to jump down on the trio for their lack of concern, knock them over, and crush them all into the ground. "Your belated worry for other people isn't touching. You should be ashamed. Your behavior is unforgivable."

As soon as she said it, regret assailed Evelyn. One of them still had a concealed derringer, and if he'd been serious about using it once, there was no stopping him from using it twice. This time on her.

Quickly, she proceeded in a softer tone. "Our driver has been shot and he needs medical aid." Turning, she addressed the prone man. "Sir, are you in a lot of pain?"

He lifted his head and looked down over the box railing. His hat had fallen off and the threads of gray in his hair were mussed. "Which one of you is the sum-bitch who shot me?"

"Filbert never meant to," Marcella said. "He was angry with me."

"And I'm still seething with anger about your little tryst, *my dove*. But I'll save all that for when we get home to Sweetwater."

"We're not going to Sweetwater," the driver managed. "Not with nobody to drive these horses. One of you has to unhitch that piebald at the lead, ride into Abilene and round up a doctor and a fresh horse."

Filbert held onto his arm by the elbow. "I have a busted arm."

"Oh, for crying out loud." The driver motioned to Gregory. "Then you get on that horse."

Gregory limped while shaking his head. "I don't ride."

"*Not horses,*" Filbert shot back with the same intensity as a bullet from his derringer, "but you rode my wife!"

The next thing Evelyn knew, both men were locked in a battle of flailing arms and blows to the bodies. Punches thrown. Groans. Curses. All while Marcella hollered at them to stop.

"Lady," the driver said to Evelyn. She turned her attention away from the brothers.

"Yes?"

"You're slight, but I think you could unhitch that horse from the line if I tell you exactly how to do it. What these here men did to me is a criminal offense— I don't give a blazes if it was an accident. Shooting a stage driver is grounds for arrest. I intend to see the both of them put behind bars. I need a sheriff out here." He licked his dry lips. "I know I shouldn't be asking a fine lady like yourself something like this, but can you ride into Abilene and get a lawman to come out here, along with a doc?"

"Yes, certainly. Of course I can ride."

"Problem is, I don't have a saddle—"

"Mister—"

"Tate," he offered somewhat solemnly.

The corners of her mouth curved in tenderness. "Mr. Tate, I'm a fine horsewoman and I know I can ride without a saddle."

"That's good to hear. I figure I can make out okay

on my own for a while. It beats all how they're carrying on down there."

"Are you sure you'll be all right—with them?"

"Got no other choice. I don't think they mean to do me in, but by the time the law comes back"—*smack, wallop, punch*—"one of them might be done for."

"You just lay here and try to keep calm. You can count on me."

In detailed step-by-step language, he gave her instructions on how to remove the gelding's tandem harness and hame. "Give him enough tension on the reins. You'll have more than you need. He doesn't have a riding bit, but the driving one should do."

"Yes, it should." She went to turn, but her teeth caught the inside of her lip. Unsettled, she thought about her father. He was wealthy and relentless, using his power to gain him fast results. As far-reaching as his connections were, there was no doubt in Evelyn's mind that people were keeping an eye out for her. There was a distinct possibility that every law official across the state had received a notice with her description on it.

Biting on the tip of her glove in thought, she realized that when she got to Abilene the authorities would ask questions. They'd want an account of what happened from eyewitnesses. That meant her. She couldn't be a witness for anything.

"I'll be on my way now, Mr. Tate. Help will be coming soon."

"You've got about a thirty-mile ride."

Moving into action, Evelyn did what she had to do. It was only after she'd retrieved her club satchel from beneath her seat inside the coach and tied it onto the horse, that the men comprehended what was happening around them. They stopped their assault on one another and gazed at her.

"Where are you going?" Filbert asked.

"To get help."

In the poorest of taste, and timing, Marcella quipped, "A lady does not ride bareback."

"This one does."

Since she had no saddle, she needed assistance mounting the mare. She backed her up and climbed onto the fold-out footstep of the coach. That gave her just enough of a boost to get on. The reins in her hands were four times the length she needed. She wrapped them together in several large knots, and then wove the rest between her fingers.

"Help is coming." Gazing at Tate, she gave him a reassuring nod.

Then she was off.

She rode fast and hard through hip-high grass and over the prairie. She'd never gone thirty miles without a saddle. All of her riding had been done on the acreage surrounding her home in Oiler. Covering territory like that was easy. The harsh plains with rocks and a trail that was uneven in more places than it was even, was something entirely different. But she could ride through. She had to.

A cynical inner voice cut into her string of swift thoughts: *Would nothing ever go right?* She'd been out on her own for less than two days, and she'd yet to enter a town in the way she'd expected. If she kept up this kind of high-road adventure, the chances of her making it to California without some other fiascos occurring weren't looking great.

But she simply refused to give up without ever having set foot out of the state of Texas.

With her muscles burning and sore, Evelyn leaned next to the post of a closed grocery store. She was at the farthest end of Abilene's main section of town. Her cheek rested next to the rough wood, and she willed the ache in her bones to go away while her gaze stayed fixed on the end of the road. Her left arm felt weighted by the club satchel. Due to sheer exhaustion, she almost dropped it.

The night sky was ink black, visibility on the street hazy from light coming through windows without coverings. It seemed like it had taken her all day to get here. By the time she'd ridden in, the sun was merely a distant reminder. The horizon was golden and stars had begun to show. She had done exactly what she'd promised Mr. Tate. She'd notified the sheriff. Although she hadn't appeared personally, she had gotten word to him. At least that's what she was waiting to make sure of.

Within a few minutes, a youth ran toward her with a hand on his hat to hold it on his head.

"Did it!" he announced out of breath. "Gave the sheriff your note and said that it was an emergency. I told him he had to ride out with the doctor to find that man you described."

Standing tall, Evelyn put a hand over her heart. Relief flooded her. "Good. Okay. Great. That's one less worry. I appreciate the help."

"*My* pleasure. You paid me a dollar to do it."

She shifted her satchel from one hand to the other. "And did you tell the sheriff that there was a gun?"

"Uh-huh."

"And that the situation was dangerous?"

"Yep."

"Good." She tried to keep a dignified posture, but the effort proved too much. She pressed her shoulder next to the post. "You're sure the sheriff read my note?"

"Positive. I watched him."

"Thank you." Blinking several times to moisten the trail dust that had dried her eyes, she added, "And remember what I told you." She opened her purse and produced another dollar. "You haven't seen me. You don't know me. I'm just a faceless stranger."

"That's for true. I really can't see your face, lady. It's too dark in this area. When you called me over, I almost didn't come. Thought you were one of the nocturnal birds wanting me to keep company with them for ten minutes."

Puzzled for a moment over the description, the true meaning was slow to register. *Prostitutes.* "Heavens, no." She went to the hitching post. "Now, there is that one last thing you said you'd do for me. Do you remember?"

"Take the horse to my house where I water and feed her, check for pebbles in her shoes, groom her, then have her back here in the morning wearing a saddle. Then you'll give me five dollars."

She looked at him askance. "We agreed to three dollars."

She barely made out his impish smile. She did see the whites of his eyes, however, when he conceded, "Oh, that's right. But I'm telling you, for that, the saddle isn't going to be very good."

"Whatever you have will do. Now, I'll see you at precisely five. Be here with my horse ready and I'll pay you."

"All right."

Untying the reins, she gave the piebald over, and the boy and the horse went off into the night. She hated to admit how fully her mind had been congested with fear. But now that the sheriff had been notified about Mr. Tate and the others, she could secure a room at a hotel, take a hot bath, eat a warm meal, and sleep in a soft bed. She'd already found a small hotel to spend the night in. Nothing fancy. Plain and simple.

Arriving at The Presidio, she easily booked a room and received her key. She so looked forward to dropping into a sound sleep after she ate and had a bath.

In the dining room, she kept to the corner and ordered dinner. The food came in a reasonable time, and nobody paid attention to her while she ate. Even if the sheriff came in, he wouldn't know who she was.

She felt fairly certain she was safe.

Evelyn walked up the stairs and down the hallway. The desk clerk told her she had a shower bath with free-running cold and hot water. It sounded like a slice of heaven. She'd wash her hair and face and get the dust off her arms.

Lost in thought, she didn't hear anyone behind her until she slipped her key into the lock of her door and was twisting the knob.

She began to turn to see who was there—

A rough hand clamped over her open mouth from behind, and a strong arm wrapped around her waist. The attacker had her firmly by the face and middle, and her feet were lifted from beneath her. She put energy into a loud scream, but it was stopped by callused fingers. She fought as she was dragged into the dark room she had just unlocked.

Then the sliver of light from the hallway suddenly disappeared as the door was slammed closed.

9

Luke Devereaux kept his hand on the woman's mouth as he kicked the door closed with his boot. While she wasn't very tall, she did put up a good fight. Her arm swung forward, and she tried to hit him with her suitcase. She made contact, but it was about as effective as an annoying gnat. Fending off her attempts to get free were the least of his problems.

He needed answers, and he needed them now.

The room was near pitch dark. Somebody had left the roller shade up allowing for minimal light to seep through the lace curtains. He caught sight of the outline of a bed. A bureau. A small door that probably led to a water closet.

He spoke next to her ear. "I'm going to take my hand away and the only sounds I want to hear from you are the answers to my questions." She wriggled and made a strangled sound from the back of her throat. "I said don't move. And if you holler out, if you try and do anything foolish, you'll regret it." He felt the muscles in her body slacken a little. "Now, I'm going to take my hand away. But I'll still be holding onto you."

Slowly, he lowered his arm.

She took in deep drafts of air, and let out several choking gasps. "I demand—"

Gritting his teeth, he put his hand over her mouth again, thinking only for a split second that her lips were soft and moist against his fingers. She tried to jerk free of him by moving her shoulders. "I wish you wouldn't thrash around. You're in no position to demand anything. So we're going to try this again. Nice and slow. You know the rules."

He released his hold over her mouth once more, but kept her close to his chest. The curve of her behind pressed into his groin.

When she said nothing, he nodded. "Good. We're clear now."

"Who are you?"

Chagrined, Luke frowned. "I told you not to say anything unless I ask you."

"Filbert?"

Filbert? "Wrong."

"Gregory?"

Who had she involved herself with since the last time he saw her? The situation could be a lot worse than he feared. "Wrong again."

He could hear her breath hitch, then she slowly let it out. "Mrs. Smythe?"

"Yes, *dear.*"

"What are you doing here? What do you want? Let me go, you big swine. I haven't forgotten how you treated me in Dallas. Disgraceful. For a man, you're no gentleman. And even when you were Mrs. Smythe, you were no lady, either. I never said this, but you looked awful. Anyone who could honestly think—"

He pressed his hand over her mouth once more. "Don't you ever shut up?"

She made no reply. She couldn't; her lips were sealed closed by the flat of his hand. Instead, she attempted to shake her head "yes," but he found her answer more than far-fetched. Since he'd met her, he hadn't known her to be quiet. Unless it was because she was guilty of something. Or trying to hide something."

Did you get a job at the Red Crown stage lines?" He lessened his restraint on her mouth. "Answer yes or no."

"No—"

He cut off any further explanation.

"That's funny—then how can you tell me you're not a thief?" Once more, he eased back. "Tell me simply, ten words or less."

On a puff of air, she said, "Because I'm not."

"Explain why the brand on your horse is RC."

When she had the opportunity to talk up a storm, she was close-lipped.

"Anything come to mind?" he questioned. "I don't see why you would be paying a kid to feed your horse and bring her back with a saddle if she wasn't your horse. But that brand does cast you in a suspicious light. Now, if you tell me why that brand is on that horse, and how come you have her, I'd be inclined to—"

"How do you know about—"

"I'm asking the questions." Once more, he gave her the opportunity to respond.

"I'm just borrowing the horse," she said. "I fully intend to return her as soon as I—"

With a firm grasp, he spread his fingers over her middle and tugged her closer to him. Heat spread through his body but he forced it away. If the light was on, he'd remind himself who she was. Not a soft and curvy woman, but a pain in the ass. A liar and nothing but a fair amount of trouble. "Frankly, I don't care about the horse." With a dip of his head, he brought his mouth close to her ear. He wanted her to be able to hear him perfectly clear. Hear every serious note in his voice, because he meant business.

As he spoke, he felt her shiver beneath him when his lips brushed over the warm shell of her ear. "I want to know what you wrote in the note you gave to the kid."

"I . . . I didn't write any note."

"You've said that before, so I'm not buying. I saw you. And it sure as hell looked like you were passing a note."

Hesitation marked her tone. "You were watching me? Where were you?"

"Across the street buying some tobacco. It was hard not to spot you the way you were skirting around under all the awnings this side of the city as if you were being followed by Jack the Ripper. Or would that be Filbert the Ripper?"

"Filbert is as nutty as his name and if it weren't for him and his stupid brother, I'd be in Sweetwater."

"Is that so?"

"Yes," she indignantly ground out. She tried to whack him with the case once more and bumped at his knee. "Let me go."

"Not until I know what you wrote in that note. You said there was a man. Dangerous. With a gun. Were you talking about me?"

He wasn't prepared to hear her laughter. "You? You thought I was talking about you?"

"You already wrote one note about me, I don't want to be worried about another."

She shoved her elbow into his ribs. The blow had no effect on him. He let out a curse, but didn't let her go. "Don't do that."

"Does it bother you?"

"Not nearly as much as you do."

"Then why not release me, leave my room, and I won't bother you anymore?"

"Maybe I will, but I want to know why you were sending the sheriff after a dangerous man."

"If you must know, I was fulfilling a promise to the driver of the Red Crown stage line who was shot in an altercation over a gun in my coach. I could have been killed by those two buffoons, but the driver was the one to be injured. I was the only one who could ride into Abilene for help. I did so. I got the sheriff, rather, that boy got him for me," she pulled in a breath, "and told him to go out and send a doctor and another horse."

Luke took perverse pleasure in agitating her. "Why didn't you tell the sheriff yourself—since you're not fencing stolen property?"

A momentary static pause filled the black room. "I answered your questions, now let me go."

He couldn't argue with that. But he did wonder whether or not to believe her. She didn't stutter and stammer her way through her story. He'd seen what she was like when she was lying. "All right."

Luke eased his arm from around her, removing his hands from her waist and shoulder. He heard her fumbling around, the bureau legs being hit and scraping over the floor. In her groping, she kicked the bed with the tip of her shoe and the frame squeaked.

"Oh for heaven's sake, where's the light switch?" she complained. "You've got me all disoriented."

Luke reached over and turned the electrical knob on the wall. Two hurricane-type wall sconces on either side of the bed came to life. It took a second or two for his eyes to adjust to the brightness. He walked to the window, grabbed the pull on the shade, and lowered it. Turning, he folded his arms over his chest and got his first good look at Eve Pierce.

She stood regally, dressed in fine clothes and a fine hat. Although the trimmings on the hat were now askew. Gloves that must have been white were covered by trail grime and the tan markings of reins. The dress she wore had to have been beautiful when she'd put it on. The rich blue suited her, as did the style of soft folds and drapes. But now the material was on the wrinkled side.

He wondered how much of her story was true and how much was pure embellishment. He couldn't find a call to question it. Being involved in a shooting seemed like something she might just get herself into.

However, he did think it unlikely that she'd ridden into Abilene without a saddle. She didn't say as much, but from the way she looked—and from his knowledge of stage lines—they didn't carry saddles on board. So she'd have had to come in bareback.

Eve stood with her arms at her sides, the satchel still in her hand. Her brows drew together in an angry frown while color tinted her cheeks in a soft pink. The vaguest impression of his hand could be seen around her mouth. He felt a fist of regret punch him in the stomach. He shouldn't have held onto her the way he had, but he'd been thinking she had done something that would jeopardize his ill-gained freedom.

"You are uncouth," she said simply. "If you only knew who I was, you never would have laid a hand on me in such a manner because you would have feared for your life. My father is—" She grimaced and the rest of what she had to say hung between them, unspoken.

"The family chauffeur," he finished for her.

"Yes, yes, yes. You're correct, as usual. Or so you think." She put her satchel on the end of the bed with its simple white iron frame and a coverlet in ivory. It was narrow and sagging in the middle, with only a single pillow at the top. "Sometimes you're wrong, you know. You were wrong to treat me the way you did in Dallas, and I can tell you this, I do not forgive you for that trolley affair. Honestly, telling me to shoplift at Neiman-Marcus."

"You look as if you took my advice."

"I didn't steal one thing."

"If you say so."

She made a face. Then she removed her gloves and hat and threw them down on the bed beside her satchel. Afterward, she turned toward him as if she'd just remembered something of monumental importance. "I answered your questions, now answer one for me—what are you doing in Abilene?"

"Getting out of it at first light."

"Don't hand me nonsense. Why is it that you turned up here to torture me?"

"You've got it backwards. You're following me."

"That's absurd. I'm on my way to someplace very important and it just so happens I have to pass through Abilene to get there."

"Same for me."

She scowled. "Get out of my room."

She went to the door and grasped the knob. But he was beside her in several easy strides and slammed his hand over the top of the door to prevent it from opening. "Not yet."

Eve looked up, her expression none too pleased. She stood beneath his arm, the top of her head almost brushing against the sleeve of his duster. "I beg your pardon? We had a deal."

"I don't make deals." He clicked the lock into place.

Backing away, she went toward the bed and sat. Thought the better of it, and stood. The tip of her shoe tapped from beneath her skirt hem as she waited.

The truth was, he'd already tempted fate far more than he should have in Abilene. Since Eve secured a room, he was going to take advantage of it in case his wanted poster had circulated this far west. His original plan had been to camp the rest of the way to Silver

City, but his horse had thrown a shoe and was in the livery overnight waiting for the smithy at first light. While talking with the stable hand, he'd spoken few words and hadn't stayed long. It would have made sense to keep to the lesser traveled streets while coming up with a place to spend the night, but Abilene's main street had something he couldn't disregard: a way of communicating with New Orleans.

It had been with the collar on his duster turned up, and his chin tucked low, that he'd gone to the Central Telephone Office to place a call to Jayce.

"The department is feeding misinformation to the newspapers, Luke," Jayce had said through the static on the line. "Paul Regale is sticking to his story that you shot those sergeants because they had proof you were taking payoffs."

"It's bullshit, Jayce. And Henry knows it."

"That's another thing. I found out Henry was making collection rounds for Sockeye."

Henry's so-called business for Captain James "Sockeye" Mullet was just as Luke thought. Months ago, he'd clashed with Henry about his dealings for the captain but Henry had given him harsh disdain. If Henry's deteriorating health was an indication of guilty culpability, it was a significant one. Henry's stomach was always giving him trouble. Like the lining was eating away at itself. He drank a lot of tonics to quiet his insides. But there were days when Henry's belly gave him so much pain, he was sick in the precinct lavatory and could barely sit at his desk. "How long was Henry in on it?"

"Six months. Maybe more."

Luke rubbed the bridge of his nose.

Jayce went on, "The new commissioner, Big Pat Ellroy, has put the heat on all precincts and is hunting for rotten apples. He's formed a special squad. Tempers are soaring and the Bayou Quarter is being cracked wide open."

"Any whistle blowers?"

"Not yet. Ellroy has put the pinch on everyone. It doesn't matter the rank. But he's got a judge in his corner who's on the up and up so things are going to turn around. Convictions are sure for some bad eggs who cooked the books. New warrants are being served every day, but none so far for Regale and Mullet."

"They're buying off insiders and anyone else who knows too much."

"You can bet Henry was one of them. He sure padded the hoof."

The patrolman's expression referred to leaving a crime scene as quietly as possible. The ink on Henry's pay settlements hadn't even dried when Henry had disappeared. Quiet and quick.

A startling thought jarred Luke. "You don't think Sockeye killed him and Boyd's body is somewhere at the bottom of the Mississippi?"

"I don't know—I can't imagine the captain going that far. But things are so crazy here, Luke, you wouldn't believe it. Reporters are everywhere trying to get the scoop. They even set up a camp at our mother's house."

"Dammit, can you get rid of them?"

"Phillipe did once. They came back the next day."

"How's she doing?"

"She's resilient. I asked her to move in with me and Kate until all this blows over and she refused. She said she wasn't leaving her home and giving a false sense of shame to the press." The telephone line had gone scratchy for a moment as Jayce continued, "The other day, she was out in the garden with the reporters right on the other side of the fence. She invited them onto the verandah for some mint juleps."

Luke hadn't been able to refrain from chuckling.

"No takers," Jayce had supplied with an equal amount of humor in his tone. The only bright light to their conversation.

Pulling himself back to the present, Luke gazed at Eve and ran a hand through his hair. He'd lost his hat in the jump from the train, and he hadn't been able to get another one.

On a glance to the mirror above the bureau, he saw that his hair rested on his shoulders; he'd never worn it this length and almost didn't recognize himself. The ever-deepening tan on his face made him seem more formidable. Creases at the corners of his eyes due to squinting into the sun gave him a harsh exterior. He resembled little of Lieutenant Luke Devereaux, which wasn't altogether bad right now.

"You really look different as a man."

Luke saw Eve in the mirror from where she stood behind him. He noted the way she took in the features of his face. "I'd hope so." He spoke to her reflection. "Like you kindly pointed out, I didn't make a very good woman."

"No, you didn't."

Facing her, he rubbed his jaw. "I suppose I'm taking

my life in my own hands here, but I must admit curiosity can't let me drop it."

She gazed at him through eyes that were slightly narrowed with distrust. "Hmm?"

"How *did* you come up with the money to buy the duds *and* a stage coach ticket?"

"Not with any help from you, that's for sure."

"Point taken."

She sat once more and scooted back onto the coverlet to open the latch on her satchel. "I have a brain. I used it."

"Look, Eve, I'm sorry about Dallas. The trolley and all."

She slanted him a dubious look.

He went on, "We have to be careful who we deal with and how. In fact, we shouldn't trust anyone."

"I agree."

"But you can trust me."

"You're more of a liar than I gave you credit for," she commented, pulling out a map from her traveling bag. His own bag was still hanging snugly over his shoulder, and he decided to set it on the floor.

Eve unfolded her Texas map, and as she did so, he saw blood on the cuff of her dress. Before he could think, he reacted. He grabbed her wrist. He couldn't explain the sudden full-blown hostility that had arisen in him. "Did somebody try and hurt you?"

Puzzled, she replied, "Ah, yes, you. But you weren't successful."

"Whose blood is that?"

"Mr. Tate's, the stage coach driver."

"The man who was shot?"

"Yes, I believe we covered that." She refocused on the map. He caught a glimpse of the state of Texas on the front.

He considered her for a moment, almost wishing they'd met under different circumstances; then he said, "The livery doesn't open till first light. I need a room to stay in for a few hours so I can get some sleep. I'm thinking yours will do."

That snapped her chin up. "I'm thinking 'Not the slightest chance.' In fact, I want you out of here right now. I might accidentally scream."

"I don't think so. Not unless you want the sheriff asking who you are."

On that, she pressed her fingers over her closed eyes. He saw that she was bone tired.

"Why are you doing this to me? I've never had this kind of dissension with a man before. Most of them have just wanted to marry me."

Marry? The idea had never entered his mind in relation to Eve. He guessed since she was a chauffeur's daughter, proposals didn't come every day. Then again, maybe she wasn't who she said she was on that account either.

He gave her an easy grin. "I don't want to marry you, Eve. I just want to spend the night in your room."

"You most certainly are *not* staying here."

"Why not? We've shared a room before. I could have forced you if I wanted to."

"Yes, that's right. You forced yourself on me just fine outside my door, you scoundrel." The crinkle of paper sounded as she turned the large map upside down, then right side up. Very seriously, she scrutinized the images and markers, the lines and relief key. Looking up, she frowned. "Still here?"

Luke read the road map over her shoulder. "Where are you headed?"

"Not that it's any of your business, but if you know you can kindly take a route in the opposite direction." The light from the wall sconces played off the colors of gold in her hair as she pointed to a black dot and heavy writing. "El Paso."

Standing back, he nodded.

Proudly, she stated, "I'll be there by sunset tomorrow."

A lighthearted amusement filled him. "And how do you figure that?"

She ran her fingertip from Abilene to El Paso. "Five hours. At the most."

"Honey, it's going to take you a hell of a lot longer than five hours to get to El Paso." Effortlessly, he shrugged out of his duster and laid it over the footboard. Eve didn't notice. Her gaze was fixed on the map. "You're looking at a five-day ride over unpredictable terrain that could easily add in a day or two."

"That can't possibly be correct. It didn't take that long to get from Beaumont to Dallas. And look," she tapped a finger on the paper, "the lines are almost the same distance. About three inches here. About five inches there. See?"

"I see." Leaning into the bedpost, he removed one boot, then the other. "What I see is, you're going from fifty miles per hour over rail to eight or nine at an easy lope on a horse that'll require food and rest. You'll need extra supplies. Camping gear."

"Camping gear?"

"Sure. A bedroll, rope, canteen, mess kit, oilcloth in case it rains, knife—actually, make that a gun—for snakes. And badmen. You'll be a woman alone out there. Got to defend yourself."

Aghast, she stammered, "I-I don't have any of those things."

"Then you'd better get that kid to round you up some."

"All that is going to cost a lot of money. I don't have any to spare."

"Damn shame." He began to unbutton his shirt with one hand.

This time Eve noticed. Noticed about the same time as she noticed his Colt strapped to his thigh within his easy reach. She shot off the bed. After a hasty search, she ended up grabbing a Bible off the bureau.

"You don't have to hit me with the Good Book to send me to hell. I've got plenty of people already hoping to put me there."

He'd unfastened his shirt to the bottom and the hem hung open to his hips. He wore nothing underneath it. He watched Eve avert her gaze from his chest.

"I don't want you doing anything to me." A tremor caught in her voice. "I don't even know your name."

Lifting his travel bag, he thought that over for a moment. Hell, she had enough on him already. "Luke. My name's Luke."

He went into the water closet and shut the door. He was going to take a bath and let her think things over about that El Paso trip. His being in her room was the least of her problems. But he wasn't so sure about his. She had him thinking about that bed and her in it.

The night was going to be long.

When Luke came out of her water closet, she'd be ready for him. Firmly held in one hand was her pencil with the sharp point, and in her other hand, her long hatpin. They may not have been lethal enough weapons to maim, but they could do damage.

Evelyn could have run down and told the manager to come up and throw him out, but she wouldn't. Couldn't. *Damn* Luke Whoever. Oh, dear—she'd sworn. That, too, she reasoned was his fault.

Camping equipment. A gun for snakes . . . and badmen.

She didn't have a single piece of gear, and he had to know that. He used her lack of preparation against her, making her worry and become sick at heart. How could she safely get to El Paso by her own means? The chances were highly unlikely.

All these years of collecting maps hadn't done her any good. Since she'd never put a map to the test, she'd miscalculated mileage. Another thing Luke not-so-kindly pointed out to her.

She'd gotten over her shock at finding *Luke*—the name suited him, as it sounded hard and unyielding—in her hotel. Of all the people to show up. She never would have guessed they'd run into each other. Or maybe she shouldn't have been surprised.

When he'd stood before her, his shirt unbuttoned, she'd had to hold onto every ounce of courage she had. She was so startled to see his bare chest, she'd nearly been rendered speechless. Of all the men who pursued her over the years, none had ever gotten out of line. None had made ardent overtures toward her.

The man in her water closet, in the bathtub—she could hear the water sloshing—was nothing like she'd ever encountered before in a person of the opposite sex. She should have been scared senseless of him. But there was something about him . . . something she couldn't pinpoint. He didn't act like a notorious thief or killer. He was just . . . more than his share of over-bearing and daring. . . .

He'd left nothing in the room for her to search aside from his boots and his duster. Both were empty. Nothing hidden. As she was setting his coat back on the bed, she paused. The vague traces of tobacco clung to it. That, and dust and . . . man.

Unbidden, she lifted the coat to her nose and lightly breathed in. Her delicate sensibilities should have been offended, but Evelyn was anything but. She closed her eyes and wondered about all the places he'd worn the duster. All the things he'd done and seen while wearing it. He'd probably had more adventures than anything she'd ever do or see in her lifetime. She wondered about the man himself. His past. Who he really was. Indeed, if Luke was really his name. She couldn't blame him if he'd lied.

The door to the closet opened, and he came out with his black hair wet and combed away from his clean-shaven face. He wore a fresh shirt and clean duck pants. He was minus the revolver and socks.

She was struck by how handsome he was. She hadn't wanted to admit it before, but she didn't entirely find him vulgar. In fact, that's what irritated her most. He was both attractive and infuriating.

"Feel better?" she quipped, thinking it should have been her in that bath instead of him.

"As a matter of fact, I do."

"Well, I'm so glad you were able to make yourself at home."

"Don't mention it."

He laid his travel bag in the corner—within easy reach if he needed it. She saw that ominous gun sticking up through the bag's opening. Giving her a questioning shrug, he asked, "What do you intend to do with those deadly weapons? Poke out my liver?"

She looked at the pencil and pin in her hands. That he could be so glib, set her teeth on edge. "All right, you've had your fun and games and bath for the evening. I want you out of my room. Right now."

"I can't get a room, Eve. I explained that to you."

"And I explained to you, that I don't want you here." A headache was beginning at the base of her neck. He could be so tiresome to her. *She* was tired. Tired of going rounds with him. Tired of thinking about how she would cope with tomorrow.

The whole El Paso thing had her upset. Distressed. She could not give up. Not now. She refused to end things here. Like this. In a hotel room with a man who thought he was so smart. So much in the know about camping equipment, and mess kits and—

Evelyn paused mid-thought. A brilliant idea struck her and she almost bubbled over with excitement. She lowered her arms, returned the hatpin into her hat and deposited the pencil into her satchel.

In an easy manner, she confronted him. "Yes, I think your staying can be of some benefit to me. Actually, quite a lot of benefit."

"I think you should stop yourself now, because whatever you're going to say next, I'm not going to like it."

His declaration didn't dampen her mood. "Because I'm such an understanding woman, I'm going to let you take me to El Paso to work off the debt you owe me."

"What debt?" he shot back.

"One thousand four hundred and fifty-six dollars and thirty-nine cents, because if you hadn't yanked me off that train—"

"—hell, this again—"

"—I wouldn't have lost my money on the Lone Star Limited." She was elated over her smart thinking. "It's only fair you attempt to repay me."

"I see where this is going, Eve, and it's not going to work. I thought Vanderhoff was trying to hurt you. That's the only reason I pulled you off that train."

"Exactly." She vehemently shook her head, went to the window and yanked up the shade. A twisting fear held her, but she had to take the risk as warm summer air rolled into the room. She stood before the open frame and looked over her shoulder. In a voice calmer than she felt, she said, "I'll give you the chance to—"

"Don't scream, Eve."

Disregarding him, she faced forward and opened her mouth. Drawing in a large breath, she prepared to scream for help. She secretly pleaded for him to come over and stop her. The pounding of her blood pumped through her brain.

"Eve. Stop it."

There was no going back as she released the air in her lungs on a cry. "Heeell—"

But before the word formed, she was knocked away from the window and a hot mouth covered hers.

10

A strong hold on her arms braced Evelyn against the window frame. She was too stunned to breathe, much less move. She hadn't been prepared for the searing heat of Luke's kiss. A fiery ribbon swept through her body, igniting and pooling in her stomach. She could hardly think; only feel. The velvet warmth of his mouth covering hers was a slow exploration of her lips. Shock tingled across her skin, and her knees trembled. She felt the hardness of his thighs pressed into the soft folds of her skirt as the clean smell of his skin filled her lungs. A heady sensation claimed her senses and she tried to pull herself out of it. Out of his arms. But she couldn't.

She was transported to a place she knew virtually nothing about. It was foreign territory, much like the lines on her maps. She'd never traveled down a road like this—the journey was unexpected.

She grew aware that her hands rested on his shoulders, her fingers lightly clinging to him. She could feel the tension of firm muscle in response. She let him kiss her for an endless moment. Reality set in as a carriage rattled by on the street down below. Then she remembered where she was. In a hotel room. Alone. With a stranger.

Evelyn immediately broke free. While she caught her breath, his eyes held hers. Her first kiss had left her reeling.

Hot air drifting into the hotel room sluiced over Luke. He wished it were a blast of winter chill instead. He damn well needed cooling off. His body was still responding to Eve, still remembering how she fit next to him. Once he'd silenced her, he shouldn't have stood there enjoying the kiss. But he had. He still did. The memory pulsed in his mind, strong and still wanting.

"W-Why did you do that?" Eve asked, her voice shaky.

Luke shoved his hair off his forehead and reached for the cord on the roller shade. Trying to keep a steady hand, he yanked it down over halfway. "I got you to shut up, didn't I?"

"I'll call for help again."

"No you won't."

"What makes you so sure?"

He took in the sight of her hair, the way tiny wisps clung to her cheeks. Cheeks that were flushed. Her lips were parted, still damp from his own. "Nothing in life is sure, but let's just say I have a hunch."

Slightly trembling, she sat on the bed and reined in

the map she had fanned out, pointedly folding it. He sensed she was doing it to curb her reaction to his kiss. "You really aren't leaving."

"No."

Quietly, she rose and gathered her belongings, taking them into the water closet. Moments later, he heard water running as she drew a bath.

Luke was sitting in one of the chairs when Evelyn came out wearing the same dress, only free of trail dust and some of the wrinkles. Her hair was free of its pins and falling softly over her shoulders in wet curls; he let himself imagine what it would be like to bury his hands in all that thick hair. Wet, it was a darker shade. Not so much golden, but more of a deep honey.

"Since you insist on staying, I want your word," she said as she put her satchel on the floor.

"Word on what?"

"You know exactly what I'm referring to. For the next eight hours—"

"That'll have to be six."

"Whatever the case, you have to be on your best behavior."

"You're saying that kiss wasn't my best?"

She held her chin high. "You're insufferable."

He only grinned. He knew her meaning quite clearly. "Toss me a pillow."

Her brow arched.

"Unless you want me to sleep in the bed with you."

A flash of plump white sailed toward him and he caught the feather pillow with one hand.

"Would you care for a blanket?"

"Too hot."

On that, her cheeks colored while her lashes lowered. "Let's just turn out the light and try to get some sleep."

The room was once again bathed in darkness as Luke situated himself on the floor in front of the door, his gun by his side. The bed frame creaked; the rustle of the coverlet and sheets sounded.

The tick of a wall clock seemed louder than normal as they settled in for the night. Neither of them moved—as if by not moving they implied an instant sleep the other wasn't enjoying.

After a while, Eve's soft voice broke into the steady tick-tock.

"What are you *really* doing in Abilene?" she asked.

Luke stirred, adjusting the pillow beneath his head by punching it with his fist. The hard floor beneath him was saved from being unbearable by a braided rug. "Just passing through like you."

"On your way to El Paso, too?"

His teeth clenched tightly together. "Yeah, I need to pass through there on the way to where I'm going."

"I knew it. You can take me and earn off the money you owe me."

"Eve, I don't owe you squat."

"You most surely do." She shifted, the mattress springs squeaking. "I won't be left behind. I'm doing you a favor by letting you stay here tonight."

"Quit talking. It's time to go to sleep."

"I agree. Because we have a full day ahead of us

tomorrow. When the sun rises, we're riding straight for El Paso."

"When the sun rises, I'll be on my way while you're trying to figure out the difference between a canteen and a tent."

11

The desert sun beat down on Luke, but the brim of his hat shaded its harsh glare from his eyes. The Stetson was nothing ordinary—fine black felt with a silver conch band. Too flashy for his tastes, but there weren't any other styles in the store. At six in the morning, a man in need of a hat didn't have options.

Since leaving Abilene, he'd ridden through Taylor County and just under half of Nolan. Noon was hitting straight up and the day promised to be a scorcher. Buffalo Gap had been to the south, while they were coming up on Sweetwater Creek to the west. Every now and then, herds of cattle could be seen grazing on the meager mesquite brush that grew over the rough terrain. Grasses were rising taller the closer they came to the town of Sweetwater.

He'd taken off his duster hours ago and held the reins in a single grip in his right hand. Astride the four-year-old flea-bitten gray he'd bought in Dallas, he loped in an easy gait. He slanted his gaze to the woman beside him.

The sun changed the blue threads of her dress to an almost iridescent shimmer. If anything, she knew how to hold herself in a saddle like a lady; and it didn't appear forced for his benefit.

Luke told himself he was taking Eve to El Paso because he did owe her something for pulling her off that train—not almost fifteen hundred dollars—but a margin of help.

But he didn't have to like it that she was tagging along—on a stolen horse, no less. Hell, horse stealing could still be a hanging offense in some parts of Texas.

"What kind of outlaw are you?" Eve's jarring question pulled him from his thoughts. The tilt of her nose was pert, as were the curves in the corners of her mouth. She was deadly serious. "What's your specialty? Banks, safes, railroads?"

He frowned at the idiocy of such an inquiry, given he was a veteran on a police force. She was so far off, she wouldn't have believed him if he said he *caught* robbers.

"It's railroads. That's why you jumped."

"You're really something, Eve." Blue sky and a few puffs of clouds marked the way to the river ahead. He could see a glimpse of its surface as it wavered just beyond a stand of lone scrub. "If Eve is your name," he tacked on, just to rile her a little. He rather liked when she put some fire in her eyes.

"Yes, it is," she defended. "I can honestly say my Grandfather Jimmy called me Eve." Drawing up next to him so that their horses were in sync, she eased up a little on her reins. "Is yours really Luke?"

"Maybe if you call for me some time, you'll figure out whether or not I'm being honest with you on that account."

A wedge of incompatible silence put a wall between them. A mile later, she proceeded as if they hadn't been quiet.

"You infuriate me, you know. Like a bee when I'm gardening and I—"

"The chauffeur's daughter gardens?"

"Why not?"

"I'd've figured you'd be helping Daddy keep all those automobiles shined up for the mister of the house."

Her satchel bounced a little at the horse's rump where it was tied on by a piece of rope. Miss Eve's own rump bounced a little, too, as she said, "As a matter of fact, I know a lot about automobiles."

"That so?"

In New Orleans, they were plentiful. Most everyone who lived in the Garden District had a Ford or a hand crank. Automobiles were a part of life. The city ran on electricity—the trolleys and the buildings and houses. Filling stations were starting to sprout up, and there was talk of outfitting the entire fire department with motorized vehicles.

"Yes, it is so." With her free hand, Eve adjusted the angle of her hat to ward off the sun. He liked that big hat with the roses and things on it, but he kept his eyes on the trail when she said, "We've got two Cadillac Model 4 Touring cars, a Buick of some kind—

I think it's a Model 19—it has tufted tan leather uphol-stery and cherrywood on it. A 1909 Rolls-Royce Silver Ghost. And the most recent is a Pierce-Arrow 66-QQ just off the assembly. I know because that's all my father talked about for weeks before its arrival. He bragged, 'It's got six cylinders of the most expensive engine in all of Texas, making it seven thousand two hundred dollars' worth of envy.' "

"Whereabouts in Texas do you live?"

"I–I never said I lived in Texas."

"Sure you did. A second ago. And even then, you wouldn't have had to tell me. *Accent.*" He mimicked the "Texas" tone to her voice.

"Oh. Well . . . yes, then I have to admit it. But it doesn't matter what city."

They were headed into that territory again—duck-ing and dodging the finer parts of truths. "Your dad works for a real rich guy in Texas, huh?"

"You don't know how rich."

"Filthy?"

"As dirty as money can get."

"Cattleman?"

"He's got some on the property."

"Big spread?"

"Endless."

"You live there all your life?"

"Yes."

"Never been anyplace else?"

"No, not really . . ." Dejection caught in her reply.

The river beat a path before them, turning and twisting a mold in the creek bed. They drew the horses up to the water, and let them take a drink. The depth of the creek didn't pose a problem crossing. A ribbon of muddy blue panned out to the left, while the right disappeared behind a rocky wall.

"Do you swim, or am I going to have to drag you out if you fall in?" he asked.

"You won't have to drag me out."

"So is that a yes or a no?"

"It's a 'Quit doubting me.' "

"All right, then. Let's go."

He kneed his horse, sitting high in the saddle. They both sloshed through the water, churning it under their animals' hooves. Droplets splashed high on the horses' knees and shoulders, spraying the bottom of his pants while spotting Eve's dress. In the arid climate, he dried almost immediately. But the water that came up felt refreshing while it lasted.

Eve held her hand out and let the water hit her glove. She ran her fingers over her mouth and beneath her chin. He watched, caught in the way something so simple held his attention. She had to be hot and tired. She hadn't given him one complaint, and for that, he admired her.

Once they were on the other side of the creek, the morning passed by in relative silence. Every now and then, he'd point out a rabbit or a prairie dog den. Common snakes. A diamondback coiling under a slit in a rock. She cringed, but she didn't get silly or hysterical on him. In fact, she seemed more than interested in everything around her. It was too hot for the coyotes. They'd be out as soon as the sun went down.

They stayed to the outskirts of Sweetwater. There was no reason to cut through. The Texas Pacific ran into the cattle town, bringing with it people from places he probably didn't care to know. Some ten miles out of the city limits, they stopped for a light meal.

He'd bought Eve her own canteen and blanket. Aside from that, he had whatever else she needed. He'd stocked up on water, bought more hardtack, tins of meat, coffee, and other foodstuff that would keep in his travel bag. He'd made a roll with his blanket, stuck in a mess kit, and fit it over the back of his saddle. The canteen was looped over his chest on a belt. His .38 Super fit snugly next to his thigh. He traveled light, but he traveled prepared.

As they shared a lunch of dry crackers and beef jerky, Eve chewed on hers with a dissatisfied expression. For once, it wasn't aimed at him.

"A Texas Steer Sandwich," she mentioned. "I saw it listed on the hotel menu last night. At the time, I thought it sounded terrible so I ordered the chicken special. Right now, I'd like to find out how terrible a steer sandwich is."

"Naw, you wouldn't like it."

"Why not?"

"It's made from oysters." That wasn't true, but the forlorn look on her face made him feel sorry for her. Something she probably wouldn't want from him, but she got it just the same. There were moments when she looked so innocent. As if she hadn't ever seen a rabbit in the desert or a menu in a hotel restaurant.

"Oysters—like the castrated kind from steers?"

"Working for a cattleman, I'd've figured you'd have known that."

"Yes, but where I live, they don't call those 'steer sandwiches.' They call them cow fries. And I can promise you, I've never been tempted even though I have a weakness for fried chicken."

Luke couldn't help himself. He laughed so hard, his rib bones kind of ached. But not in an unpleasant way. No, not at all.

The night fire was banked low. The crackle of the few pieces of fuel Luke had found burned with a lot of smoke. They sat upwind of the fire. He'd thrown on a patty or two of cow droppings. She never knew that something icky like that could be used to burn.

Stars had risen into the sky. They blazed in deep clusters here and there, like a twinkling blanket of wonder; only small pockets of deep black were visible.

Evelyn lay back on her bedroll, legs crossed at the knees, and looked up for the longest time, thinking she'd never seen anything so beautiful. Nor had she ever tasted a dinner so good—one out of a can. Some kind of ham preparation she'd thought would be vile. On the contrary. The cured meat went well with Boston crackers and strong black coffee. She usually drank English tea with plenty of sugar and cream. Oddly, she found the roasted beans perked over a campfire more than satisfying. But then again, she'd been so ravenous, she could have eaten almost anything.

Told to curry the horses, she'd stayed back and watched Luke fix their dinner without a falter in efficient speed. She could take care of horses, and was glad he entrusted that end to her. She couldn't take care of dinner. So it came as a surprise that Luke offered to cook without knowing this. To her knowledge, she'd never eaten anything prepared by a man. Their cook was a woman. She'd always assumed the chefs in restaurants were women, too.

When she'd finished with the horses, she'd sat and observed all the little things Luke did. He had a can opener. Interesting device. Effortlessly, he used a steel blade with a handle, and some kind of guide, around the can's tiny circumference. As she studied him, she thought it sad that she'd never once opened a can. How many people had opened cans and she hadn't? It should have been taught in school. Can opening. Coffee making. That, too, had proved to be a lesson.

He had a small coffeepot to which he added grounds and water. Not a lot of water. He placed the pot on the fire until it boiled. Then after about five minutes, he added more water before pulling the pot off the direct heat of the fire and letting it sit for a few minutes. How did he know how to do that? Did he have a mother who taught him? Sisters?

Dangerous thoughts pulled her toward a place she shouldn't go. She shouldn't be interested in anything about Luke Whoever. They were merely travel companions to El Paso. In five or so days from now, they'd never see each other again.

And yet . . . she couldn't forget the touch of his lips over hers. She'd never experienced anything like it; soft and demanding yet gently arousing. She'd been thinking a lot about that night in Abilene. About the way Luke had kissed her. She'd relived the moment more than she would ever admit to. Even now, there were times when she looked at him and she wanted him to kiss her again. To make her feel—

She quickly blinked the thought from her mind.

The odor of tobacco smoke drifted to her. Evelyn lifted herself onto her elbows. Careful not to spill the coffee in the bent cup in her hand, she took a drink and looked over the rim to stare at Luke.

He leaned his back into the curve of his saddle, one leg straight out in front of him, and the other bent. The outline he made against the sky was powerful and devilishly attractive. The cigarette between his fingers burned as he drew on it; the reddish glow of the ash illuminated his face. He seemed relaxed, but his features were tense. The set of his jaw suggested he was bothered by something. There were touches of worry around the corners of his mouth.

"What's after El Paso?" she asked quietly.

At first, she thought he didn't hear her. Then he looked her way. "New Mexico."

"Oh."

Resting his arm on his knee, he asked, "What's after El Paso for you?"

In that moment, Evelyn made a decision. She'd had few friends in her life. Mostly acquaintances except for Pinkie, who had gotten married years ago; regretfully, their correspondences had slowed to a trickle. Aside from that, every woman she was associated with knew who she was. What she stood for. So special little snippets of shared life experiences weren't really valued between them. It was more about who they were, what they were, who they were to be married to when the time came. Evelyn had never seen any usefulness to that kind of relationship. It seemed petty and superficial. In all its sadness—she'd never had a best friend.

Not that she was mulling over Luke's potential as a friend, but he had no clue as to who she was; she felt safe in telling him a small piece of her reality. Simply because in less than a week's time, and given how they'd traveled and what she knew about him, he couldn't really care less who she was. He had his own agenda.

"I'm going to California," she stated, then sipped some of the warm coffee. She'd drunk one cup already; this was her second. The more she had, the smoother it went down. And the more wide awake she felt. "I want to see the Pacific Ocean. And lemon groves. Palm trees. All the things that Texas doesn't have."

Thoughtfully nodding, he silently offered her a cigarette with a half smile that spoke louder than any teasing words could have. She declined, never again willing to have the gray smoke choke the air from her lungs and make her sick to her stomach. She'd only tried smoking to be fashionable. Out here, there was nobody to be fashionable for. Just her, Luke and . . .

"I've never been to California," he offered.

"Where have you been?"

He hesitated a moment. "Most every part of Louisiana, some cities in Oklahoma and Mississippi. My folks took me to Chicago once to see the World's Fair when I was fifteen."

"It must have been wonderful."

"Yeah, it was pretty great. My dad got a big kick out of it. He dragged me and my brothers with him to see the water fountain dancers four times."

Smiling softly, Evelyn said in an equally soft voice, "Well, it doesn't sound like you minded. You're very lucky to have a father like that who wants you to go with him. Mine would never make time for a fair, much less watch women dance in water."

"My dad died three years later, and yes, I was lucky to have him as long as I did."

"I'm sorry."

"No—it's all right. He lived a good life. He accomplished a lot."

She drank the rest of her coffee, then rubbed sand inside the cup like she'd observed Luke do. Water was too valuable to waste on washing dishes so they had to find another method. "How many brothers do you have?"

His eyes met hers; the white of his teeth was visible as he gave her a fast smile. "We should turn in. We've got a long day tomorrow."

"I'm not sleepy."

"Force yourself, Eve." He shuffled the gear beside him, pulling out things from his bag. He unrolled his blanket to make a bed. Using his smoothly tanned saddle as a pillow, he drew a second blanket up to his broad shoulders. He was no more than several feet away from her, yet she felt a little frightened. As if he were miles away. What if a snake slithered into the camp? She'd put on a brave front when he'd pointed them out today. But she'd been petrified.

With his back to her, he settled in. "Lay back and close your eyes. You'll drift off."

She didn't think so. She was more wide awake than she'd been in days. Evelyn made up her own bed in the same manner. She could do it herself. She was realizing she could do a lot of things herself. It was a nice sense of accomplishment to take care of personal needs. All her life she'd had people do for her. Now she was doing for herself.

As she lay down, she tried to tuck as much of the blanket around her as possible to keep crawly things off her. Her eyes refused to close. She thought she heard things. Noises. Scratching and ruffling through the pops of the slowly dying fire.

In the distance came a bay. Like from a dog. Then a yip. No wind stirred the air. Everything seemed to hang thickly. The fire smoke, the noises, the sound of her breathing.

Evelyn rolled onto her other side. Now, she faced Luke's back. Big mistake. She definitely couldn't close her eyes. They remained focused on the breadth of shoulders, the outline of a hip naturally cocked against the hard ground. The black hair that rested on his collar. His duster was wadded into a ball on top of the saddle. By his side, the gun was within reach. Although it wasn't visible to her now, she'd seen him put it there after dinner.

Drawing in a sigh, she reasoned she was interested in him because he was something she could never have. Even if she went home, her father would never allow her to be courted by a man who was eluding the authorities. Luke was an outlaw. A rough frontiersman. But it was those forbidden things about Luke that fascinated her.

His hand came up to absently scratch his neck. Was

he still awake? She was in the mood to talk, but she didn't want to disturb him. She bit her fingernail and willed herself to get sleepy. Time seemed endless. As the minutes ticked off, her mind began to drift. Then things grew dark.

Darker . . .

At first, Evelyn didn't know what woke her. She didn't even think she'd been asleep. Because when her eyes flew open, she was instantly aware of her surroundings. And a pain in her leg from where a rock poked her. Shifting, she ran her hand over the blanket and moved the offending piece out.

Urrr! Yeyeye! Yip! Yip!

She stiffened, eyes wide. There it was again! The scary noise out in the dark. She'd heard it in her sleep. She'd been dreaming the wild whoops were her father joyfully calling out when the 1019 Gusher hit pay dirt at one thousand nineteen feet.

Looking at Luke's silhouette, she was hoping he'd move so she wouldn't have to be alone with her fears. But he didn't give the slightest indication he was awake.

Urrr! Yeyeye! Yip! Yip!

Evelyn put her fingers over her mouth and lay quietly. Alone with her worries that wild animals were preparing to descend on them and eat the flesh right off their bones. She put the scratchy wool blanket over her head and tried to blot out the cries. They didn't go away. They seemed to grow louder.

About five minutes later, she became aware of something that she simply couldn't will away. She had a strong need for the water closet. But there was no way she was going into the bushes on her own. So she'd wait. Until morning when the sun was up and the—

Urrr! Yeyeye! Yip! Yip!

—nighttime animals were gone.

She closed her eyes. For all of thirty seconds. No question, she was not going to make it until morning. Of all the unfortunate timing. She was loath to wake up Luke. But there was nothing else she could do.

"Um—Luke?"

Nothing.

"Luke, I need to get up for a moment."

Mumbles came her way. "Go ahead."

While she was relieved he was now awake, she was also distressed by having to clarify what she needed him for. "Yes, but I can't without you."

"Why not?"

"I . . . that is, I need you to stand guard for me."

"For what?" he muttered, stirring.

He was making her spell it out. "Well, I have to . . . that is . . ." She couldn't say it. She was mortified. Surely, her cheeks were as red as the heat she felt on them. "I have to . . ." she tried once more, but trailed the words. "I need to . . . there are wild animals out there or I wouldn't be asking. But I really don't want to be taken by surprise and be something's evening meal."

Rolling over, he stared at her while shoving a strand of hair from his eyes. "What in the hell are you talking about?"

She clamped her lips tightly together, opened them, closed them, then finally said, "I drank too much coffee."

He let out a long, tired sigh but he didn't give her an indication he thought she was hideously vulgar for bringing up such a private matter. "You couldn't have taken care of this before I fell asleep?"

"I didn't have to then."

He stifled a yawn. "Fine." But the word didn't sound so *fine* when he uttered it. "Let me put my boots on."

"Thank you," she murmured, overwhelmed by embarrassment. It was the first situation of its kind she'd been in. And she hoped never to face such a thing again.

Within a few moments, Luke stood holding onto his gun. He didn't even bother to strap on the holster. He held onto the revolver's grip and aimed the barrel at the ground. "I saw some brush over there."

With his chin, he motioned in the direction of the yapping noises.

"I don't know about that. Wouldn't over there be better?"

"No. It's too rocky."

"I don't mind rocks," she said with optimism.

"These rocks have snakes in them that love to slither into boots."

"Over the way you said will do just fine." She quickly retracted her earlier opinion.

They walked into the darkness with the campfire embers barely aiding them. It didn't take long before the ground grew awfully black. Luke led the way, and if she walked any closer, she'd slam into him. Although it was an exceptionally warm night, she shivered.

"Right here. I'll turn my back."

Evelyn dared to take five large steps away from him so he couldn't hear her, then made fast work of what she had to do. Efficiently, she put herself in order.

As she pushed down her skirts, *Urrr! Yeyeye! Yip! Yip!* practically sounded directly into her ear. Gulping, she slowly turned around and gazed into two glowing eyes.

Evelyn let out a petrified scream and followed it with, "Luke!"

12

Luke had the hammer of his .38 cocked and was instantly beside Eve. In the immediate distance, the skitter of pebbles sounded and his trained eyes recognized the vague outline of a coyote as it took off in a run. Releasing the hammer back to safety, he lowered the gun. Then focused his attention on the woman holding on to him.

As he breathed in, he could smell last night's soap in her hair.

"Honey, if I'd known you were coming to pay a call," Luke spoke as Eve burrowed herself next to him, "I would have washed up in that creek we passed about fourteen miles ago." Pressed so close to him, the curves of her body seemed to fit just right.

He brought his arm over her shoulder and tucked her head beneath his chin, his Colt resting in his hand and pointing away from them.

"I don't care about that," she frantically replied. "Th-There was a wild animal right there. Where I was. I saw glowing eyes. Didn't you hear it yapping?"

"I did, but there's no reason to get all excited about it."

"Is it gone?" With a forced optimism in her voice, she asked, "For good, do you think?"

"Maybe."

"You don't think for sure?"

"Couldn't say."

"Oh." Then he felt her stiffen. As if she just figured out where she was. Following the tensing of her muscles came a murmured, "Oh . . . I'm sorry. I didn't mean to jump at you."

With the nice fragrance of her hair clouding around them, he said, "You can jump at me any time."

He could barely make out her face.

"I don't think it will be necessary again," she replied softly. "Thank you for the rescue. I appreciate it."

"Not a problem. Is this where I get a kiss of gratitude?"

He never thought she'd do it, but she reached up on tiptoes and kissed him on the cheek. A brief and chaste brush of her lips, but it heated him just the same. With her face still within inches of his, she slowly lowered herself and stood considerably shorter than he once again. Before she moved any farther, he slipped his hands around her waist and pulled her back to take full possession of her mouth.

He caught her unbound hair in his hand, feeling its softness as he tasted her sweetness. He pulsed with heat and wanting. She molded herself to him; his muscles burned where they touched. Wrapping her arms around his neck, her full breasts crushed into his chest. It took everything he had not to bring her down to the ground and make her his. He resisted, but his desire didn't dim. A tormented groan escaped him while he changed the slant of their kiss. There was a reckless abandon to it as he caressed her mouth.

Luke's whole consciousness focused on her. His hands moved down the length of her back, bringing her closer. She curled into him. Her body melted against his and brought him a pleasure that was explosive.

Time ceased as the passion built between them. The kiss deepened and the very air around them seemed electrified. He traced the seam of her closed lips, but felt her muscles tense in response. She gasped, then slid her hand up his chest and abruptly tore her mouth from his while gulping for air.

She wrenched herself away, looking down, then drawing her hand to her temple as if to steady her balance. "I-I'm all right now. We can go back to the fire."

The fire inside Luke was already raging and, as far as he was concerned, they were standing in the middle of the conflagration. He told himself it was just a kiss, but he knew there was something more than that. The realization instantly sobered him.

"All right," Luke finally managed to say. "We'll go back."

They started walking. The low ember light fanned out before them, and as if to erase what had just happened, Eve lightly mentioned, "You came when I called out your name. It's really Luke."

His thoughts were still not as clear as they should be. "Yeah, it's really Luke."

They returned to their bedrolls. Eve huddled deep into her blanket as if to shield herself from him. Maybe from her own feelings of discovering the strong passion of need.

Lying there, she faced him while he still sat. He wished like hell she'd turn the other way as he tried to shove aside the awareness of her watching him. The warmth of her mouth remained at the forefront of his mind. He battled against the effects of her close scrutiny, against taking her in his arms once more and damning the consequences. She bothered him in ways he hadn't anticipated; as if he needed to measure up.

He wondered what she was thinking, then thought better. He didn't want to know. Because he didn't want to think about how good she'd felt in his arms.

Luke wasn't sleepy anymore. He'd been out cold before Eve woke him. He was the type of sleeper that once he was awake, he could forget about falling back off. There would be no more shut-eye for him tonight.

Extending his hand toward the firelight, he glanced at the time on his watch dial. A glare made him tilt his wrist forward in order to read the position of the hands. Sunrise wouldn't break on the horizon for at least another two hours.

"What time is it?" Eve asked from her woolen den.

"Three thirty-seven."

"Is that the kind of watch I think it is?"

He raised his arm to show her. "What? A wristwatch?"

"Yes. I've never seen one on a man before."

"They make them for men if that's what you're wondering. I have a half dozen pocket watches, but they aren't as handy as this. Having the time readily available to me on a wristband beats digging for a pocket watch while driving."

"Driving?" She scooted up. "You know how to drive an automobile?"

He lay down and lit a cigarette. "I *own* an automobile. A Torpedo Roadster that sits sweet and low with a rather rakish-looking windshield frame."

"I've never seen a Roadster. Are they terribly expensive?"

He was real proud of that car. It might not have been any Cadillac, but the vehicle was a modern convenience that he appreciated; he kept her parked in a garage he'd had built special at the back of his townhouse. "Maybe not for your father's boss cattleman, but for me it was. That Roadster set me back seven hundred big ones. That's a lot of hours of police work."

"Police?"

Ah, hell. For a moment, his jaw clamped down as he did some fast thinking. "Sure—police work. The work it takes to dodge the flatfoots from trailing me in the robberies I commit. After a heist, I have to be careful where I stash my"—the Cajun-style explanation rolled off his tongue as if he were C. C. Savoy, a rounder who was in and out of the Sixty-second Precinct on bunko charges—"picayune."

"What's picayune?"

"Boodle?"

"What's—"

"Stolen money."

"What's a flatfoot?"

"Policeman." Luke bent his arm and rested his head on his elbow. "That part of Texas where you're from must be nothing but sagebrush country, because you don't know a lot about the outside world, do you?"

"It all depends on the subject," she said, the tension from the aftermath of their kiss waning to where she challenged him. "I've learned lots by, uh . . . observing. Yes, by observing and listening to household conversation. Ask me anything about etiquette, letter writing, clothing styles and floral language."

"I'll pass."

"Well, if you did ask me, you'd see that I'm quite knowledgeable."

"But how often do you really need to know those things? Wouldn't you rather know five different words for police officer? Given your line of work—stolen stage line horses, and all. You'd better know what law words to look out for when you're being pursued."

"I'd never thought about that." She sat up, her glorious hair falling over her shoulders in a cascade of golden curls. He tamed his thoughts before they could get the better of him. The blanket had fallen beside her lap, and shadows on her face traced delicate contours and curves. She was definitely beautiful to look at. "Okay, what are some?"

Luke didn't normally—in fact, he never had—enlightened people on the jargon associated with his job. "Well, you've got flatfoot, long arm of the law,

muldoon, bluecoat, and my least personal favorite—
roach."

"I wouldn't like roach either."

"So there you go. You just learned five new words."

Her lips parted in a smile. Looking at her made him
feel good. "Thank you, Luke, that was most informa-
tive."

Eve collected her hair in one hand, ran her fingers
through the soft tangles, then braided it. The gesture
was simple, but new to him. He'd never watched a
woman braid her hair. He'd taken hair down, pulling
out the pins, but he'd never paid attention to it going
up. While he'd never envied his brothers their mar-
riages, right now, he did think about them. The intimacies they were able to share each day. All three had
fine wives. He was the oldest, and so far, no woman
had made him want to step up to an altar.

Luke had been the first of his brothers to join the
department. Proudly, he'd worked his way up to lieutenant over years of hard work and dedication. He
took on the toughest beats, tackled the hardest cases,
and invested long hours. He probably threw too much
of himself into the job. Jayce, Chandler and Phillipe
were able to carve solid careers for themselves, but
they also met the women who would become the
focus of their lives. His brothers would rib him about
finding a wife of his own but since he never lacked
female company, he didn't feel he was missing anything.

He told himself he was happy. Completely devoted
to his job, he liked keeping the peace. Liked walking
the beat when he had to. Seeing old faces. Meeting

new. He liked driving his Roadster down to the Bayou Quarter for some beignets and talking with the fishermen sitting at the docks.

With the corruption shaking through precincts, the explosion coming from the Sixty-sixth, he'd been rethinking a lot of things. Being away from New Orleans had allowed him time to acknowledge that life was short, and perhaps he had not been living it to its truest end.

He'd begun to wonder if he'd missed out on experiences that would have made him a better man. He didn't want to reach old age with regrets.

"I can't fall back asleep," Eve said with a wistfulness that broke into his thoughts.

"You should try. You'll regret it tomorrow."

"It's already tomorrow. Maybe we should saddle the horses and get an early start."

"Nope." He pitched his smoke into the fire and poked around the coals with a stick. Several shoots of tiny flames sprang to life within the rock border. "We can't ride out until the sun comes up. I don't know this terrain. I've never ridden it. Could be sandy, could be rocky. I need to see things clearly."

"I've been studying my map," she continued, "and I figured out you had us walking into Dallas backwards. It would have been faster to just go in a straight line, but no. We went out of our way. How come?"

"Because you never travel how somebody expects you to."

"What do you mean?"

"Like our going to El Paso, for example. Anyone

would think either ride the train or on horseback and directly follow the Texas Pacific. We haven't been doing either. I've cut us through gullies and washes. We're four miles south of Roscoe. It wouldn't have taken us long to get there to have a hot meal and a decent bed for the night. But doing that would have been too risky."

"You're pretty expert on this dodging flatfoots thing. You've had a lot of practice."

On the flatfoot side. "Uh, yeah." He went for the coffeepot, felt if there was any left, and was able to pour himself a half cup. "I can make another pot, if you want."

"No, that's all right." She brought her knees together, draping the blanket over her legs. "But you wouldn't happen to have any tea, would you?"

Teasing her, he returned, "I didn't pack any this time."

While sipping his coffee, a falling star shot through the sky. One of the horses nickered. And somewhere over the east ridge, a lone coyote howled.

"Do you play cards?" Eve suddenly asked through the coyote's cry, the high pitch in her tone failing to mask fear.

"It depends."

"I have a deck I got from the hotel. Would you care to play?"

"Not at this hour."

"It would be fun, really. We both can't sleep so it'll help to pass the time."

"I can sleep," he lied.

"No you can't. You said so yourself, and if you could, you'd be doing so right now."

"Well, maybe I will. I'll just turn over and—"

"*Please*. Please play cards with me. Those coyotes are making me restless and I—I did drink too much of that blasted coffee you made. So I'll probably have to go visit the . . . you know, once more. We can play whatever game you'd like."

He'd never played cards with a woman. The opportunity had never presented itself. He liked a good game of faro or poker, but parlor games weren't his specialty. His family played them—introduced by the wives, much to his mother's joy. She was a whist player. Had a club of ladies who were in the house once a week for tournaments.

With a brightness in her eyes, Eve said, "I'm quite adept at Toad in the Hole, Puss in the Corner, Demon, Beleaguered Castle and Windmill."

"Never heard of them."

Loosely joining her slender fingers together, she lowered her chin. "They're all solitary games."

"Spend a lot of time alone?"

As if holding a hurtful emotion in check, she simply sighed. "I do."

Facing her, he folded his arms over his chest to give her a curious gaze. Perhaps she was so talkative because she apparently rarely got the chance to converse; she spent a lot of time on her own.

Without a moon, the night was clear and windless. Warmth rose from the ground and radiated from the small campfire. There was no sign of dawn spreading over the eastern flatlands. He should make her rest. He hadn't missed how she arched and rubbed her back after she'd dismounted. The stiffness and pain of being in a saddle for seven hours. How she maneuvered herself on her bedroll with slow and deliberate motions so as not to tax her muscles.

While he might not have minded playing cards, he knew she should be thinking of relaxing her body before entertaining her mind.

Luke pressed his hands over his knees. "I don't know how to play any of the popular card games. Just poker."

"Then you could show me how to play poker?"

"It would take too long."

"But you said yourself, we can't leave until the sun comes up. That would give us an hour or more of nothing to do. I'm quite certain I could catch on rather quickly. Then tomorrow night, after dinner, we could amuse ourselves with games until we get tired."

Looking at the sparkle come to life in her eyes made him think of other ways they could amuse themselves. Killing a few hours watching her arrange cards would be pleasing on his eyes.

He flexed his fingers. "Get out your cards."

"Wonderful!"

In seconds, she produced a deck of cards and over the course of the early morning, as the sky began to streak with fragments of daylight, he taught her card lingo and the manner in which poker was played. To her credit, she never lost interest in his explanation of suits and flushes. She grasped the concept, and in fact, was very good at building a hand.

As they packed up the camp at sunrise and saddled the horses for another full day, Luke wondered what else Eve would be good at.

13

Swaying with the motion of the horse beneath her, Evelyn had never felt a dry heat so hot. The relentless rays of the sun pressed down on her head and shoulders like a flatiron. While her hat was of some relief, its brim couldn't ward off the stifling air hitting her in the face. Against all that was proper, she'd undone the buttons at the cuffs of her sleeves and rolled them to her elbows. The skin on her arms was turning pink, but she didn't care. She still felt faint from wearing too many layers of clothing. What she wouldn't give to sit in a watering hole.

She took another drink from her canteen and moistened the end of a bandanna Luke had given her. Using the damp material as a compress, she laid it on her forehead with one hand, while the other held onto the reins. She'd given up on wearing her gloves miles ago and the chafing between her fingers was worsening.

Luke rode in front of her down a marginal grade of rocky ground. She kept in line behind him, trying to keep her mind from the heat. Each time she thought of a distraction, it came back to one thing: last night's kiss.

She couldn't believe she'd taken him up on his dare for a kiss. What had started out as innocent, and admittedly flirtatious, had turned dangerous. As soon as he'd taken command of the kiss, her complete response to him had come as a shocking thrill. Suddenly and swiftly, she'd longed for more than just an obligatory token of appreciation. Where those thoughts had come from, she couldn't fathom. And yet, when he'd moved to slip his tongue inside her mouth, she'd gotten scared. Everything had gone so fast.

She wasn't prepared for this. To have these feelings of confusion. If only she wasn't who she was and he wasn't who he was and they weren't in the middle of—

A wave of heat threatened her balance and brought on nausea. *Don't think about how hot you are.* Keep your mind on other things.

No, not on Luke.

She went rounds in her mind with the facts and figures of poker. Five card draw. Knave, ace, deuce. Three of a kind beat two pair. A straight in the same suit is called a straight flush. Three of a kind and two pair is valued as a full house.

She moved the bandanna down the side of her face and onto the back of her neck. She could almost swear she saw a large expanse of water ahead. It appeared to go on for miles and miles. A lake.

A lake.

Evelyn's elation surged through her body, bringing

her back to life in a way that she felt giddy. She licked her dry lips and was so glad, she began to laugh at their good fortune.

"I for one intend to soak myself through in that body of water," she said, feeling a bit of renewed strength. "I don't know how you found that lake and I don't care."

Over his shoulder, he asked, "What lake?"

"That one straight ahead. It's not on my map. Have we gone very far outside of West Brook?"

Luke faced forward and drew in on his reins so he could wait up for her. Once she was beside him, he leaned forward in his saddle. Resting his elbow on the saddle horn, he used his thumb to adjust the angle of his hat so the sun wouldn't be in his eyes when he spoke to her. "Honey, I hate to tell you this, but there's no lake out there."

"But there is. I see it." She looked out to the expanse of land in front of them, scattered with cattle-size boulders and scrubs—and the shimmering stretch of a large lake. "How can you not see it?"

"I never said I didn't see water—I do."

Relief once more held her. "Oh good. I knew it. We can cool off and—"

"Eve, it's a mirage."

"I don't care what kind of lake it is. I'll sit in it."

Rubbing the muscles behind his neck with his leather-gloved hand, he shook his head. "A mirage is an optical illusion. You're seeing what's not really there."

"That can't be. I know what I see." She squinted hard and sharp just to make sure. "It's water. Lots of it."

"No, there isn't any. It's a trick of vision."

"But I . . ."

The sober inflection in his tone told her he wasn't kidding. There really was no lake.

Her eyes fluttered closed, and she felt as if she could fall right out of the saddle and just wither up. Give up. Go home. This was the worst form of torture. Endless desert that felt like it had no air, and with heat ripples off the desert floor. She'd never been so hot and tired and dirty in all her life.

"Whoa," Luke called out, invading the black space that had pulled at her. She blinked as a steady hand gripped her upper arm. "I almost lost you."

Her mouth fell open, and she exhaled, looking into the concerned depths of gray eyes; they'd deepened to a hue of blue. Smythe Blue. She couldn't focus on anything but his eyes. They filled her with tranquillity. Luke's heavenly eyes that caused her to speak what was on her mind, no matter what. Perhaps she really was in some kind of delirium, because she began to ramble.

"I want . . . I want a cool bath with my favorite rose smelling salts and a glass of lemonade with ice and lemon slices." Then the strangest thing happened— she suddenly grew cold. "The spring issue of *Harper's Bazaar* where they illustrate the Easter hats." Her palms went from dry to clammy and it was an effort to breathe. The unrelenting stays of her corset constricted her ribs from expanding. "I want an electric fan on my windowsill and fresh linen sheets on my bed. To wear my boudoir gown. The dainty white lawn one with the nice white embroidery medallion and beaded ribbons."

"That's it. You're getting off your horse."

"But I'm not finished telling you want I want."

"You're finished. Give me those reins."

She didn't remember relinquishing them. Simply riding beside him until they reached the bottom of the hill they'd been ascending. Once at its base, he dismounted and came around to reach up for her.

She gazed into his face, his arms extended. "Come on."

"Do you have the lemonade ready?"

She received no answer. He must have fisted the fabric of her dress skirt because she was yanked toward him. The next thing she felt were firm arms beneath hers as the sandy earth touched beneath her shoes. She allowed herself to be propelled toward a lone evergreen. How the scruffy tree got out in the middle of nowhere, she'd never guess. Its shade gave her a little respite from the blinding sun as Luke sat her down under its vague canopy.

"I've lost my bandanna. Where's my bandanna? The one you gave me. I was holding it, now I've lost it. I need that."

A canteen was shoved at her, the top screwed off. "Never mind the bandanna."

In this illusive transitional space she had no understanding of, the Trail Riding Eve evaporated into the heat ripples. She became Evelyn Thurgood-Baron in thoughts and actions. She wanted to be pampered. Waited on. Made comfortable. "Be a dear, would you, and pour me a glass of lemonade."

"I want you to take a sip. *A small sip*. You got that— *small*."

"You said it twice."

"And I meant it twice."

"Where's the lemonade?"

"You can have the lemonade when you're done with the water."

"Oh, very well then." She did as she was told. One small sip. As soon as the warm liquid touched her parched tongue, she knew she had to have another sip. Just a quick one. She lifted the canteen—

"*Small.*"

"But I'm thirsty," she pouted.

She felt tugging and pulling at her feet. "If you drink some more, you're going to puke."

"I haven't thrown up in years, not since I ate an entire box of Pitney's chocolate covered cherries to relieve my—"

Whoops! She'd been on the verge of revealing a female malady she suffered from, and her requirement for a large quantity of candy to make her feel remotely human. "Never mind why I ate the chocolate. My mother knows why. That was one of the few things we understood about each other." Evelyn heaved a sigh. "Go get her for me . . . I want to talk to her."

A feeling of loneliness and despair settled deeply inside her. Suddenly, she wanted to be back home. To hear her mother's voice and be comforted by her. She missed the sound of her father's gruff laughter. Seeing him at the breakfast table in the morning reading the newspaper. Melancholy tugged at her heart.

"More water," she managed, shoving her reflections aside. Her mouth was so dry she could barely speak. "Please. Aside from an overindulgence of Pitney's, I have a very dependable stomach."

"You still can't drink any more water."

"Why not?"

But her question hung between them as she gazed down to see a pair of tanned hands at the throat of her dress—unbuttoning it. Aghast, she locked her jaw, then coughed in surprise. "I don't think . . . that is, I feel much better now."

She weakly batted at his insistent hands when he didn't cease parting her bodice. What he was doing to her was not only shameful and humiliating, but exciting and thrilling. The way she had felt when she'd reached up to kiss his cheek last night.

Oh, don't think about that again, Evelyn.

Her gaze fixed on his lips and their firm outline. The rough bark of the tree's trunk behind her didn't feel so uncomfortable anymore. It felt as if she were floating a little. Kind of on a cloud. A bit light-headed, but not in the way she had felt earlier.

"You're choking on fluff," he said, reaching behind her neck. She grew aware of an article of a highly personal nature being removed from her.

For reasons unknown to her, the pursuit to retain her modesty had failed as soon as his rough knuckles had brushed over the hollow of her throat. Without blushing, she corrected, "That's my bust ruffle."

He shoved the lace at her. "It's your handkerchief now. Get it wet in the water from the canteen. Try not to spill any. Once you've got it wet, put the ruffle behind your neck."

"It would feel much better over my bust," she

quipped, unable to believe such a comment came from her. She truly was ill. Some desert fever had set itself deep into the marrow of her bones.

With hands that were not all that confident, she poured some of the water and got the lace damp enough. Then she did as Luke had told her. She put the cool cloth behind her neck where the fine hairs on her nape met at her collar's edge. The quenching respite she felt was instantly replaced by a bolt of consciousness over where Luke's ministrations had taken him.

To her waist. To the very exposure of her corset cover, the suffocating corset, and beyond to her snowy white underskirt. Dear heaven. He was undressing her down to the skin.

"My head hurts," she complained. "Maybe I am going to be sick."

If he was planning on ravishing her, why had he waited so long?

The hooks in the front of her corset were plucked from their eyes one by one with quick flicks of his fingers.

"Luke—I never meant for this . . . last night . . . I'm not what you think I am. Or who for that matter. Reconsider what you're doing. I know you can be reasonable. You taught me poker when I asked."

The dress was removed despite her argument; the corset came next in a quick jerk out from behind her back. How he'd managed that, she couldn't be sure. One minute the items were on her body, the next they were off and she was sitting against a spruce in her cambric corset cover and underskirt with its deep flounce. All the blood inside her seemed to freeze.

Having grown numb in the position in which she sat, she moved her legs; then became aware of yet another disgrace—he'd taken off her shoes as well.

"You're going to have to sit like this for a while. In another ten or so minutes, I'm going to have you drink a sip of water again." Luke sat back on his heels, crouched in front of her, his face appearing handsome and bronzed by the baking sun.

"W-Why do I have to sit in my . . . unmention-ables?"

"You've got heat exhaustion."

His hands reached out, closer toward her collar-bone. She waited for him to grab her shoulders and kiss her on the mouth like he had before. She closed her eyes, warring with two different reactions to him. No and . . . *yes*.

The prolonged stillness was unbearable. When she cautiously opened her eyes, she could see Luke was adjusting the bust ruffle at her neck by sliding up the skimpy lace higher off her shoulders. The contact made her heart take a perilous leap and sent a cascade of shivers across her flesh.

"Don't let that slip down," he said.

When his fingertips slid over her skin as he backed away, she needed a moment to reorient herself. Once more, she lowered her lids. When she lifted them, Luke was out of reach. Not far away from where she rested, he was loosening the cinches on the horses. He checked their hooves, ran his hand down their legs, and didn't once look at her.

She didn't know whether to feel relieved . . . or dis-appointed. The latter pulled strongly.

As for her heat exhaustion, she still felt awful but slightly cooler now that she was in a state of near undress. Thinking she could put her clothes back on, she reached for her dress. Her stomach clenched, almost in an angry rebellion, as if the bottom had dropped out. Moisture beaded on her brows. Every joint in her hurt so badly, she was near tears.

Good heavens, she really wasn't herself.

"Can I have another drink now?" she asked in a hoarse voice. She tried not to let her mind wander back to days in Oiler where she'd sat on the verandah, in the chaise, with a book in her grasp. She pictured her parents sitting in side-by-side rockers, talking at the end of the day. There had been moments of good times for Seymour and Hortensia. But over the years, they had become less and less frequent. Until the household had turned cold. And bitter. With Evelyn caught in between.

"A small one," Luke replied.

But the small taste left her yearning for more. "Just another?"

"No."

"But I can't take it. I'm so thirsty. I just want—"

"No. Get your mind off it." Luke looked at her over the rump of her horse as he checked the leathers on the saddle. "Talk to the tree."

"I beg your pardon?"

"You were the one who said you could talk to flowers."

"Not *talk* to them. I know the *sentiment* attached to them."

"Then tell me what a spruce means."

While she was more versed with a floral medium, she did know the universal consent of leaves as well. "Farewell."

His head lifted. "You're not going anywhere."

"No, the spruce means farewell. If you were to make an arrangement of spruce and yellow chrysanthemums for your lady, you'd be telling her she'd slighted your love and you're bidding her farewell."

"I didn't know that."

"See—I told you I was knowledgeable."

Rounding his horse, he asked, "What's a magnolia mean?"

"What variety?"

He shot her a frown. "I don't know. The ones with the big white flowers."

"Peerless and proud. Perseverance."

"In my neighborhood, the streets are lined with magnolias."

"Your neighborhood?"

"The place I go to when I'm not . . . actively being a road agent." He had a twist of pain on his face when he spoke further. "Where my mother lives. In New Orleans."

"Ah, yes. Humid, like East Texas."

"Right."

"I wouldn't mind humid right now." She sighed. "I'd stick out my tongue and suck up the air."

His low and resonant chuckle seemed to reverberate around them. He let the horses graze on a patch of brown grass, then returned to her. On the edge of a rock beside her, he sat and put his hands on his knees, his feet spread. "How are you feeling?"

"Hot."

"It'll take a little while to cool you down. We'll be held up about an hour."

"I could move on—if we had to."

"No. We're all right." He took a drink, wiped his face with a red kerchief he kept in his trouser pocket, then gazed at the sun for a fast moment—as if to judge its ruthlessness. "So, what does a rose mean? I've given bouquets to women before."

Evelyn stared at him. His hair was thick and heavy, barely visible beneath the brim of his hat, except for the pieces that touched his white collar. While the shirt wasn't bleached nor pristine, it was rather nice; looking more like it belonged to a suit and vest than a pair of pants that were coated with mud splats at the cuffs.

He hadn't shaved this morning and the lower half of his face was dark and heavy with beard. How had she ever thought he was a woman?

For the first time, she noticed a faint scar at his cheek—left, just behind the cheekbone. She vaguely wondered how it came to be there. He moved his hands, and she looked at those, too. They were wide and strong. Hands that could crush. Or minister. Be gentle. And thoughtful.

She lifted her gaze. As their eyes met, she felt another jolt of shock race through her. This time, not in association with surprise, but more electrically charged and magnetic. She disregarded his question about roses—there were twenty-seven varieties, including three buds, and all could mean any number of things—and instead, asked a question of her own. "Have you seen a lot of ladies in their underwear?"

His black brows slightly lifted, but aside from that, he showed no hint of being startled by such a query. "A few."

"I'd bet more than a few."

"Maybe."

"Do I . . . that is . . ." It was absurd, pure and simple, but she had the burning desire to know. "Do I look like they do? Physically . . . appealing?"

This time he worked his jaw, tensing it and with a slight tick just visible below his ear. "You look nice, Eve."

"Honestly?"

"Honestly."

A knot rose in her throat, and she dared herself to speak past it. "Then why haven't you tried to kiss me again?"

He knit his fingers together, and looked skyward once more, then back at her. "I want to. And I've thought about it in more ways than you'll know. But if I kissed you right now, I'd be taking advantage."

"Maybe I really don't want you to reconsider. Maybe—"

"Don't say that."

"Well, maybe I really want you to surprise me," she went on. "To take me into your arms and just kiss me senseless until I—"

"Eve, I'm going to forget you said that."

At this particular moment, she disliked Luke's iron control. The way he could command his emotions without faltering.

A wide-winged bird soared overhead in a circle, crying in a way that made Evelyn grow reflective. She wiped her brow with her palm, unable to understand why she suddenly felt like crying again. Looking at the small line of blisters on her hands, she grew even more despondent. If her mother could see her in this condition, she'd be appalled. Her father would handcuff her to Hadley and that would be the start of her life sentence.

Bone-weary, prostrate from heat, blisters on her hands, and a burn over her arms, she was losing her bid for independence. She felt a partial defeat. A pull toward admittance that she'd been wrong to go out on her own. But she couldn't accept it. She *wouldn't* accept it.

"Let's go," she said tersely, angered by her shortcomings. She needed to be strong. "I'm done resting."

Luke put a hand on her arm. "I don't think so. You can't get up yet. You wouldn't make it ten yards."

Further irritated by her weakness and his strength, she clipped, "Then when will I be done recovering?"

"Thirty minutes."

She sighed. Waited a short while to reason with herself whether or not he was right about her or was just trying to trick her into thinking she was finished with her little attack of vapors. She sighed once more. "Give me your watch. I'm going to time it."

With a smile and a shake of his head, he did as she asked, slipping the band from his wrist. He took her hand, eliciting a shower of tingles up her arm and the curve of her neck. Where the band had covered his skin, there was a pale strip in the rich sun-touched tan.

He put the watch on her. The nickel tension band didn't fit her in any way. The watch hung on her wrist like a bracelet, but she still took comfort in its heavy warmth as she watched the second hand tick in the smaller dial within the large face.

Rising, he asked, "Happy now?"

"Yes." Her steadfast gaze didn't leave the tiny black hand that rounded the twenty-eight-second curve. In her mood, thirty minutes was going to seem like thirty hours.

"You can wash up in the creek," Luke said, handing Eve a cake of soap. The Ivory was nothing fancy—not like that rose stuff she'd been pining over earlier in the day, but the soap he had was better than none at all.

Dusk was creeping up on the day, and they'd stopped for the night at Giraud's Creek, just west of Big Spring. In consideration for Eve, he'd quit pushing their pace for the remainder of the day.

"Soap." She breathed the word as if it were worth a million bucks. "You have *soap.*"

"Sure."

Eve stood in front of him, her tiny hand grasping the Ivory until it nearly disappeared in her fingers. Strands of her blond hair were tousled at her cheeks— cheeks and the bridge of her nose that were suffering the effects of the blazing sun.

After taking off her dress and corset, he'd had her rest long enough to where she was able to ride again. And that was only because he'd refused to let her put on that damn corset. It had been hard to pretend he didn't appreciate the swells and valleys of her body as she'd lain against the tree. The skin at the top of her corset had been as pale as the soap.

When he'd helped her remount her horse after she'd drunk enough water to continue on, he'd fought against the warm sensation deep in the pit of his gut over how soft and pliable she was beneath his palms. Without the corset, she was all woman.

"And a towel?" Eve asked, breaking into his thoughts.

"No to the towel." He removed his hat and wiped the grit from his brow with the back of his hand. Sweat beaded on his forehead, and he didn't think it necessarily came from the June heat. "The air's so warm, by the time you walk from the creek bed back to the fire, you'll probably be dry."

She looked over her shoulder to the string of brush lining the creek banks. Sturdy junipers grew randomly along the water, close enough to let the roots suck up moisture. "Do you think there are any coyotes by the creek?"

"Not now."

"But there could be?"

"I guess, in a half hour or so."

"Do you think," she returned her worried gaze to his, "you could stand guard?"

"I could do that if you want."

"I'd like you to." She went a few steps, then stopped. "But don't look at me while I'm washing up."

"Now how can I watch for coyotes if I'm not looking at you?"

"Well . . . you could wait right over there"—she pointed to the closest juniper while walking to the water's edge—"and sit behind it. That way the branches would block your view but you'd still be able to watch for coyotes."

He tried not to laugh at her crazy reasoning. Not hours ago, she'd been after him to kiss her senseless. Here she was worrying about modesty after he'd already seen her in her underwear. "Yeah, sure."

She waited for him to take up his post before proceeding into the creek. He rested his weight on the balls of his feet in case he had to get up fast. He reached into the pocket of his shirt and fingered a cigarette. He lit it and while smoking, he settled in and gave the terrain a cursory exam. He'd never seen such stark beauty in desolate country. If he'd been out here for any other reason, he might have felt a sense of peace.

"Can you see anything?" Eve called up to him through the gentle splash of water.

His gaze landed on Eve. "Not a thing."

He could see everything.

What she hadn't calculated on was the juniper not being as tall as she thought. And the lower she descended into the water, the more he was able to see of her wading out in the creek.

The sunset bathed her in hues of brilliant gold and orange. She'd stripped out of her dress and stood in her underwear, the now-sheer white fabric clinging to her curves. She held the soap in one hand and ran it across her neck and shoulders. He could almost see her visibly relax. She smiled skyward, then without warning, held out her arms and let herself fall backward into the creek with a delighted cry that sounded more like a song note.

She floated for a long while, soaped some more,

scrubbed her hair and washed her dress. He tried to ignore the tightness in his groin. She made him feel like he had to protect her. Right this second, he *wanted* to protect her from anyone and everything she was running from.

Stars popped out in the blackening sky. He'd started a fire and could smell wisps of burning mesquite come to him on the faint breeze. He wished he could offer her something for dinner besides canned ham and crackers.

Squeezing the water from her blue dress, she climbed the shallow embankment to collect her shoes. The smile on her face said he'd made her happy and it felt good.

"I have never been more glad to be in water in all my life," she said as she reached him.

He rose and ground out his cigarette beneath his boot. "I'm glad to hear that." And he honestly was— glad that he'd done something to put that smile on her mouth.

Water dripped off her long hair, and down her back, and puddled at her feet. Her underclothing was near-transparent, and she was aware of it, too. She covered herself with the fold of the dress held at her neck to conceal her breasts and legs.

"You can wear my duster until your dress dries."

"Thank you."

While Eve sat by the fire brushing her hair dry, Luke washed up in the creek himself. He made a fast but efficient job of it. He returned to find Eve trying to operate the can opener. Miles ago, he'd suspected she wasn't fond of cooking.

She dropped the unopened can and gave him an

apologetic shrug. "I was going to get dinner started." The firelight touched her hair and he felt his throat swell.

"That's all right, I'll do it," he offered, and went for his traveling bag, needing to do something to get his mind off the vision of her as she'd walked toward him in her underwear after washing up.

In a tone filled with awe, she commented, "There must be a real knack to that opener. I tried, but I couldn't figure it out. I'm loath to admit my ignorance, but I . . ."

He didn't hear the rest. He couldn't take his eyes off her. The way she sat with her legs peaking out of the closed front of his duster. Beneath it, she was wearing next to nothing.

. . . *Maybe I really want you to surprise me . . . and just kiss me senseless until I—*

Luke licked his dry lips, his heartbeat racing.

"Where did you learn to use that can opener?"

"Necessity." Rising to his feet, he took long steps to the campfire.

"I suppose that would do it. I've never had the necessity. And do you know what else—I've never really appreciated the finer things in life."

He towered over her and she gazed up at him. A gap in his duster left her throat and the straps of her short chemise exposed. "W-What?"

Reaching down to Eve, he pulled her up to him.

"You wanted to be kissed senseless."

"I—ohhhh—" Her stunned cry became muffled as his mouth crushed hers, and he kissed her hard and deep.

The taste of her lips was like honey, soft and sweet.

He had tried, and been unsuccessful, in ignoring the ache in his body when he held her. When he kissed her. He slanted his lips across hers, their pliant softness warming and arousing the blood that still bolted through him. She aroused a hunger in him that timing had misplaced. Of all the women, of all the moments, to feel such desire. But the reality of a dead end to any kind of romance—him on his way to New Mexico and she on her way to California—didn't stop him from holding her tighter. The stiff surprise in her body slowly melted away. Her arms reached up. Then he felt her hands on his shoulders and she was kissing him back.

Eve's uneven breathing brushed at his lips, the sensation making his pulse jump. He ran his palms down the sides of her arms, teasing the bare skin that was summer warm. He wanted to explore the sensitive skin at the base of her throat. Cup her breasts in his hands.

Lost in the moment, he didn't hear anything around them until the call of a deep, male voice intruded into their embrace.

"Buenos noches, amigos."

14

The heat coursing through Luke's body swiftly cooled. He carefully set Eve away from him, but still held onto her.

"*Amor. Amor. Amor—eh?*" came a guttural laugh.

Two men rode toward the shallow circle of light created by the fire. As they did, Luke missed the weighted feel of his Colt against his thigh. How could he have let his guard down? *Dammit.* He'd broken a cardinal rule of the department: Your gun is your life, without it you're dead.

He made a quick assessment of the armed pair as they sat high in their saddles—the stirrups accented with flashy silver trimming. From the way they were dressed, Luke could see they weren't your average cowboys. Both wore all black. Their bolo ties had ornamental silver clasps while silver beading decorated the pockets of their shirts. Near-identical black pants with silver conches sewn down the outer seams covered their legs.

He wasn't quite sure if they were dangerous or desperate to make a good showing. Either one didn't sit well with him.

"The law of the land is to share," the taller of the two spoke in a heavy Mexican accent. He had a mustache that stopped halfway up his lip.

"You share your coffee and fire," the second stated in an accent that equaled the first man's, "and we will share our hen." Without being invited, he tossed a dead prairie hen beside the campfire.

Both men dismounted in a jangle of silver spurs and silver accents.

Luke spoke to Eve with his eyes.

Do not say a word.

He lowered his hands from her, taking both sides of his duster and bringing them over her breasts.

Then he approached the men. "Evenin', gentlemen."

"*Buenos noches, señor.*" The taller removed his hat in a sweeping gesture, his gaze on Luke. "*Don* Roberto Martínez *y* Vanegas." Motioning to his partner, he added, "And this is my *compadre.*"

"*Don* Ramon Montalvo *y* Gómez." The shorter of the two wore a thin goatee that was trimmed to look like a horseshoe on his chin. "But there is no need to be so formal. You can call me Ramon, and my partner—Roberto."

Luke didn't call either one of them anything. His thoughts were on one thing—his Colt, which rested on top of his travel bag, some ten feet from where he stood. He couldn't just walk on over, get it, and strap it on. He sized the weapons Roberto and Ramon had, at least the visible ones. In holsters, Colt .44-40 and Army .45—both grips carved with Mexican eagles. Two rifles in saddle scabbards. Possible Bowie knife.

"And you are *señor y señora*—?"

He came up with the first name that popped into his head, and he hoped it would work in his favor. If the pair recognized it, they weren't badlands men with no idea of civilized culture. If they didn't, then he had more to be worried about. Men cut off from the real world were a dangerous breed.

"Langtry," Luke offered. "Mr. and Mrs. Langtry."

"Like the singer?" Roberto asked with a quirk of his head.

"Yes."

He'd never thought it would mean anything to him, but his father had had a harmless love affair with Lillie Langtry—her on the wall of his study, and him sitting behind his desk admiring the playbill.

Ramon's eyes glittered with interest. "Are you a relation to Miss Langtry?"

"No."

"Pity."

Roberto took his hat off as he approached Eve. "*Señora* Langtry, it is a pleasure."

Wide-eyed, Eve stood there, both hands crossed over her breasts in defense. The muscles in Luke's legs jumped; a tick at his jaw made him clamp down on his back teeth. He took a protective step in front of Eve.

"I have some extra cups," he offered, even though he didn't. "I can pour you boys some coffee." He'd barely taken a step to his travel bag when Ramon called out.

"It is not necessary to arm yourself, *Señor* Langtry. We haven't come to do you and your wife any harm— but if it would make you feel better to wear your gun, you are welcome to do so. It is, after all, your camp." He licked his fingertip and wet the edges of his mustache in an alternate smoothing motion. "We do not need your cups." He grinned, the pearly flash of teeth against dark skin. "But it was a good excuse to get your Colt." He snapped his fingers and tilted his head toward their horses. "Ramon, *mí amigo*, the cups."

Ramon went to the horses and came back with two engraved silver cups that he proudly held up. "What kind of coffee blend do you have in the pot, *Señor* Langtry? Indian or Colombian?"

Luke went straight for his bag and Colt. He answered while strapping on his revolver and feeling instant relief. "Just plain ground coffee."

"A shame." Roberto shrugged and exchanged woeful glances with Ramon.

While the two men claimed they were here on friendly terms, Luke wasn't going to give them an opportunity to prove otherwise. If they so much as suggested differently or laid one hand on Eve, he'd react. And without a moment's hesitation.

He had a full chamber, and he could discharge six shots in half the time. Three probable impacts. A bullet from his opponents might hit him, but he could kill either Ramon or Roberto.

Kill.

As a veteran of the New Orleans police force, he had never shot a man. He'd used his gun when called for, but prided himself on his ability to bring suspects in without firing the weapon in confrontation.

Right now, something clicked in his brain the minute he'd felt the heavy metal weight of his Colt on his hip. The slain officers' memories came to Luke with a full awareness. Sergeant Cook and Sergeant Bashioum were dead. The repercussions of that night's raid had fallen apart so quickly, he'd had no time to express his grief. Cook and Bashioum had been his associates, two men he'd shared drinks and conversations with. They were gone forever.

And here his premeditated thoughts were those of killing in earnest.

"*Señora* Langtry," Ramon said, "if you would be so kind as to pluck the hen so we can eat. *Muchas gracias.*"

Eve gazed hard at Luke but she didn't move. She held herself so tightly together, she would have snapped if the right breeze came along.

She'd buttoned his duster down to the last hole; its hem dragged on the dirt, and she held onto the middle of it to prevent herself from tripping on ends.

"I'll do that for you, darling. You can sit over there and rest on the blanket." Then to the men he explained, "My wife isn't feeling very well—the family way."

Thankfully, Eve didn't utter any kind of gasp of surprise over his lie. In fact, she mumbled, "I threw up on my dress. I'm in the family way."

That was good, Eve. Now don't say anything else.

"But I washed the dress in the creek," she went on in an anxiety-edged tone, "that's why I'm not dressed. In my, uh, blue dress."

"*Dear,* you really need to rest. You're sounding feverish."

She dropped onto the blanket and folded her hands in her lap.

Ramon chuckled. "Not need to explain, *señor*. Roberto's wife, she is expecting their eighth child. He has seven daughters. Perhaps he will have a son this time."

"If I had a son," Roberto said with a flare of his nostrils and a high lift to his brows, "I would sleep with my Bible and thank the good Lord at least once a week."

"You should do that now."

"I should—*eh?*" Once more rubbing his mustache, he added, "I will start thanking Him tomorrow. And when my son arrives, I will thank Him every day."

"My Anita thinks your Teresa is carrying a son."

"If I had a son, I would take him with me when we do business. No offense, *amigo*, but I think we need to round out our company."

Ramon shrugged with indifference, then addressed Luke. "We get tired of only talking to each other."

The kind of business they did wasn't the kind Luke wanted hanging around his campfire. The sooner they ate, the sooner they could be on their way.

Luke lifted the coffeepot and poured them each a full cup. Then he took the hen by its feet. Before he'd washed up in the creek, he'd set a pot of water on the fire to heat so he could shave. There was an open spot in the flames where he held the bird above the fire to singe the feathers. Smoke curls rose off the hen as he turned it a quarter turn over the coals. He was grateful his mother had insisted he learn how to dress and clean a chicken, as well as cook one. She'd said no son of hers would ever be hungry in their own home as long as they were capable of boiling water and knew how to handle a knife.

"Are you and your wife visitors to this part of our country?" Ramon asked as he sat back on his haunches and drank coffee.

"We're just passing through." Luke moved slowly, and with clear intent, to the knife sticking out of his mess kit. He didn't want either man to get trigger happy over something that wasn't a threat. Once he grasped the handle, he inched back to the fire with equally slow motion. He plucked as many feathers off as he could get, then made a clean slice at the neck to remove the head. Next, he cut through the skin around the legs, below the leg joint. In a clean snap of bone, he pulled the feet off.

"Oh . . . dear," came Eve's distressed cry.

He gave her a cursory glance. "It was dead, darling. It didn't feel a thing." Then to Ramon and Roberto: "My wife, she's not a cook."

"Neither is my Teresa," Roberto commented. "But I would never tell her that. She would shoot me. She has a temper as fiery as a chili."

Ramon laughed. "My Anita, she cooks like an angel."

Eve listened to the men, her gaze going from one to the other. Luke hoped she would just stay quiet. He gutted the hen, then quartered it into four sections; then washed the pieces in a pail of drinking water. Once they were clean, he dumped the bird into the depths of boiling water.

"Your wife, she has a burn from the sun on her

face," Roberto said. His observation made Luke's palms tingle and itch in the creases. He kept his arm slightly bowed outward, the wrist cocked at an angle for a quick draw if need be. Because if Roberto was looking at her face with that much interest, he had to be looking at other things, too.

"You should gently rub linseed oil on her skin to soothe it," he said in suggestion to Luke. "I would offer you a tin, but I do not have any."

"We have no need for sun repellent," Ramon put in. "Our work is done in the early dawn or the late dusk. We do not ride during the sunny hours of the day."

Roberto put in, "Bad for business."

"Sí, bad for our business," Ramon concurred.

The fire snapped and an ember popped. The greasy odor of boiling prairie hen worked the fringes of the air. Somewhere out in the desert came the insistent howls from a pack of coyotes.

"What is it that the two of you do in the dark?"

Eve's innocuous question hovered over the four of them like a cloud ready to break free with a torrential downpour. Luke's blood pulsed through his brain in a deep and throbbing ache.

"Never mind, sweetheart." Luke picked up a fork and moved a breast and drumstick in the boiling broth. "Dinner shouldn't be long."

Roberto Martínez assumed an air of bravado and didn't seem to mind answering Eve's question at all. "We are *bandidos, señora.* Lawless men of the West."

"We mostly steal cattle," Ramon clarified, drinking his coffee.

"*Sí.* We have fifty head of longhorns—a small

evening's work—down by the bend in the creek not a half mile away."

Ramon licked his lips. "Fifty head and a big mule."

Roberto smiled and explained to Luke, "His Teresa—she wanted a big mule this time."

"My wife—I get her whatever she wants. I love her."

"All we need is something special for my Anita." Roberto set his cup down and looked pointedly at Eve. "I see we have shocked you. I can assure you, *señora*, we are not heartless bastards. You would not understand the way of the land out in Texas. You are not from around here, that is evident from the way you talk. But here in the desert we make our own rules. Our own laws. We govern this land the way we have to. We only use our guns if we are prevented from conducting our business. Most of the time we are peaceful thieves, but we are also smart thieves and we will shoot if we have to." He smoothed his black mustache, as was his habit. "Again, you would not understand this."

His hand fell on the top of his revolver handle, and Luke's was on his just as quickly as he pulled the Colt from his holster and aimed it at Roberto.

Without any evidence of offense, Roberto gave Luke a frown but didn't make the slightest move for his weapon—because Ramon had drawn in the split second after Luke and had his Army .45 trained on Luke's chest. "*Señor*, I had no intention of firing at you—I was getting out my watch. But if you keep acting so jittery, *mí amigo*, I might react before thinking you are nothing but a greenhorn." Using his thumbnail, he opened a watch case, briefly studied the time, then slipped the timepiece back into his pocket. "Your distrust is an insult to my honor."

"W-We don't d-distrust you by any m-means," Eve's words tripped over one another. "Why, I think you both possess an air of dignity and refinement. For lawless cattle thieves, you're very nice."

The muscles in Luke's body locked tightly around his bones. He shot Eve a warning glare not to say another word. He slid his Colt back into his holster. "I'll make another pot of coffee. Dear, you just sit tight and let me entertain our guests."

"But I'm just trying to tell them, they need not fear us divulging their occupation. We don't want any trouble, *amigos*."

Ramon cracked a smile. "She speaks Spanish."

"*Sí*." Roberto chuckled. "She called us friends."

"Well, aren't you?" The worry in her tone rose.

"Cigarette?" Luke quickly produced several from his shirt pocket and extended his arm to Ramon. "Take two."

"*No, gracias*. We roll our own weed, *señor*, but thank you for the offer." On that, he came out with a cigarillo and lit it. "Your wife," he said, waving out his match, "is a charming woman. For someone who seems very refined but . . . off-kilter."

"Is dinner almost done?" she asked with a squeak to her tone. "I'm starving."

"Get the plates," Luke said stiffly.

Ramon and Roberto supplied their own, as they had the cups. And like their cups, their plates were fine quality silver. They sat down with a spread before them that was worth more than everything in the camp put together—four horses, saddles and camping gear.

Both men bowed their heads and uttered prayers in what Luke assumed was Latin because it wasn't Spanish and it wasn't French.

The meal was eaten over mild conversation. Nothing significant was exchanged between them. Today's heat, the coming winter, and if more ranchers would be settling in middle Texas. The fire sputtered and kept a glow about the area while the moon rose high in the sky canopy. When all the utensils and pans were put away, and the last cup of coffee drank, Luke was ready for the two desperados to be on their way. But the men had other plans. They said it was time they turn in. At Luke and Eve's camp.

Luke asked in a stilted voice, "Don't you boys want to move on to keep an eye on your cattle?"

"No."

"No." Ramon spread out his bedroll. "We are happy to sleep here. With you and your wife, the beautiful *Señora* Langtry. I will dream a better dream knowing she is across from me. It is hard to sleep without the smell of a woman on my pillow."

Eve's fear was obvious and abrupt at the compliment. Her face flushed and her hands began to tremble.

Apparently seeing the stark fright in her eyes, Roberto said, "Do not worry, *señora*, we have no intentions of violating you. We are both married."

"Th-That would stop you?" Eve asked in a near stutter.

"Of course." The seriousness in Ramon was not forced, but quite firm.

"*Sí.*" Roberto followed Ramon by arranging his bedroll across the fire from where Luke had laid out his and Eve's. "The divine priest in my church is somebody I respect. I go to confession. I could never tell him I was with another woman."

A curve caught at the corners of Ramon's mouth. "But we can tell him we steal cattle. He said the Lord taketh and the Lord giveth. Padre Rojas has an order with us for ten head. He is expanding the church."

Luke sat down beside Eve, whose mouth had fallen open. He didn't want her to say another word the rest of the night. She'd said enough already.

"Let's turn in, sweet gal." His arm came down over her shoulder, and he steered her toward his bedroll. He motioned for her to lay down, and he was right behind her. He covered them with a blanket.

Facing him within the woolen confines, she whispered, "They make me nervous. I wish they'd go away."

"It'll be all right. We have no cattle to steal and our horses aren't worth a damn."

Uncertainty filled her eyes. "What about our belongings? They might want the few things we have. There's a little money in my satchel."

"It doesn't matter if they search my bag. They won't find anything of value in it. I'm wearing my billfold."

"But if they do take our pitiful horses . . . we could be left out here to . . . die."

"I won't let that happen."

She settled her head into the crook of his arm. His duster enveloped her, giving her figure a slighter appearance. But not frail. Eve was proving herself to be strong.

"What are we going to do?" she said with a dismal sigh.

"You're going to get some sleep. I'm going to keep a watch on them."

"But you'll be tired tomorrow."

"I'll be fine."

"We can take turns staying up."

"No. Get some sleep."

"I'm not sleepy."

"Then just close your eyes."

He stroked her back to relax her, and after a while, her breathing came evenly.

The howls of the coyote pack echoed over the plains. Insects made noises and one of the *bandidos* began to snore.

They lay there, the night sounds playing around them. The feel of her beside him made Luke wish they were alone so that he could finish the kiss they had started before their uninvited guests had arrived. The smell of her hair was sweet and its texture equally so as he wrapped a curl around his finger. Soon, the steady and even sound of her breathing came to him as she drifted off to sleep.

Luke couldn't have closed his eyes, even if he wanted to. Because he wanted something far more necessary than sleep.

He wanted to savor the feel of her in his arms.

*　　　*　　　*

Luke woke with a jolt. He must have drifted into a light doze. There was a fragmented second he took to get his bearings and cursed the fact he'd fallen asleep.

As soon as his eyes shot open to the sound of movement in the camp, his hand gripped his Colt, he saw *Don* Roberto Martínez *y* Vanegas had already trained his gun's long barrel at a sleeping Eve and said, "*Buenos días, señor.* Show me your hands. And do so quickly."

Eve stirred as Luke slipped his free arm from her and slowly raised both hands over the edge of the blanket.

"*Excelente.* Now your revolver, *señor.* Only for a moment"—he said with an apologetic lift of his brows—"during our little transaction. Nice and slow. Pull down the blanket so I can see it in your holster."

Luke did so and Eve sleepily murmured, "What's the matter?"

He ignored her and did as he was told, handing it over and sitting up. Once the Colt was out of his possession, Roberto handed the gun to Ramon who set it beside the cold campfire.

There was barely a tint of predawn gold to the sky, but enough of it so that Luke could see clearly. Ramon came toward them and stopped, his gun holstered but Roberto's still on Eve. "Your money, *por favor.*"

With the blanket half-covering her, Eve had sat up as well. "We don't have any money."

The hammer clicked in a deadly note as Roberto pulled it back. "I do not wish to shoot you, *señora.* But we are trying to conduct business. Stand up. No, *señor,* you'll stay here. You, *señora*, go to the travel bags, and I want you to dump out their contents."

Eve looked at Luke. "Do like he says."

After their belongings were laid in the dirt in a pile, Ramon swore. "There's nothing in his. She has a few coins."

Roberto gritted, "Now it is time to empty your pockets."

Luke dragged in a sharp and angry breath.

"First your wife," Roberto instructed.

Eve's face paled.

"She doesn't have anything on her," Luke ground out.

"She has on a coat and underthings," Ramon corrected in a level tone that showed none of the warmth from the prior night. "Remove the duster, *señora*. Slowly."

Eve looked at Luke once again. His mind was sharply engaged on what she had been instructed to do and how he would lunge forward if either man laid a hand on her. Belying a calm he didn't feel, he replied, "Go ahead."

He could see her swallow as she stood and began to unfasten each of the buttons and shrug out of his coat. Ramon took it, felt through all the pockets and came up empty-handed. Eve trembled, wearing nothing but thin white undergarments. Her arms had come up to cover her breasts, and she kept her legs firmly together.

"Turn around," Roberto ordered, the gun never wavering. "Slowly. Move. Stand right there."

He'd ordered her to stand in line with the sun that

was creeping up the horizon. It lent enough of a ray that caused the hem of her petticoat to be made sheer enough to see through. She made quarter turns as was instructed and then she was told to sit back down.

A sweep of Luke was next. He stood and Ramon stuck his finger into his shirt pocket, tossing the cigarettes onto the bedroll. Then the bandit shoved a hand into his trouser pockets, making a quick pull of the lining in each. Luke had to grit his teeth to keep from moving. The back left produced what Ramon was seeking. He hit pay dirt with his billfold.

As Ramon fingered the paper currency and coins, he nodded his approval. *"Muchos gracias."* For show, he tossed the leather wallet high into the air, and as it came down, caught it in his fist. "This will buy my Anita her little something."

"Well, *señor y señora*, it was a pleasure doing business with you." Roberto picked up Luke's gun and threw it into the desert as far as it would fly. "We have to leave now with our cattle."

"And our big mule." Ramon went to saddle their horses and Roberto stood guard.

Roberto kept his gun trained on them, unwavering and steady. "We would take your horses, but they aren't worth their hides in cheap boots. Pitiful. And one has a stage line brand on it. It would seem you're in the lawless business yourselves. I would suggest you be more selective about your merchandise. Even your saddles are a disgrace."

Luke's gaze held fast.

"It is an interesting country out here, do you not

think?" Roberto went on. *"Bandidos y bandidas.* Texas is full of robbers."

Ramon called for his partner, and Roberto gave them a parting comment as he mounted, "We suggest you do not attempt to follow us."

"No." Ramon followed suit. "Because we will shoot."

With that, they rode off.

The minute they were out of sight, Luke ran to look for his Colt. He quickly found it and shoved the gun barrel into his holster as he went to the campfire. He angrily kicked the coffeepot. The enamel pot bounced across the camp and clunked against a large rock. He raked his hair back, swore, then lowered himself by the pit and lifted a blackened rock. Beneath it was the two dollars in dimes and half-nickels he'd hidden. At the time, he hadn't figured robbers coming into their camp was high on his list, but he'd known the possibility existed and he didn't want to be caught empty-handed. It was a good thing he'd been overly cautious because he was going to need every last cent.

"Where did that come from?" Eve questioned, her voice choppy.

"Me. I put it here when we made camp."

"How did you know?"

"I didn't." He began to gather up the cooking gear. "Get dressed and pack your stuff."

She knelt down and began to put her things back into her satchel.

He threw his mess kit into his bag, then rolled his blankets. "We're going to have to go into Midland and see if I can get some more money."

"At a bank?"

"No." Although he had money in an account and it could be wired to him, the funds would tip off his whereabouts.

Eve bent to get her blanket, and in a short while, they were packed and ready to mount the horses. As he helped Eve plant her foot in the stirrup and get a leg over, the sunrise caught in her curls. The day already promised to be hotter than a griddle; she'd left the top two buttons on her bodice unfastened, exposing a slight hint of her throat.

Then something dawned on him.

"Hey, where'd you stash that gold and diamond locket of yours?"

She faced him, as if knowing what his thoughts were. She gave him a long sigh, then said, "I'm wearing it . . . but not around my neck."

His teeth clenched and he spoke through a tightness in his jaw. "Great. Really great."

Turning away, he scratched the bristled underside of his unshaven jaw as he acknowledged the reality: They were both nearly cleaned out down to their last dimes.

15

The trail leading into Midland wound down a
steep mountainside of what Evelyn thought
looked like shale. Rock shards slid beneath her
horse's hooves, sometimes slipping over the road's
edge in a scatter that echoed to somewhere unseen.
Dry spruces grew out of the crevices. In the flatland
below, a vein of water ran through large patches of
green that indicated irrigated ranches nearby. Jagged-
topped plateaus sprung up west of the city, while a
blanket of high, thick clouds rose over the modest
stretch of populated area.

Once they were at the bottom of the mountain, they
merged onto a well-traveled road with other horses
and horse-drawn traffic. A group of men on strutting
bays tipped their hats to her as they passed, their
gazes lingering longer than polite. She knew that she
was a sight. After getting it wet in the creek, her dress
had lost its shape and tiny wrinkles were everywhere
in the fabric.

Loping forward to stay in line with Luke's horse, she noted his chiseled jaw was set in the same hard clench it had been for miles. The *bandidos* had not only taken most of his money, but a piece of his pride. She'd known he was angry with himself over the turn of events, and she'd been thinking of ways she could help to make some money. So far, nothing brilliant had struck her.

At the intersection where Main Street started, a sign was posted.

MIDLAND
THE WINDMILL TOWN
POPULATION 2,177
WE SHIP CATTLE

The smell of fresh lumber, mortar and paint scented the air. A tall stack of bricks and boards were at the corner of the First National Bank of Midland. The building next to it was hollowed out and black inside a glassless window. A yellowing notice was posted on a lamppost in front of the *Midland Gazette*.

FUTURE SITE OF THE MIDLAND FIRE DEPARTMENT
LET NO FIRE DESTROY OUR CENTRAL
BUSINESS DISTRICT AGAIN.
—YOUR 1910 CITY LEADERS

There were several reputable businesses lined up and down the street, then they thinned to those that were dishonorable. Saloons, dance halls and what Evelyn was certain was a brothel by the sign painted above the entrance door: ROOMS BY THE HOUR.

Luke stopped just before the last honest establishment on the block. Miss Tindale's Down-Home Eatery and Bakery. Once at the hitching post, he dismounted and came around to help her down. She gazed at his richly tanned face for any sign of softening around his edges. All she saw were hard creases at the corners of his eyes, and the start of a dark beard on his chin.

"I want you to sit on the boardwalk and wait for me." She was backed up next to its height, built tall enough that three steps had to be used in order to reach the eatery.

"Why can't I come with you?"

"Because I don't want you to." He picked her up beneath the arms, lifted her off her feet and propped her onto the planks. Her tender behind took a bruising by the way he deposited her on the hard wood.

"Where are you going?"

"I'm going to find a way to get some money. I'd put you in a hotel room if I had the means, but I don't." He nudged his hat up with his thumb, then looked up and down the street. "I'm going to be back as soon as I can. You've got the canteen and you've got a tin of crackers if you get hungry."

"You don't have to do this, you know," she called out as he started to turn away. "I can make my own way. I don't have to be your concern. You don't have to be mad at me."

"I'm not mad at you. I'm mad at myself for having a gun pointed in my face. I don't make mistakes like I did back there. So I'm not going to make any more. You told me I owed you. That I had to bring you to El Paso to pay you back." He adjusted the angle of his hat. "So I'm responsible for you until we get there. After that, you can go wherever you want."

She clamped her lips together and said nothing more as he disappeared around the corner to the bad side of town.

Watching where he turned, she hoped she would find Luke coming back to her. But he didn't, and she grew increasingly uncomfortable about him going where trouble most likely was behind a bar.

She looked at the people who walked past, staring out of curiosity as they went in and out of the restaurant behind her. She hoped the owner wouldn't come out and tell her to move along. Matrons raised their brows at her; one had the nerve to give her a loud *tsk*. Evelyn fought the compulsion to raise her nose at her.

She gazed at the poles across the street and knew they stretched to the outskirts for miles and miles. Some homes had a spur of the wire attached to their roofs, so perhaps the cable was telephone line. She couldn't be sure. Of that, or anything. She thought it strange that every house had a windmill in its yard.

Pulling in a sigh, she drummed her fingernails on the boards and watched a boy whack a can down the center of the street with a stick. He didn't even give her a look. Following him were a pair of women. Definitely not town matrons. They were dressed in what she called siesta clothing. Flowing shirts and colorful red skirts.

They were barely out of view when another three women ran after them, one carrying sheets of paper. A sheaf fell from her arms and blew across the road and landed facedown. Evelyn stared at it. A horse and rider came trotting out of the opposite direction. The paper was stirred beneath the horse's hooves and it sailed up into the air and floated in a soft twist.

The paper landed several yards from where her feet dangled over the boardwalk. A mahogany-paneled delivery wagon for Seminole Beer pulled by two black horses trampled the leaflet, stirring it from its resting place and creating enough of a draft to send it close enough to Evelyn where she could read it even though it was torn at the corner now.

There was a drawing of a woman with printed words above her. The advertisement read:

Drinking. Dancing.
Singing competition at the El Rey this evening.
All invited. Top prize is $100.00 in cash and a room at the Red Banana for the night or
$110.00 in an ante at any poker table of your choice.

Evelyn brought her fingertip to her mouth. One hundred dollars and a free hotel room. She thought back to the ten dollars she'd won at the Dime Box. Could she do something like that again?

I want you to sit on the boardwalk and wait for me.

Indecision held her still, but the lure of one hundred dollars made her lean forward for a better look at that flyer.

Why can't I come with you?

Because I don't want you to.

Did he think her completely inept?

One hundred dollars was a small fortune given their dire straits.

Where was the El Rey? What time was it? Where could she put the horses? They might be stolen if she left them. Or maybe not. They'd been tethered at the hitching post for a half hour and nobody gave them half a glance. Luke's travel bag was cinched behind his saddle, entrusted to her care. She wouldn't leave it behind. Nor her—

What was she thinking?

She had to stay.

Luke played cards with six men of dubious character. But he didn't care which side of the crib they'd been born on—he just wanted to stay in the game and keep his money growing. His measly two dollars had been enough to ante him into this poker table.

The house band at the front of the elongated room burst out lively and loud notes. The men seated around him were distracted by singers on the stage in some sort of competition. He had no time or interest in the performances. Under other circumstances, he would have been irritated by the distraction; now it served him well. He'd won the last two hands.

"I'm in." The man wearing a rattlesnake skin necktie had been in every hand tonight, not folding once. And not winning once. Either he was as dense as a piece of wood or he was setting them up for something. Not being a regular poker player, Luke couldn't be sure which one. He didn't intend on sticking around long enough to find out.

After tossing in a quarter eagle ante, he glanced at

his watch. The time was closing in on eight. He hadn't counted on being gone over two hours, but he was up to three hundred and sixty dollars in a high stakes, fast betting game. He couldn't walk. If he won this game, he'd be richer by another fifty-two. He had to stay and play. Then he'd collect Eve.

He hoped he'd made himself clear she had to stay put. The idea of her still sitting on a boardwalk with night beginning to fall disturbed him. He shouldn't have been short with her. He hadn't anticipated being here so long with two men constantly ordering drinks and barmaids interrupting the game to collect money for rounds of whiskey, three diverting their attention to the scantily dressed dancing girls who walked around the tables, and the one complaining he was suffering from a bad case of heat rash.

"I'll call," added one of the gamblers; then he grinned at a barmaid who wove her way through the tables holding a tray of liquor.

A second man drank the rest of the whiskey in his shot glass. "Me, too." He bottomed-up the glass on the table, slamming it down on the rim. Motioning toward the barkeep, he called out, "Another whiskey!"

"I'll pass." The man tossed his cards facedown and scratched his arm.

Luke read his cards. Two tens—clubs and spades, a queen of clubs, a club deuce and five of hearts. When the dealer asked him how many he wanted, he tossed down all but the tens. Then the dealer moved on and dealt a second round of cards around the table.

Observing each expression on the six men, Luke tried to read their hands through the way they rose brows, lowered brows, rubbed an eye, licked a lip, or inched back in their chair.

He looked at his own cards, still facedown in front of him. He had to make this one count so he could get the hell out of here. Sliding them forward, he picked them up and slowly fanned them out in his hand.

"What do you think you're doing?" the women asked Evelyn. "This isn't a joy house. If you want to do that, you have to go next door to my cousin's bordello, the Red Banana."

Evelyn kept inching her dress off her shoulders so she could appear provocative. She had to fix her mistake by doing *something* to become more appealing. She'd ruined the bodice by splashing water on it. She'd thought that would help with the wrinkles, but it had only served to put unsightly spots in the delicate fabric.

So here she was, tugging and pulling the sleeves off her shoulders after having unbuttoned the top five buttons of her bodice to show her cleavage.

"Hey—*estúpido!* I told you the El Rey isn't your place."

The woman's shiny black hair was slicked away from her face, anchored by decorative combs at the top of her head. She bore a striking resemblance to someone Evelyn couldn't place. It couldn't be possible she'd know this—what was her name—? Conchita. That's how she'd been addressed by the heavyset man who'd let Evelyn pass through the velvet curtains of dressing rooms.

Evelyn ignored Conchita, willing—but not want-

ing—to go out on that stage like this. She had to gar-
ner the judge's unbridled attention. Between the
exposed skin delving low at her throat and the red
cactus flowers she'd stuck into her hair, she may just
have a chance.

Maybe . . . if the judges were dim-sighted.

"I understand what you're saying," Evelyn said in
a tart tone, "but I'm not here to do anything but sing.
And win the prize."

A hand curled into her shoulder to prevent her
from moving. "And I say, you should give up your
attempt at looking sexy. You look awful."

Evelyn shrugged out from Conchita's hold. She put
her hands on her hips. She stood behind the stage of
the El Rey, off to the side and hidden from public
view. A bustle of activity went on around them as one
singer, then the next, departed the stage after their
performances. Both men and women had been com-
peting for the prize money. So far, Evelyn hadn't
heard one of them that was worth their weight in one
hundred dollars and a hotel room—except for a gar-
ishly dressed man who sang better as a soprano than a
woman.

"Miss Conchita, I really need to win this money."

"*Chica*, everyone needs to win the money."

"But nobody needs to win it more than me."

The band was winding down, and Evelyn was to be
the last singer of the evening. The talent performer
before her was attempting to finish his song amid
jeers and hisses. Despite her need to win, she felt
badly for him. She could wow the crowd if she could
go out there looking suggestive and inviting. Not that

she was comfortable doing so. It didn't thrill her to expose so much skin. But she had to do everything she could to enhance her chances.

She made a final adjustment of her sleeves where they rode off her shoulders. She picked up her skirt and hiked it up enough to show her knees.

"You are *loco*," Conchita said. "That's it. I'm getting my cousin, Jorge, to throw you out."

"If I were somebody important like—like—" Within seconds, a name popped into her head. "—Rosita Carmichael, you wouldn't be standing here threatening to throw me out and telling me what to do. So—"

"Rosita?" Conchita tilted her head back and postured a surprised stance. "You know Rosita?"

Evelyn stopped fussing with her clothing to stare into large brown eyes. She was baffled, but at the same time, encouraged over Conchita's abrupt mood swing. "Why, yes, I know Rosita Carmichael. We met at a hotel in Beaumont, then again at the Dime Box."

Conchita rattled off Spanish, then lifted her hands. "*Aiy!* Rosita does indeed work at the Dime Box. She is my cousin."

"I thought your cousin owned the Red Banana."

"Yes—that is my cousin Ferdinand. My other cousin, Jorge, he is the strong arm here at the El Rey. And my other beloved cousin, she is Rosita *mía*."

The confirmation brought an idea to Evelyn. "It's a small country, isn't it? Do you know, I thought Miss Carmichael was one of the most lovely women I've ever met," Evelyn remarked, hoping that by her knowing Rosita, it could get her a shot on the stage dressed like a . . . she hated to use the word . . . floozy.

"How was Rosita?" Conchita asked. "Was she with Castillo?"

Further encouraged, Evelyn replied, "As a matter of fact, yes."

"Bastardo!"

Evelyn cringed. Apparently, she shouldn't have said that. She fought to come up with something that would smooth things over. "Yes, she was with him, but there was a problem. He brought her to the hotel where I was staying and Mr. Castillo wanted to go to his room. *But,* they never did. Rosita told him she had to sing at the Dime Box so she left."

That was a half-truth. But if it would soothe Conchita's temper, she was willing to use whatever she could.

"That is good to know." She uttered more Spanish, then said, "In that case, you definitely cannot go onto the stage such as you are."

"Can't I?" Evelyn asked, desperate. "But I just—"

"No." Conchita took her by the arm and steered her to one of the private rooms. "You will go on wearing," she swung the door inward and stood back, "this."

Luke upped the ante in the current pot by five dollars. He would have put in more but it might have caused suspicion. He'd been playing with caution all night.

Snakeskin necktie called, "I'm in." Then he made a dry smack of his mouth. "Another whiskey!"

"I'll take some of that." The itching man added his own five piece.

"All right, gentlemen, show up your hands." The dealer laid down a pair of jacks. Next to follow were three at the table who folded, their hands too inferior to compete. The man with the rash studied the two jacks, as if looking for finger marks on them.

"I don't know. I don't like it. Something ain't adding up." Itching his chin, he shook his head. "I don't like it."

The necktie pursed his lips. "If you don't like it, prickly heat, then get the hell out of the game and call your losses. All you've done for the past several hours is scratch your ass and I'm getting damn tired of it. You're contaminatin' the cards."

"I thought that myself," the dealer commented, gazing at his cards with a grimace. "Is what you got catching?"

"Gentlemen," Luke broke in, "I'd like to finish this game."

"Yeah, we'll finish it, when he tells me what's going on with them jacks." The man scratched his chest, then the top of his hand, his face growing blotchy and red. "Now I've been watching how the hands have been dealt, and we ain't due up for no damn pair of jacks."

"Are you accusing me of cheating, mister?" Necktie snorted.

"I ain't accusing you of anything until you let me examine them cards in your hand."

Luke switched his cards from his right hand to his left, making his trigger hand available if need be. He didn't like the ugly turn of events. He tried to take on a lighter tone. "Let's show our cards and be done with this, boys. I've got a woman waiting for me."

"We all got women waiting for us," one of the drunkards laughed, leaning so far back on his Windsor chair, he fell over and his cards flew off the table with him.

The other two drunks laughed with him, pointing and guffawing until they were teary-eyed. Luke wanted to get out right now, but he was riding on a good deal of money, and he had a hand to win it.

"Showing cards," Luke said and fanned his out in front of him in an effort to move things along.

His two tens and three eights beamed up at him like a dollar sign. He started to slide the money in the middle of the table toward him.

"Not so fast." The man with the rash shot to his feet and fumbled in his pocket.

Five arms rose, with five guns pointed at him.

The man's red face paled to ash as he slowly produced a small glass magnifier. His Adam's apple bobbed as he explained, "I-I was g-going to check for fingernail marks in his cards."

The guns were lowered, hammers uncocked. Luke had to wipe the sweat on his forehead that had immediately popped out with the drawing of five guns. The charged scene reminded him of something else, and the bottom of his stomach had clenched tight. For several seconds, he'd been inside the Pontchartrain Club waiting for the smoke to clear.

Lowering his arm, the cuff on his shirt damp from his skin, he stared at the winning pot that he'd swept toward him. He swallowed the thickness in his throat. He had several hundred dollars just waiting to be tucked into his pocket and have him on his way.

He drummed his fingertips over the green felt-cloth covered table. "I won, gentlemen. There's been no argument all evening about marked cards. I'm sorry to have to do this, but I'm leaving."

"No you ain't." The magnifier in his hand shook. "I just need a moment to—"

"Would ya'll shut the hell up over there!" another man at the next table barked in a disgruntled tone. "We're trying to listen to the lady!"

Luke grew vaguely aware of a woman singing. His gaze went to the stage for an instant, then back on the table. "Let's settle this—"

His eyes shot back to the stage where shell lights illuminated a woman. Not her face, but her body. Her face was hidden by a trick angle of light from above, as if to tease and dramatize the seducing effect.

She had enough ivory cleavage showing to start a riot in the house. A loose-fitting blouse fell softly off at her shoulders—it was one of those Mexican ones with the embroidery and near-sheer white fabric. The calf-length skirt was vivid red silk with black stitching across the bottom and a hint of snowy petticoat showing. She wore translucent black stockings and high-heeled shoes with bows.

Singing her heart out, she kicked up her feet in an artful dance, her skirt lifted to show a tease of her thigh. He'd bet half the men in the El Rey would be lining up to see how much she cost by the hour when she was done with her number.

As she went into the chorus, the light above was snapped on. The room went into an uproar.

The first thing he noticed was her wealth of golden hair piled in loose curls. Her full mouth was painted a red so seductive that—

To hell with that.

He was going to kill her.

16

Evelyn hit the last high note in her rendition of "The Lovely Ladies from Texas," and held it as long as she could through the cheers and cat-whistles. As she finished, the smile she felt was genuine. She gazed across the room as she nodded and mouthed her thanks to those who were on their feet clapping.

She had impressed them. She'd won them over. That hundred dollars was as surely hers as—

A man in the crowd caught her attention, and her mouth suddenly went dry. *Uh-oh.* There in the near-center of the room stood Luke. He cut her to the quick with a glare that could have melted a two-hundred-year-old glacier. She hadn't planned on him finding out like this.

She had it all figured out—she was going to show him the money and hand him the free hotel room key, and when he was happy about it, she'd mention she did a little singing to secure them.

She gave him her most flattering smile and hoped he would give her one back.

Nothing.

Her smile faltered, then looking past him, she acknowledged the other men whooping it up in the El Rey. She curtseyed and left the stage to a waiting Conchita.

Conchita embraced her hands and squeezed them. *"Dios mío!* You were wonderful, *chica!"*

"Thank you."

"You won, there is no question. My cousin Jorge is the judge and I had told him to vote for my other cousin, Juanita, but I changed my mind because of Rosita. But, really, you sang the best. Juanita is going to slap me—I'll give her one hundred dollars anyway."

Evelyn tried to follow the fast dialogue while catching her breath.

Conchita said, "The reason I didn't want you to go out on the stage had nothing to do with your dress and what you were doing with it. I heard you singing a few notes to warm up and I knew Juanita would lose if you sang."

"I'm glad you gave me the opportunity."

Other competitors came by to offer congratulations, some to shrug and give her a look-over. The male soprano snubbed her with a lift of his chin that had been powdered heavily with stage makeup. Juanita came up to Conchita and pouted, then smiled.

"You were better than me," Juanita said to Evelyn.

Evelyn felt a bit numb. She was grateful beyond words for the loan of the blouse and skirt that had

been a success, too. Grateful that she was now one
hundred dollars richer.

"Thank you," Evelyn said as stagehands rushed past
them, some bumping into her. They were readying for
the next event of the evening. Some kind of acrobatic
troupe with animals. Yapping dogs darted by.

A burly man carrying a plank of wood bumped
into her and didn't even mutter an apology.

"I don't mean to be hasty, Miss Conchita, but when
could I have my money? There's a gentleman in the
audience waiting for me." *Not that I'm anxious to face
him.*

"Ah, yes. A man." Conchita secretively winked,
then motioned for Evelyn to follow her back into her
dressing room where the decorative skirt and blouse
had been displayed over a dressing screen. The articles of clothing she wore belonged to Conchita.

At the outside of the door, Evelyn sized up who she
believed to be Jorge standing guard. "Hello," she
offered.

He grunted, "Good song."

Once they were in the small room, Conchita closed
the door. "Now, I have the money in my safe."

"I'll give you back your clothing."

"No, no." Conchita waved her off. "You can keep
them. I have my share of beautiful dresses. I saw how
the men looked at you. You'll have a good time
tonight with your man."

The false assumption would have been laughable if
Evelyn felt like laughing.

Conchita lowered herself behind the dressing
screen; the whirl of a safe dial spinning and clicking

sounded through the room. Evelyn thought about the night she'd cracked her father's safe. Beyond a doubt, by now he'd figured out his money was missing. Unless Mr. Vanderhoff had returned it with her valise. Oh, why did she have to go and think about that? About the whole nightmare on the train and the likelihood of Cecil Woodworth after her.

The safe slammed closed.

"I didn't ask before," Conchita began, "but did you want to have the one hundred and ten to play poker, or just the one hundred and the room at the Red Banana?"

Evelyn paused, a thought holding her still. "Didn't you say your cousin Ferdinand ran the Red Banana and that it was a . . . house of ill repute?"

"I called it a bordello."

"Oh, well . . ." She wondered if maybe she should give Luke the money to play poker with. Or if she should accept the room at the *bordello* and the cash.

After a short moment, she made up her mind. "The one hundred and the room will do."

Conchita stood and handed Evelyn bills that she counted out. They looked glorious in her open palm. "Thank you."

"I will send immediate word to Ferdinand that you and your gentleman friend will be our guests for the evening in the Lover's Suite at the Red Banana."

The Lover's Suite . . .

She gave an anxious little cough. "That's not necessary. Just a regular room will do."

"No, the Lover's Suite was part of the prize. I'll have your bags brought over. You just need to bring

your man to the room." Conchita broke into a grin
that flashed briefly and contrasted pleasantly with her
warm complexion. "And I will see to it that you are
made more comfortable than you can imagine."

Evelyn found it peculiar that Ferdinand and
Conchita, who made their livings from sporting and
gaming houses, could find fault in Rosita's dalliance
with Mr. Castillo. But she wasn't about to ask questions.

She swallowed once more, unable to argue the
point. "Well . . . all right. I suppose . . ."

Given its name, she needn't ask if the Lover's Suite
came with two beds rather than one. She'd have to
contend with beds later. Maybe the room was furnished with a nice divan that she could sleep on.
Hopefully, the fact that they had the suite's use for the
night at no charge would deflate the angry tension
that had gripped Luke when he'd stared at her.
Although somehow, she doubted that.

Minutes later, Evelyn walked onto the main floor of
the El Rey still wearing Conchita's costume. Her once-
elegant blue dress and matching hat had mysteriously
disappeared. She would have preferred to wear a
wrinkled dress rather than the skimpy blouse and
skirt. Although she had to admit, she loved the silky,
airy feel of the fabrics. Only their soft and wispy flow
about her arms and calves wasn't appropriate to enter
into a roomful of men who wolfishly admired her. She
didn't encourage the attention she attracted and kept
her focus on finding Luke.

She saw him immediately, and he saw her at about
the same time. He still stood at the table she'd seen

him at while on the stage. Several men held up cards and shouted to one another. A pile of money on the table was shoved toward Luke.

As she wove her way through the tables, she bit her lip, then began to change direction. Just as she did, Luke shook his head, that hat of his a beacon in a crowd because he was so tall. Slowly he shook his head once more. Signaling a—"No, don't do that." As she froze, he then gave her another nod—"Yes, come here."

She pulled a breath and forced a cheery smile.

As she continued, men seemed to come at her from different places and touch her. On the arm. The hand. The neck. She tried to shy away from their petting, ducking and keeping her walk steady. She forced a smile she didn't feel, and thanked those who told her they liked the song she'd sang. One cowboy appeared out of nowhere and grabbed her about the waist. She pushed him away with her elbow.

When Evelyn looked up, Luke was no longer at the table. A thread of panic ran jagged through her heartbeat.

"Lady, I'm in love with you," the cowboy said, low and close to her ear.

She turned, only to get a strong blast of liquored-up breath against her face. Frightened, she didn't know what to do.

"Th-Thank you, sir. Now I must go on."

But a hand was around her waist once more, tightly gripping her and shoving her next to his—

"Hands off," came a dangerous growl. "The lady is my wife."

Evelyn jumped at the sound of the familiar voice,

its low and deep quality reassuring. "Y-Yes, that's my husband. Darling! I'm so happy to see you."

And she was. So happy, in fact, that when she was untangled from the cowboy and brought flush against the full length of Luke's body for a hot kiss, not one of her muscles resisted him. She didn't have a moment to think about the unexpected kiss that held her captive. Leaning into him, she heaved a sigh of pleasure. There was no question—Luke could kiss her senseless.

His mouth was hard and demanding on hers, then vanished altogether. The kiss ended as abruptly as it began.

When she caught her breath and looked into his face, his gaze wasn't even on her, but on the men surrounding them. "My wife is one hell of a singer and I'm going to make her sing me a song right now, boys. Under the sheets of a bed." Then to her, "Come on, honey. Let's go."

She allowed him to drag her toward the back of the El Rey.

"Luke, I need to explain," she tried to say through the noise in the gaming house. "I didn't mean to have you find out like this. But I have to say—I won some money and a free room for us to stay tonight."

His mouth was firmly set, his profile stubborn with hard lines that made her a little queasy. He was mad, all right.

"One hundred dollars," she explained, hoping to snap him out of the taut expression. "In usable cash, not certificates or anything . . ."

She held off a wince as strong fingers dug into her soft flesh when he steered her clear of a loud group of men. In a second, chairs flew and wooden legs shattered. Glass broke. A punch was thrown.

"I left a card table," Luke said next to her ear. "Do you know what happens when you do that?" He gave her no opportunity to reply. "You don't have any more claim to your money."

"I'm sorry, but I—"

"I'm sorry, too. Because I took what was in front of me and when those men find out what's missing, they're going to come gunning after us. We have to get the hell out of Midland right now."

"If the money was in front of you, wasn't it yours?"

"It should be. But those *gentlemen* were disputing who was the rightful owner. They don't cool down before reacting. At least three of them were fully loaded and ready to aim."

The significance of his words finally sunk in. They were going to be shot at—no second chances given or questions asked.

Luke flung the exit door to the El Rey open and immediately the fresh, warm night air assaulted them. The tight press of people in the gambling house had been one big cloud of smoke and an offending odor of liquor.

The narrow alleyway had only one way out— through the bad part of town. To their right, the highwall dead end was blocked with crates, barrels and broken windmills.

"Wait." She held back, unmoving when he tried to proceed with a jerky stride. "We can't ride out of town. It's dark. You said yourself, no night riding."

The brim of his black hat hid his face as he turned toward her. All she could see were the outlined traces of his chin and mouth. His white teeth were barely visible in the shadows when he spoke. "We can't stay here and have them shaking down the hotels."

"They won't find us." A curl fell against her neck, and she pushed the annoying piece of hair away. "Because I know of a place better than a hotel. Trust me. I really know."

She didn't wait for him to tell her to forget her idea. She took his hand and went to the end of the alley and directly to the building on the immediate right—the Red Banana. Looking both ways to see if the coast was clear, she proceeded to the double red front doors. She didn't bother to knock, and instead, went right into the foyer.

And what a foyer.

The carpets were red and gold diamond–patterned, and they went right up to the high base-boards. A stairwell was straight ahead, and on its opposite side was a long, single row of marble statues—of naked men and women engaged in . . . various positions of . . . Paintings of exotic-looking women hung on the walls, while a white marble-topped receiving bureau table held a huge vase of fresh-cut red roses, white peonies and yellow mums. A chandelier dripping with more gold than Evelyn had ever seen hung directly overhead, its electric light burning brightly. While she was aware of the stunning infusion of light, she was also aware of the luscious fragrances of perfumes. In the parlor room off to the side with closed French glass doors, beauti-fully made-up women entertained a host of men wearing finely tailored suits.

A dark-haired man dressed in black evening attire came toward them from a rear chamber. His brows were swarthy and his complexion vaguely hinted of pox scars. "I've been expecting you both."

"You must be Ferdinand."

"Yes. The Lover's Suite has been made ready for you."

She blurted, "That was quick."

"We operate by the hour here. Nothing is too quick to prepare in a short amount of time."

"Lover's Suite?" Luke said, giving her a sideways glance. "What is he talking about?"

"It's our room. Where we can stay for the night. Conchita set it up for us."

"Who's Conchita?"

Ferdinand replied, "My cousin."

"Wasn't that nice of her?" Evelyn infused an airiness in her voice but one look at Luke told her it wasn't working. He appeared as morose as a man who'd sunk his last dollar into yet another rig that failed to strike it rich. "Don't worry." Enthusiastically, she hooked her arm through his muscular arm that remained flexed at his side. "We'll be just fine here. Ferdinand is known for his discretion, aren't you, Ferdinand?"

"I am, *señorita*."

"No one will know we're here, right?"

"No, *señorita*."

"See? There's nothing to worry about."

Luke shifted his weight on his feet, folding his arms over his chest. "Where are the horses?"

"Where you left them."

"Great. They won't be there tomorrow—if they're still there at all."

"*Señor*," Ferdinand said in an even tone, "allow me. I'll send someone to look for them and take them to my private livery."

Luke's eyes turned hard as he narrowed them. "Where's my travel bag? Don't tell me you left that behind, too? Dammit all, Eve."

"I most certainly did not," Evelyn interjected tartly, not caring to be spoken to as if she were a half-wit. "I brought them with me to the El Rey and Conchita kept them safely for me while I sang. When we made the arrangements for . . . here, she said she'd have them brought over."

"They are in the suite waiting for you." Bowing, Ferdinand made a sweeping gesture to the gilt-edged stairs. "If you would like to see your accommodations now."

"That would be wonderful." Inadvertently, her gaze landed on the statue nearest to her with the gentleman who had one hand on a lady's lush breast and the other on her lap in no way that was decent. Their legs were wrapped around one another in a way that . . .

Forced determination kept Evelyn's heart from foolishly beating at her ribs. Whatever lurid décor was in that Lover's Suite, she was going to act maturely and calmly about it. Not even make a single mention of anything naked or suggestive.

Ferdinand took the steps first and led them down a long hallway with elegant runners. He stopped at the double doors at the far end of the corridor.

"The suite," he said, then opened the doors. He stepped aside and gave them entrance.

Evelyn didn't turn around, but she heard the doors close behind her. She was too stunned to move. She felt Luke draw up beside her. So this was the Lover's Suite.

Everything was black lacquer and gold. The bedstead, which was the most outstanding feature in the room, had a very large headboard with carvings and spindles, while the footboard repeated its design, only on a smaller scale. There was a matching bureau with a wide mirror flanked by two tiny side mirrors. Exquisite lamps were placed before each smaller reflective glass and their light cast a soft glow that muted the walls.

The walls themselves were a hue of gold that shone as if it were a real precious metal. Pictures were framed in black lacquer while a side chair and settee were gold brocade. An Oriental rug spread out so wide, the entire bed and then some was positioned over its detailed lotus pattern. She'd seen such a thing once in one of her mother's decorating magazines.

"You know how to pick them," Luke said, his voice almost startling her. For a moment, she'd forgotten he was there. But how could she? It was going to be a long night, made longer by the two of them sharing the rich confines in a bordello.

There was a room off to the left of the bedstead. She could see a large claw-footed tub and all the fringe and trim that draped the bathing room.

"I'll bet it comes with rose bath salts like you

wanted." Luke went forward to view the intimate atmosphere of the lavatory.

"How did you know I liked rose bath salts?"

"The day I propped you under a tree you babbled it."

Evelyn didn't remember. Had she said anything else of note?

The bedroom color scheme carried through to the bathing room, which was a nice size. The walls were covered in gold wallpaper with a small linear oak-leaf pattern. The same print continued in the heavily fringed curtains over the tub that imposed a sense of decorum and stateliness in a room clearly built for non-decorous behavior. A bolster before the seat of the pull-chain commode didn't fit with the surroundings, but it was matched in color to the rest of the furnishings. Sponges and scented soaps in floral shapes, as well as oils and perfumes rested on a tray that crossed over the interior of the tub.

"Nice bathtub. Nice smelling stuff. And nice—" Luke's arm reached out, and he touched a dressing gown and robe of rose gossamer that had been draped over a bar on the wall, "—this." He startled her by brushing her cheek with the back of his hand. "Maybe this place is more than adequate after all."

When Eve finally came out of the bathroom, she was wearing the filmy rose nightgown and robe—but with a large towel thrown over her shoulders, and her hands held the edges together at her breasts in order to cover as much as she could.

Luke lay on the massive bed, his back and head

supported by half a dozen velvet pillows with tassels.
A bountiful spread of food was beside him. He didn't
know what most of the dishes were, but they tasted
good. The meal had come with Mexican beer and con-
fectionaries, as well as a box of chocolates.

Eve asked, "What's all this?"

"Dinner."

As she nervously moved to the other side of the
room, ceiling light played off the gold in her hair and
made it shimmer. She'd left the long length unbound;
the ends fell to her hips. "Where did it come from?"

A corner of his mouth lifted. "The dinner fairy."

She scowled at him, sitting down on the chair, fussing with the wide black towel, primping and settling
it over herself just right.

Drawing up his leg, he leisurely rested his hand on
his knee. "I've seen you sleeping in a frilly nightgown
before."

"That was when I thought you were a woman."

"Don't make a mistake about that—I'm no woman."

"I know." Her gaze drifted across him, and he
could almost feel it caressing his skin.

She turned away from him, then prudently studied
a painting on the wall. It was nothing special. Just an
oil portrait of a woman.

"I know her," Eve said. "That's Rosita Carmichael."

"She's pretty."

"Yes. Even prettier in person. I met her once. In
Beaumont when I entered a singing contest. She
encouraged me."

"So this isn't your first time?"

"W-What do you mean?"

Her mind was definitely preoccupied.

Clarifying, he rephrased, "Your first time singing on a stage in front of rowdy men?"

"No . . ." Her eyes were still fixed on the portrait. "But I only did it to win the prize money."

"Same as before?"

"Actually, no. Before I did it to prove to myself I could."

"You can."

Eve drew in a breath, then faced him. "You couldn't even hear me from where you were."

"I heard some. Enough to know how good you are."

Watching her walk through the room, Luke admitted he liked her. More than what was good for him. When he'd seen that cowboy's hands on her, he'd wanted to beat the man into the ground. A fierce stab of jealousy had almost pushed him over the edge.

"Where did you get those clothes you're wearing?" she asked.

The black trousers were finely tailored out of a lightweight worsted wool. He'd slipped into a white shirt of ground sateen with gold chameleon cuff studs and buttons. He'd neglected to tuck the tail in, nor close the bottom button and the three at the neck. Beneath everything, he wore no undervest or socks, just a pair of merino drawers.

Ferdinand had brought the fancy clothes to him and asked if there was anything else he needed. Luke hesitated for a long moment, then replied yes. The dark man's expression held a perceptive note of trustworthiness to it. He struck Luke as the kind of person who wouldn't sell out even if the price was more than right. He'd asked Ferdinand to inquire around town if there had been a man passing through recently who matched Henry Boyd's description. Ferdinand had said he'd take care of it right away.

"Ferdinand gave me the duds," Luke replied. "He keeps a stockpile of new stuff in a clothing room. Your hair's different colors when it's damp. It looks pretty."

She blushed.

"Do you want me to brush it for you? I saw one in the bathroom." The question came out before he could stop it. He didn't *want* to stop it.

She sat so stiffly, she could have broken in half. "I think I prefer it when you boss me around rather than . . . um, flirt."

At that, his low laughter floated across the room. "I don't flirt."

Before she could remark, he patted the expanse of bed beside him.

"Come here and have some dinner. It's still hot."

She didn't move. She didn't say anything. She just stared, first at him, then at the bed, then at the food. "I'll have something to eat. Over here."

She rose and scooted the chair to the bureau's edge so it could act as a table. In the process of rearranging the furniture, her towel cape fell off. She went to pick it up.

"Don't bother, Eve."

She straightened.

The towel remained on the floor.

She brought her full lips together and licked them.

"What is there for dinner? I'm starving and I don't care if you know."

"Why would I care?"

"A lady never divulges her innermost feelings in mixed company. They're reserved for private meditations within her journal or shared with her . . . and even then, they're most likely kept to herself."

"Shared with her who? Her lover?"

Slanting him a look, she licked her lips once more. "Husband."

He brought his arms back and rested his neck in the cradle of his hands. "I don't mind hearing your innermost feelings."

"The only innermost feeling I have now is the fact that I could eat everything on that bed."

Luke nearly choked on the myriad of feelings that erupted in him without warning, his mind clearly elsewhere. "Be my guest."

She gave no hint of comprehending his double meaning. She took tentative steps toward the bed, the bureau not being but mere steps away from it anyway. Once there, she selected a plate of browned rice, some meat-wraps rolled up in what looked like pancakes but didn't taste at all like them, and some melon slices. He held out his hand and gave her a utensil.

"It's all yours. I haven't used it."

"Thank you."

Sitting down, she kept her profile to him. He watched her daintily eat, even though he could hear her stomach rumbling from where he lay.

"While you were in the tub, I left to see if they found our horses."

Her brows raised. "And?"

"They were where you left them. Now they're in Ferdinand's private livery. After I talked with him, he showed me to a room at the opposite end of the hall that had a shower bath. I cleaned up in there."

"I wonder where all these clothes come from?" She ran her palm down across the fine fabric of her robe. "Why are they here?" She slid the fork over the plate, spearing a slice of melon but pausing as she brought it to her mouth. "I'm aware of the fact," a hot blush fanned across her cheeks, "of what goes on here, but don't people come wearing their own clothes?"

"Brothels are all fantasy houses. This is one of the nicer ones I've seen."

"You've seen others?" Her fingertips looked cold around the fork. "I figured men liked them . . . but I didn't think of you as a frequent . . . I mean, so you've seen lots of places like this before?"

For reasons he didn't care to examine, he didn't like her thinking less of him as if she thought him immoral and without a single pang of consciousness in his bones. Like he enjoyed paying for rousing sex. Like he *had* to.

The truth was, he'd been in more whorehouses than he could ever count. Working the street beat, he'd been called out to stop prostitutes from being roughed up by intoxicated or indignant johns. To charge madams with assault and battery for keeping young girls against their will. Drunkards needed to be hauled away and arrested for disorderly conduct.

And, yes, he'd gone to brothels for his own pleasure, too.

"I wasn't a frequent visitor," he denounced, "and my meaning isn't what you think."

"Then what is it?"

He felt his freshly shaven jaw, dragging his blunt fingertips under his chin and down his neck to the base of his throat. Telling her that he was a police officer would be simple, but it wouldn't be wise. Days of road travel still spread out ahead of them, and nothing had changed to give him a reason to reveal the truth. He was still a hunted man; she was still unforeseen trouble.

A woman he hadn't counted on coming into his life at the wrong time. If he'd met her someplace else, things would be different. Luke found himself wanting to involve himself romantically with this woman. He fought against telling her truths that would help make sense of everything. But it was the strong sense he felt toward protecting her that kept him silent. The less she knew, the better off she'd be.

"It is what it is," he supplied. "And that's all."

From the quirk to the corner of her mouth, she digested his words, then let the subject die.

A humidor rested on the bedside table, and he leaned over to pull on one of the gilt handles of a drawer. The aromatic scent of Cuban tobacco filled his nose. He took out a finely rolled cigar, smelled it, and then put it back.

"I don't mind if you smoke that in here," Eve commented as she discreetly chewed behind her napkin.

"I might have one later," he replied. Spying a snifter beside the humidor, he did concede, "But I'll have a glass of whiskey now." He slid off the bed to pour himself a drink in one of the two available glasses. "Want one?"

The napkin was lowered onto her lap. She studied the pear-shaped curve of the snifter, then cleared her throat. "Yes, thank you."

He half-filled two glasses and brought one to her.

"This could be a nice evening, Luke." Their fingers brushed. "I mean, you don't have to hate it here. I did do something right."

"You did. Very admirable."

"No, resourceful."

Heat spread through him, and he could barely cling to a thin thread of control. He wanted to pull her up to him on his level, press himself into the soft folds of her body and hold her with his kiss.

The kiss in the El Rey had left him yearning for more than false displays of lust. He felt more than that. The desire he had for her was quite real, and he had a hard time pushing it away.

She took the glass, and for a short moment, their fingers touched. He became instantly aroused, his blood coursing at a heated pace.

Since he couldn't stay where he was without imagining her in his arms, naked and wanting, he ended up sitting on the windowsill. He rested the heel of his foot on his knee. The hems of his pants hiked, further exposing his bare feet.

She glimpsed at him, and he had to wonder if she'd ever seen a man's naked feet before. Because she blushed once again, then turned back to her dinner.

Her innocence, her ability to make him smile, and the wonder with which she viewed the world, entranced him. When he looked at her, his entire body came alive. She appealed to him. She charmed him. He barely knew her; he wanted to know more.

But whatever he thought or felt about Eve couldn't be explored. In less than a week they'd be in El Paso.

17

~~∽∾~~

Evelyn lay on the tufted settee, curled on her side with her palms pressed together beneath her cheek. The gold flocked walls were bathed in semidarkness. Through a tiny seam in the velvet window treatments where the two panels didn't meet all the way, a strong line of lamplight cut through the room and sliced its way across the bureau where she'd eaten her dinner.

Somewhere, probably on one of the bedside tables, echoed the tick from Luke's watch. Its movements seemed to pulse, slow and even, not at all like the beat of her own heart that tripped and snagged with each breath she took.

She had no idea of the hour, but she most certainly wasn't the only one up at the Red Banana. Filtering through the walls came the sounds of operettas and popular songs being played on a phonograph. Glasses clinked. Laughter rose in volume, then lowered to whispers. Once in a while, somebody walked through the hallway. Someone had hit their door, not intentionally like a knock, but as if two people were engaged in a heated embrace on the other side. She assumed that because she could hear moaning, then a door opening and closing. Then dead silence. But the silence only lasted for minutes before other noises fell into the night patterns once more.

She sighed, trying to do so quietly so as not to wake Luke. Being taller and larger than she was, she'd insisted he take the bed. He was sprawled out on it and took up its length from head to toe. The sight brought an ache in her heart. That ache came with physical awareness bringing heat and deep quivers to her body. She tried not to show it. Did everything she could to stave off these feelings and remain a proper lady, and yet, when she'd exited that bathing room and saw him reposed on that bed . . .

Never had she felt such feelings at the sight of a man wearing a simple white shirt, gold studs, and black trousers—and without a stitch of anything else remotely to be called respectable. Good heavens, he hadn't buttoned the shirt properly nor wore socks. What was so special about Luke that she'd barely been able to look at him without wanting to throw herself into his arms and beg him to kiss her?

It was silly. Ridiculous. She should be sleeping. She should ignore the voices outside. The tinkles of laughter and the low thuds that hit the wall. Sometimes they came in slow movements, others in rapid thumps and moans. She knew what they were doing. And she wanted to die from knowing. Wanted to close her ears and drown all the lurid behavior out of her mind, because with it came lurid thoughts of her own.

She attempted to roll over, reposition herself on the settee so she could get comfortable enough to fall asleep. The sunburn on her cheeks tingled. The tops of her wrists stung where they had been exposed to the burning sun, as well as a narrow place behind her neck, just above her dress collar. The chafing was made worse wherever anything touched against her bare skin. While the blankets Luke had torn off the bed and given to her were soft crêpe de Chine, they were slippery and hard to cocoon into without sliding over the surface of the settee.

She quit her adjusting, willing herself to fall into a sleep. Closing her eyes, she waited for oblivion to claim her.

The watch ticked, seemingly louder with each secondhand beat.

More suggestive laughter.

Her sunburn hurt.

She moved her leg. Her back was to the small divan's back, so she switched positions to face the camelback rest. In doing so, she slipped off the satiny-feeling blankets and spilled onto the floor in a tangle of sheet and nightgown.

"Can't sleep?" came the low-toned question.

If Evelyn thought her heartbeat was erratic before, it now careened into a frenzied staccato.

Luke was awake.

The hour was uncivilized. She wore a nothing robe and gown. He wore only a pair of trousers to bed that hugged his thigh muscles; his bare chest was broad and defined, while a light curling of hair covered its expanse. Things seemed so different in the dark. And things were definitely different in a "lover's suite" rather than an open range where a dirt bed and campfire were the only comforts. This place was, as Luke put it, sheer fantasy. From the oversize bed to the bathing tub, and the slick, seductive feel of superfine blankets and sheets.

Evelyn climbed back onto the settee, dragging the bedclothes with her. "I was sleeping. I turned over and fell. I'm sorry I woke you."

"I haven't been asleep. And neither have you."

She thought about voicing a denial, then reasoned why bother. It was apparent she'd been awake by all the tossing and turning she'd been doing. "The music is keeping me up. When do you think they'll shut it off?"

"Maybe sunrise."

"Great. We'll be out of here at sunrise."

"Don't you like the songs?" A teasing amusement filtered into his drawl.

"It's not really the songs, it's the—" She shoved a pillow firmly beneath her head. *It's the lascivious acts that bang at the wall.* "—shouting." *Moaning.*

The rustle of sheets on the big bed made her ears prickle. She held her breath, waiting in long dreadful seconds to find out whether or not Luke was getting up.

When he spoke next, by the direction of his voice, she knew he was still reclining in the bed. "You get used to the noise when you live in the city."

Tucking the blanket to her chin, she brought up her

knees. "Do you like it? I've never known anything but wide open land and smelly oil pumps, rather, um cattle."

"Yeah, I like it well enough. That's where my family lives."

Thoughtfully she recalled his mention of brothers, but not how many and that his mother— The thought broke mid-stream and another took its place, spurred by the word "family." "Luke, are you married?"

Without hesitation, he replied, "If I were married, I wouldn't be kissing you or any other woman."

She remained quiet for a moment, thinking over his declaration. The firm implicitness of it made her wistful. Made her long for a man who'd think that way about her if she was his wife. "That's very honorable of you."

"Yeah, well—I *am* honorable." She heard him punch his pillow to a new plumpness. "It's true I don't want to be found right now, but I'm not what or who you think I am."

"Then who are you?" The darkness around them made her feel secure in asking him for an answer to the unknown that had shrouded him since first seeing him as Mrs. Smythe. "What's in New Mexico?"

She could hear him moving over the mattress. "I'm looking for a guy."

Quietly, she asked, "What for?"

His answer wasn't forthcoming so she didn't think he would reply. When at last he did, she was surprised. "I'm pretty sure he's involved in some killings back in New Orleans. I need to know his side, but he's disappeared. He used to be a friend of mine."

Remorseful compassion struck a chord in her. "I'm sorry, Luke."

Fresh laughter sounded outside their suite door, seeping through the panels. Kisses were passionately loud, sucking sounds of mouths dancing together could easily be heard.

Bump. Their door was slid across by two bodies fused together in a lock of arms and legs. Surely that was what was transpiring. Mere yards from where she nestled in blankets, a couple—the woman bought for her sexual expertise—were entertaining one another with hands and mouths with an inevitable outcome in a room across the hall.

"Don't rush," came a woman's purr. "You've got me for an hour."

A man's gravelly voice responded, "And I'm going to get my hour's worth, darlin'."

"Ohhhhhhh . . . do that again, lover." The low, feminine moan was drawn out and didn't sound fabricated. "Yes. Right there. Touch me."

Thump.

A grinding motion rattled the door frame, then more hungry kisses and moans. Finally, a slide of silk and petticoats, and the click of a door opening and closing.

"Sweet Judas." Luke's feet pounded over the floor. "You want another whiskey? I need one."

She was already flushed and excited, and feeling as if her skin had been wickedly turned inside out. To her complete mortification, the couple outside the door had ignited an arousal she couldn't explain. Her body longed to be stroked such as the woman's in the hall had been—and she hadn't even watched them.

Did she want another whiskey? She'd already had a little, but that was hours ago. Or was it only minutes ago? How long had she been lying here? Listening to Luke talk. To lust knocking at the door in the hall. She'd lost all track of time.

She wasn't herself right now. Everything inside her pooled in a hot darting point at her unbound breasts, making them feel unusually heavy, that even the friction of nightgown across her skin sent forth gooseflesh.

She didn't feel any aftereffects of the whiskey she'd drunk earlier, nor did she feel the slightest bit impaired by her indulgence.

While deciding whether or not to have another drink, a match was struck and a taper in a gold holder was lit on the bureau. A flame wavered to life, and Luke's shadow went from deep grays to a milky cast of light until she could see him almost perfectly.

The pectoral muscles stretching across his chest were defined with hard strength. Earlier, he'd unbuttoned the shirt he'd worn, and she'd watched as the expensive white fabric was parted with his deft fingers as he'd removed it before bed. Now, ridges of muscle created a solid wall of chest that he had no false modesty about exposing. She wondered whether or not he knew he was so beautifully made.

Below his navel, a darker line of hair fell into the waistband of his trousers. His stomach at which the pants rode was washboard flat and stretched taut.

"Do you want one?" He moved toward the opposite bedside table, leaving the candle where it was.

Did she want . . . ?

"Yes"—she shook herself from the warm fog that had enveloped her—"since you are."

The chink of glass and snifter sounded melodic. In a brief minute, he came to her and extended his hand. She wordlessly took the whiskey and drank a sip. She fought against the same initial sputtering as she had earlier in the evening. She didn't want to embarrass herself and let him see her eyes watering.

Luke tossed his drink down in one swallow, then went back for a second while she remained on the settee. She scooted as far up as she could to view him from its curving back. In doing so, her hair caught beneath her and tugged, the lace collar of her robe scratching at the tender skin at her nape.

"Ooooww." The automatic response to her sudden pain escaped her.

"What's the matter?" Luke towered above her, standing so close at the edge of the divan, she grew momentarily dizzy looking up at him.

"My skin hurts where it's burned."

"I've got something that'll help." He was gone, and she could hear him rummaging around in his traveling bag. In his wake, the clean scent of his bathing soap pleasantly distracted her from the discomfort of her burn.

Confined in the dark room with such a larger-than-life man made her arms and legs feel limp. The glass in her hand sagged in a cool and heavy weight. She brought the rim to her lips and took another sample.

Then opted to drain the entire contents for fortification. Instantly, the liquor trailed a burning path throughout her body, charging to life every nook and curve, hidden and exposed. Like the golden puddle of wax forming at the base of the candle, she was melting too.

Luke soon returned with a bottle of salve. "Linseed oil."

"Oh." He stood so close, his knee met hers.

Before she could react, he was sitting down next to her. "Thanks, I'll—"

He disregarded her outstretched hand, the other firmly holding the empty glass. "You can't reach your neck."

Of course she could. "I can do it if you take my glass."

"Empty already?" A black shock of hair fell at his temple, and she could just make out the surprised gleam that lit in his eyes. "I'll rub the linseed in. You can barely keep from swaying."

His words sounded like they ran together in a breath clinging hard to control. She wasn't swaying. But the room did seem to tilt a bit.

He unscrewed the metal cap, poured some oil into his palm and set the vial on the floor. With his motions, his body heat curled around her, filling her with deft swirls of temptation. All thoughts fled her mind—except for one: She shouldn't have drunk the whiskey so quickly.

"I'm not swaying," she insisted. The muffled thud of glass hitting thick carpet didn't immediately register—until she realized she was without her glass. One minute it was there, the next it was gone. With a frown, she stared at her fingers. "I can put my own sunburn oil on."

The plea was ignored while she was turned around on the brocade, then slid forward to fit between his open legs behind her. Their position was anything but proper. She could almost feel herself leaning toward him. She pulled in big drafts of air, willing herself to clear her head.

She blinked, rapidly and quickly, ordering away the liquid warmth fanning below her waist.

"I can't seem to—" Her mind fluttered.

Her long hair was lifted from her trembling shoulders, caught in a large hand that was considerate of her discomfort. Warm, gentle fingers grazed her nape as he twisted the length of her hair and handed the full skein of bound curls to her. "Hold that up."

She was helpless not to do as he bid. In fact, she wanted to do what he told her. She wanted . . .

Evelyn squeezed her eyes closed.

The impression of his thighs against the swell of her behind left her breathless. The measure of material between them was almost nonexistent. Without a warning from Luke, oil spilled on her burning skin, making her jolt at its cooler temperature. But the second his fingers glided across her flesh to let the linseed soak in, she moaned.

That moan persisted deep into her thoughts—long after she felt his initial touch. She kept her voice locked tightly inside, not wanting him to hear how he could make her feel. His massage was sensual and she felt as if she were falling while sitting. Falling over the edge of a cliff she had never before stepped this close to.

Her eyelids were still closed tight, blocking out any light and any resistance she met to keep from trembling. A song filled her head—the one that currently played on the phonograph down the hall. Its words were suggestive and colorful. She mouthed the lyrics while languishing in the ministrations of Luke as he, in calculated placements of his hands, kneaded the tension from every fiber of every muscle connected anywhere to her neck and shoulders.

"Kiss me once. Kiss me twice. Kiss me till I cry your name." Her eyelids flew open, and her mouth parted in stunned surprise. She must have uttered a phrase, or two, to that ribald song. Oh dear. She'd been singing.

An unrecognizable growl of humor came to her. Warm breath caught on the delicate shell of her ear. Hands, the fingers splayed, caught on either side of her neck, and moved up and down the column of her spine. Slowly skimming, massaging. A shower of fiery sparks, such as those from a large bloom of fireworks, spread across her scalp, making each strand of hair stand up in uncontested delight.

"You're drunk, Eve." The whisper mixed into her hair which she'd some time ago released and let fall over her breast.

"I-I'm not drunk . . ." she managed, coming to her own conclusions. "I'm just a little . . . marinated. I think."

A strand of her hair caught on his lips as he brushed the side of her neck to whisper, "Turn around."

Momentarily dazed by his command, she inched her way around to face him. She barely had a second to breathe short, choppy gasps when he took her hand. Where the skin was chafed and red at the back of her wrist, he spread the mineral-scented oil. She studied the fit of her hand in his. His was so large, so powerful. His grip could crush her bones to dust, but the way in which he held her was definitely mild, and dear.

"I should have done this days ago," he said in the darkness.

She wondered if he meant touch her in such a manner, or put the oil on her sunburn. The question hovered at the fringes of her mind, but it evaporated when the pads of his callused thumbs captured her face.

In a slow, circular motion, he massaged in the oil high on top of her cheekbones and into the depression beneath. The therapeutic pressure of thumbs and palms froze the breath in her throat. Her eyelids became heavy, her lips parted, her nipples darted to hard points.

She could feel herself gravitating toward him. She couldn't invite him any more than if she stood naked in front of him. She desperately wanted him to kiss her.

She licked her lips, looked into his face, the dark lines and shadows of swarthy manliness.

"Eve." Her name came out in a gravelly monosyllable that brought a silent appeal into her eyes. She knew it as surely as she was looking at the same appeal in Luke's. "Do you know what you're doing?"

"Do you know what you're doing to me?" Her soft reply was more a dare to her sensibilities. By acknowledging his power over her, she was in essence telling him she would surrender without a fight.

"Yes." His mouth swooped down over hers in a hungry possession. The kiss was all that she wanted, and more. Hot and moist. She kissed him back, but her kiss was the only thing she freely yielded. As for touching him, bringing him close, shyness kept her still.

She swallowed, her lips closed and damp from his kiss. He had to have sensed her inexperience. The heat of his breath touched her as he spoke, "Open your mouth."

Open her mouth the way she hadn't before.

She did so this time. And as soon as she did, his tongue delved deeply into her, unexpectedly. Beneath her tiny cry of surprise, she was cautious, not knowing what to do. There was no need for her to wonder. As the breath was driven from her lungs, her mind and body took over. She instinctively reached out as his hands cupped her cheeks; her fingers curled around his wrists. Slightly tentative at first, but stronger in their grasp as his tongue swirled through her, stroking and tasting.

She let him explore the cavern of her mouth in a kiss so intimate, it was indescribable. Her arms went up to his chest, feeling his heated skin that she'd admired in the candlelight. He was everything and more than she imagined. Smooth as marble, hard as steel. The power in his body was so strong it took her breath away.

His hands left her cheeks, slowly roaming over her shoulders and grazing the sides of her breasts. She trembled in anticipation. Lower, his hands came to rest on her waist, sliding up and down, feeling the contours of her hips and breasts. Breasts that held back her heartbeat from pelting through her rib cage. Oh, how she ached for . . . more than this. Ached for him to touch her where she touched him—on bare skin.

The shock of heat from his skin made her fingertips tremble. She felt no embarrassment, no shy restraint. Just glory.

Their kiss ripened with her eagerness to explore, to spar with his tongue. She was sliding over an edge to an unseen place, shuddering in new sensations. Beneath her roaming caress, his nipples were hard little nubs, and he growled when she ran her thumb across one, feeling it pucker even tighter.

Then his hands were on her breasts, the rub of fabric over them maddening. She would have taken the robe and gown off. She wasn't thinking clearly, or rationally. Nor did she want to. While she touched the warmth of his skin, his hands and fingers were on her, touching, feeling. His mouth fused an even harder bond with hers, his tongue slanting and dancing to the same rhythm as her own.

Her heartbeat was beyond slowing. Her mind was completely empty of conscious thought aside from his touch, his mouth, his hands, and the burning desire to press herself into him for more. More than kisses and touches—the full act of possession.

How could she be thinking such a thing? She'd

been taught to save herself for her wedding night, and she had planned on it. But she had made up her mind not to marry. There would be no special night. No—

Luke's mouth left hers, and she felt an instant's loss. Moaning her displeasure, she touched his jaw, trying to bring him back. He ignored a silent plea she sent him. Instead, his kisses traced a path over the curve of her shoulder at her neck, lower, kissing her skin, the full round of her breast at the edge of her nightgown. Even though the fabric covered her, she could feel the heat from his mouth as surely as if she were without a stitch.

In a single pull, he tugged on the ribbon at her throat, and let the robe part, quickly unfastening the top of the gown as well to expose her fully. A current of air brushed at her bare skin, the high rounded edges of her breasts now revealed. She could stop this now. Tell him no more. She still had her wits about her and they hadn't come so far she couldn't turn back. Even though her gown was unfastened and her robe had fallen off her arms, her modesty was still intact. Nothing was exposed for his view.

Nothing had happened. She could stop him. . . .

The satin blankets and fine sheets were slippery beneath her, sliding against the settee's brocade. While indecision plagued her, she reached out and brought Luke to her for a kiss. A kiss that would help her to decide what to do. As he leaned forward, she felt herself slipping over the edge and before she knew what had happened, they were on the floor, his full weight on top of her.

Their lips broke apart, the heaviness of his body

removed from her at almost the same time as he rolled onto his side. His hand was on her breast, warm and unmoving, while his face was burrowed into the crook of her neck. Neither of them moved.

She exhaled her breath in the same tempo as her beating heart. Perhaps it was a blind salvation that the blankets had shifted on them, jarring her back to a reality she'd not wanted to contend with.

In the darkness of the room, with just the light given from the candle flame, she murmured, "I've only kissed you a handful of times, and here I'm wanting to do more. And I'm letting you, and I know it's . . ."

"It's not right," he finished for her. Then added, "But sometimes what's not right isn't necessarily wrong, either." He propped himself onto his elbow and gazed down at her face. With a surprisingly gentle touch, he brushed her hair from her brow, and tucked it behind her ear. His breath was ragged like hers, his pulse pumping double-time. She could feel how it sped through his body where his thigh touched hers.

For a long moment, a quiet stillness held them. It afforded her a space of time to think about how she felt about him. Honestly. They'd been traveling with each other long enough that they were bound by an undefinable sense of duty toward one another. At least that's how she felt about him. She had to confront her growing feelings for him. They both scared and amazed her. But she knew they would still part ways. There were no promises. No hope for more.

Given that, she felt she owed him one truth. One that counted.

"My real name is Evelyn."

"Evelyn," he said thoughtfully, testing it and bringing delightful chills over her bare arms.

"But I don't mind when you call me Eve. You say it so divinely, the sound of your voice makes me shiver sometimes."

From out in the hallway, the sound of a door slammed across the way and a woman's laughter followed a man's heavy footfalls down the narrow corridor.

Luke moved, and she was dismayed by the sudden loss of his body heat beside her. She loved being nestled next to him.

Lifting up, Luke pulled her robe and nightgown together with fingers that couldn't quite manage the delicate bows. All the while, she held herself still, refraining from bringing him down on top of her for more kisses. More delightful and wonderful kisses.

He held out his hand. "Come on—Evelyn, you're going to get into the bed and sleep. We've got to make it to Monahan tomorrow with two rivers to cross on the way. You'll need your rest."

She took his offering, his fingers firmly circling hers. Standing and letting him propel her to the bed, she protested, "But what about you?"

"I'll sit in the chair by the window. I'll doze off, don't worry."

"But—"

"Not buts. You need to sleep. You can't do it on that tiny divan."

The covers were flung aside, and she was directed beneath them. She did so, only because he stood over her to make sure. Once she was nestled into the satiny confines, he gave her a kiss that ended before it began. Chaste and sweet.

She saw him go to the humidor on the bedside table, then a minute later, he lit a cigar from the candle flame. Getting comfortable was next to impossible. How could she sleep when he was so near? Just on the other side of the room.

He sat beside the window in silhouette. The curtains were parted at the bottom of the sill, the window lifted open. Smoke curled in front of the pane, then drifted low and outside. The red tip of his cigar burned brighter as he puffed.

She sighed, unable to sleep any more than she could take her eyes from him.

"Luke . . ." she ventured. "I'm not running away from home per se, but rather a situation. My father wants me to marry a man he chose for me. I can't go through with it."

After a thoughtful puff that gave no indication of how he felt about what she had just said, he commented, "He can't make you."

"Yes," she insisted. "He can. That's why I can't go home. That's why I'm going to California. To see what I've been missing all my life. Finding you wasn't something I counted on. It's been . . . nice."

Then Evelyn lowered her head and turned away onto her side, afraid of what he might say in response. With the blankets tight in her fists, she held her breath.

But she needn't have worried.

Because he said nothing at all.

18

~~~~~

Luke recognized Jude Bienville at once.

Milling around the front of the general store buying gasoline in two-gallon containers, the former inmate in the Sixty-sixth Precinct jail cell still looked like a bayou hoodlum. His near-white blond hair was oiled back from his short forehead, and a piece of straw was indolently stuck between his lips. He wore a pair of overalls and low-heeled boots; a button on his suspender was missing, leaving the bib down at one corner. His hamlike arms were stuffed into a faded and frayed red shirt with the sleeves rolled past his elbows. For a man who appeared to be down on his luck, Luke thought it a strange coincidence Jude was fueling the tank of a blue Model T Touring car that, aside from dust clouding the long ribbed running boards and fenders, didn't have a scratch on the glossy paint. The automobile must have just been purchased—if indeed it was bought.

The windshield was folded down, an indication

Jude wasn't passing through. If he were taking the vehicle out on the open highway of Texas desert, he'd be eating bugs. Not to mention repairing tires every mile or so. Then again, the way curiosity seekers gathered around the shiny car, the Ford was a novelty in a town that wasn't big enough for the railroads to construct a stop. Jude may have just rolled in. For what, and why he had that automobile, was Luke's guess.

Jude Bienville was back in the grand larceny business.

Not good timing for Luke. Jude could finger him in an instant if he spotted him. Soured up ex-cons were the first to seek revenge against the police officers who'd locked them behind bars. More than once. Which Luke had. Eight times, to be exact. He and Bienville were not on the best of terms the last they spoke—which, given their situation, who'd want to be friendly?

Laughing at something the clerk said while he exchanged an empty tank for a full, Jude propped his leg onto the rear tire. His cocky stance was that of a real big man. The general store proprietor, along with men who'd stepped out of the iron forge barn next door, eyed the touring car as if it were cast in bronze.

Luke turned away, damning his timing. Of all the days, of all the precise minutes, to have been stuck in Ysleta, Texas.

Walking the side of the main street, he kept his hat low to ward off the blinding midday sun. He'd left Eve at the Nook and Crook café. She wanted to come with him to buy another horse, but he'd insisted she stay there and get something to eat. He'd join her now and grab something for himself. They hadn't had a decent hot meal in five days; not since leaving Midland.

That night in the Red Banana seemed so far off, but the feel and taste of Eve still remained firmly in place in his head. The silky touch of her skin, the hot moistness of her mouth. He'd been willing, she'd been willing. But he'd known all the while as he kissed her, touched the soft curves of her breasts, that doing more was doing harm to Evelyn.

Evelyn.

She'd said her true name was Evelyn.

Evelyn B.? He reasoned it mattered as much as his own last name mattered to her. A detail that was inconsequential. Just like knowing who she was supposed to marry and why.

In many ways, he envied her freedom. She knew what she wanted and she was getting closer to it. While all that his future held for him right now were uncertainties. But it was a strong possibility that gave him a fragment of hope he was on the right trail.

Ferdinand's scouts had turned up something significant.

Henry Boyd had been in Midland the week before. Luke had listened attentively as Ferdinand had relayed the details. Henry had come into town, gambled and drank heavily in a bar. Somewhere around three o'clock in the morning, a doctor was summoned to attend to Henry, who'd gotten so sick he'd vomited blood. He was taken to the doctor's office where he spent the rest of the evening on a cot, then left at dawn after paying for services rendered.

The doctor told Ferdinand's man that he'd treated Henry for a severe stomach ulcer and abnormalcies of the bowels. He'd given Henry a bottle of pills and urged him to quit drinking. When Luke pressed, Ferdinand said he hadn't learned anything about Henry going to Silver City, New Mexico. Even if Luke didn't have that sure piece of information, he did have the knowledge that Henry Boyd was headed in that direction.

Since then, Luke's thoughts had been focused on getting closer to El Paso as fast as he could. The only trouble was, at the moment he didn't have a sound horse to keep going.

His died this morning about five miles out of Socorro. The horse hadn't shown signs of colic until late in the night. Blessedly, the animal's death had been quick. Eve had been horribly upset, reluctant to leave the horse behind, knowing what would become of it in the desert. But there was nothing Luke could do.

They'd ridden double on her horse, his saddle and bridle strapped over his back, and entered Ysleta where he put up her mare at the livery—which was a dicey thing given the brand on its rump. Service horses were bought at auctions all the time, and that's the explanation he'd give if asked. He hoped they weren't asked because he had no bill of sale to prove it.

They only had twelve miles left to El Paso, and he needed to buy a horse with his poker winnings from Midland. At the livery, there hadn't been a one that looked sound enough to ride across the street, much less to El Paso. So on a tip from the livery owner, who apologized for poor stock, Luke was going to head out a half mile on foot and check out what a local rancher had to offer. He had to tell Eve what he was doing and make sure she'd be all right when he was gone. Having Bienville in town concerned him, but he didn't want to alarm Eve.

Climbing the steps to the café, he saw her sitting beside a window in the front. He paused, momentarily taking in her appearance in the soft light. She'd bought a simple green calico dress in Wild Horse. While he loved that white Mexican blouse and red skirt on her, they weren't what he'd call going-to-town clothes.

They'd had to veer into Wild Horse, and two days later, Rio Grande for more supplies. His canned goods had run low and the canteen he was using developed a ding and leak at the metal seam on the bottom. In a store in Rio, he'd bought her a small box of chocolates, as well as a bar of rose soap. He'd never seen a woman's face light up so bright.

Opening the café's door, he ducked a notch beneath the entryway and went for her table. He pulled out a chair and sat down across from her.

"I don't see anything hitched outside with you," she commented, a plate of ham and eggs before her. She'd eaten half the biscuit slathered with strawberry jam.

"No horse." He eased back in his seat, glad for a view of the street and Jude Bienville, if he had the inclination to come down this way. The café was a stretch from the general store, but he wouldn't put it past the man to ride through town in the Ford, tooting the horn. "None any good. All I saw were cracked heels, inflamed hocks and double flanks." He removed his hat and rested it on his knee.

Her hair was in a dainty twist and her sunburn, having faded to a light golden tan, complemented her hair color. The two warm tones brought out the blue of her eyes, enhancing her features. "What are we going to do?"

"There's a ranch about a quarter mile out. I'm going to walk over and see what they have." He noted the tiny spot of red jam at the corner of her mouth. The smudge endeared him to her.

"We could take a stagecoach," Eve suggested.

"I checked. One doesn't run through until tomorrow noon. We need to move along as soon as possible."

Holding the biscuit in her hand, she paused and looked at the fluff of flaky white and jam, then at him. "You should really eat before you go."

In spite of the tension winding through him, the corners of his mouth lifted. "Did you leave anything in the kitchen?"

A short moment passed before she understood his quip. "Of course I did."

"I don't know, you devoured two boxes of chocolate on the way over out in that desert."

"I *indulged* in two boxes. A lady never devours anything."

"The finer points of deportment," he said in a teasing manner.

"Yes, actually."

The waitress came to the table, and he ordered steak and eggs and black coffee. His gaze wandered to the street on occasion, and he found it sleepy. Every once in a while, a horse and wagon rolled by. A rider on horseback. A cart with lumber. Milk dray.

Adobe was prevalent in building construction, and the population predominantly Tigua Indians, who congregated at the rebuilt mission on the other side of town. The pueblo smelled of baking bread, and the fuel of burning mesquite roots. He'd checked and there was no town sheriff, just what they called a *mayordomo*—a captain who kept the peace.

Luke hoped that the peace would stay that way. He didn't need a surprise face-to-face with Jude. The sooner they could get out of Ysleta, the better.

His meal came, and he ate quickly without savoring the home-cooked flavors. Sunlight hit the window and warmed his left shoulder and cast a beam across the table with its oilcloth cover.

"When do you think we'll make it to El Paso?" Eve asked, sipping her coffee after her plate had been cleared.

"If we can get out of here in about an hour, I'd say we'd be well to get there three hours after sunset."

He didn't like traveling at night but since Midland, he'd been filled with a sense of urgency he'd tried not to let overpower him. Not to mention, the closer they got to going their own ways, the more he wondered how he could say good-bye to a woman who'd been stealing her way into his heart, but he'd never see again.

Eve's wistful comment broke into his thoughts. "I

keep thinking about that poor horse and how he died."

"Didn't you ever come across a newly born calf that didn't make it?"

"No. I spent most of my time in the garage with the automobiles. I used to sit behind the steering wheel and pretend I was driving to . . ." She gave him a shrug and sigh, a hint of self-conscious color tinting her cheeks. "It sounds silly now. But I'd imagine I was driving all the way to Atlanta or New York."

"I'll bet you've seen your fair share of fancy automobiles."

"Hmm. Yes." She tucked a wisp of hair behind her ear. "Did you see that Ford at the general store? My father has one just like that—I mean," she cleared her throat, "the man who he works for has one. It's two years old and neglected already. It hasn't been driven in ages. It's such a waste of money. I never thought about it until these past weeks, but there's a tremendous flow of cash out of that house—and for what? Automobiles that don't get more than a second look. It's all for show. To be the best."

An alarm went off in his head. He didn't need her heading over to that general store to get a closer look at Jude's touring car.

"Don't go hanging around that Ford, Eve." Luke chased down the last bite of his eggs with a swallow of strong coffee. "I want you to stay here while I'm gone. Get yourself a soda from the fountain." Fitting his hand into his pocket, he gave her a dollar. "Try all six flavors."

"I'd get sick."

"Drink them slow."

"I could go with you." A hopeful curve caught on her mouth. "I could tell you more about my Grandfather Jimmy."

"No. I need to travel fast and my legs are a lot longer than yours. I'll be back soon."

Luke rose with his hat, adjusted the belt of his gun holster and slung his travel bag over his arm. Her club satchel rested at her feet. Inside was the hundred bucks she'd won singing. She'd offered to pay for some of the food but he hadn't let her. She was going to need that money to see her through. He could fend for himself, but a woman alone . . . He could hardly think of her moving on alone.

His chest tightened. "I'll see you in about forty-five minutes."

She gazed at him through the fringe of her long blond lashes. "I'm only going to wait forty-five minutes, then I'll be eloping with the cook."

The cook stood behind a counter, his white hat greasy on his gray hair. At present, he held a netted fly swatter and was slamming the flat end against the wall. His fingers were fat and gnarled at the knuckles.

"Damn. I'd better hurry up."

Evelyn drank her third cherry fizz and felt waterlogged. A visit to the lavatory became a necessity. She scooted her parlor-style chair back from the table, took her satchel with her, and walked to the back of the restaurant where she followed a hand-painted sign with an arrow.

She'd never known of an establishment to advertise where the ladies' lounge was located. As she walked through a narrow corridor that led to an outside closet, she noted some of the playbills that had been tacked up on both sides. Theatrical troupes had been to town, as well as a circus at one time last year. There were other notices pinned to the whitewashed span of wall above the painted green wainscoting. Some of the papers were yellowed, showing time and age. Others were fresh white paper with bold black ink. It was such a notice that gave her pause, her heartbeat snagging in her throat.

She drew closer and gazed hard at a particular agency's stationary and the caption below.

Generous Reward!
For Information On The Whereabouts Of
Evelyn Thurgood-Baron
Read Her Description Here
She stands at five feet four inches
with light blond hair and blue eyes.
She may be traveling under an assumed
identity or being held against her will.
Last seen in Oiler, Texas, and could be
heading across the state.
Immediately contact Woodworth Detective
Agency in Beaumont by wire.
July 1, 1911—See Cecil Woodworth,
Prickly Pear Hotel

From the handwritten addition at the bottom, the notice had been posted today. That meant . . . Cecil Woodworth was at the Prickly Pear Hotel.

Right now.

Evelyn tore the notice off the wall, quickly turned away from the café tables and continued out the back door. Somebody inside could have seen her and already read the notice. There were many blond-haired women with blue eyes, but when a reward was being offered, people would be interested in anyone fitting the description. She couldn't be one of them.

The summer heat crushed her as she went outdoors. The lavatory was straight ahead and she made fast use of it, closeting herself off and trying to think of what she should do.

She had to get out of town. Fast. Or risk being discovered. But what about Luke? She'd have to leave now. She couldn't wait for him. Couldn't explain why she suddenly had to go.

Her horse from the Red Crown stage lines was in the livery, down by the general store. Luke had told her to stay here while he was gone. This wasn't how she'd imagined they'd part ways.

For the past four hundred miles, she'd ridden with him. Come to depend on him. Enjoy their time together at the campfire where they played cards, talked and grew drowsy from a long day of riding. She would always cherish that night in the Red Banana.

How could she leave today . . . this instant? And not say good-bye?

But if she stayed, and if Woodworth discovered her, he could discover Luke, too. She didn't know why he didn't want to be found or how this man in New Mexico figured into anything. But by bringing attention to herself, she might inadvertently endanger Luke.

A week ago, so determined to gain her independence, she wouldn't have cared about saving anyone but herself. She would have done what she had to do and not worried about Luke or anyone else, for that matter. But things had changed. Circumstances had changed.

Her feelings had changed.

Why now? Why did she have to realize she was falling in love with him now?

Her heartbeat swelled, her chest constricted until her throat ached. It was the most inopportune time to be thinking about Luke like this. There was no going backward. Only forward. Alone.

Love for her wasn't possible.

Not now. Not with this man.

Even knowing that, she felt bound to Luke like she had no other person in her life. The sight of him did things to her insides. She wanted to be with him. In his arms. Touch her lips to his. Stroke his skin. Watch the sunrise with him. Marvel in the vibrant oranges of a sunset. Wake up in the morning and see him sitting across from her, watching her.

But that was never meant to be. From the first day out of Beaumont, they had been two people who happened to be headed in the same direction.

That they were thrown together had been by chance.

That they were to part company was reality.

If they had made it to El Paso together, that would have been the end of things regardless of Cecil

Woodworth. But, oh, how at this moment she hated him for stealing what little time she had left with Luke.

Pressing her hands to her face, she held back a shudder. She had to go. Right now.

Evelyn went quickly to the livery, gazing intently at the Prickly Pear Hotel, which was across the street and on the corner. There was only a single thoroughfare running through Ysleta, and this was it. That meant calculated steps on the boardwalk and an alert gaze.

There was little activity on the street. Dust whirls rose in a funnel in front of the post office. A clutch of deep red chickens scratched the dirt by the Indian trading post. The livery had two large doors, both thrown open to circulate the heat in and out of the oversize barn. To the left, the general store. That Ford was still there. Empty. The owner was gone. She'd briefly seen him earlier, but didn't take a good look.

Once inside the livery office, she inquired after her horse to a man calling himself Fletcher.

"I'd like my horse saddled, please." A horse liniment calendar still held open to June hung on the wall, while a clutter of papers lay across his desk. One in particular jumped out at her. It was the Woodworth Agency notice! How many had Cecil passed out? They must be all across town. Everywhere. "Right away," she added urgently, turning her face away from him so he wouldn't take a closer look at the features so perfectly captured in black and white.

"I've got her out in the back pasture," Fletcher

replied. "It's going to take me a minute to get her. I checked her out for colic and parasites. And I gave her a vaccination for—"

"Yes, that's fine." She held back the stammer threatening her tone.

As he left the office, she followed closely at his heels. Anxiousness to get away flexed the muscles of her heart into a rapid beat.

Fletcher reached for her bridle and tack hanging on a nail in one of the livery posts. She noted Luke's saddle and blanket on the floor, right beside hers. A disquieting qualm gripped her in its cold hands; but she shoved it aside. She was doing the right thing.

You told him that if he wasn't back in forty-five minutes you weren't waiting. So he'll think that you left early. That El Paso was so close you decided to make it on your own without him. Neither of you meant to go further than that anyway. Being together was a fluke. It was time to part company. He'll understand. He may be grateful to be rid of you now.

The reasoning made her feel utterly dismal. She didn't want to believe he'd think that, but she had no choice. Convincing herself it could be true was the only way to move on.

"I did notice the brand on her," Fletcher said as he headed for the rear door. "Red Crown. How'd that come to be?"

"I bid on her at a horse auction," she automatically replied. She'd used the response Luke had told her to use; which she had already done one other time in Rio Grande when one of the mare's shoes had needed renailing.

Fletcher paused for a moment, then shrugged. "Wait here."

She did so, nervously pacing in front of the open doorway with the scorching heat of the forge at her back. She kept her gaze on the street, keeping a look out for a weasel dressed in an expensive suit. She also looked for Luke. Maybe he would come back early. She thought it had been nearly forty-five minutes. Thirty minutes at least. Maybe—

"Your horse has been stolen." The blunt statement uttered by the livery owner caused her to spin around.

"Excuse me?"

"I put that mare out in my corral and she's gone."

"How can that be?" She took fast steps to the rear door to see for herself.

Spread out before her was a weathered corral with poorly dug posts and uneven slats. A dun, a chestnut and a skewbald grazed on hay in a wooden feeding pocket; all three were sorry nags. A shored-up water trough and meager tail-feathered rooster took up the rest of the space. There wasn't a piebald among them.

Indeed, her stolen horse had been—*stolen*. Of all the gall. Or had it been taken someplace else as evidence? After all, Fletcher had inquired about the brand. The sheriff might be coming to question her.

"What bad luck," she said, forcing herself to be calm. "But these things happen. Give me a replacement horse and I won't trouble you further."

"I don't have any available."

Even though Luke had said the horses were in sad condition, she had no choice. "There are three horses in that pasture, I'll take any one."

"Them three are spoken for."

"Now, that can't possibly be true," she rebuffed, her gaze darting to the street as a buggy went by. "I know for a fact you were willing to sell one to a gentleman not more than an hour ago, but he declined."

Fletcher fanned out his chest and folded his arms over the straining buttons of his grimy shirt. "I sold these in the past fifteen minutes."

"Oh, honestly. Then I'll pay you more than you were offered."

He weighed out her words. "Fifty."

"Fifty is robbery." But she had no alternative. Gritting her teeth, she was opening the clasp of her satchel.

Footsteps sounded on the boardwalk in front, and she quickly turned. A man wearing overalls came into the livery. His white-blond hair was made even whiter by the reflection of the sun in the strands. A piece of hay was stuck between his back teeth, the fringed end sticking out of his lips.

"Howdy," he said to her in a drawl that sounded strangely familiar.

She kept her chin low so he couldn't see directly into her face.

"It's a hot one, little lady," he commented further. "As hot as the hotbox in a yard."

Those words gave her pause. What yard? A residence didn't have a hotbox, only flower boxes. A yard that had hotboxes was a—

"Yes, ma'am. Hot as the dickens."

A delayed realization came to her:

The man talked in an accent like Luke's.

*   *   *

There wasn't a horse to be bought at that ranch and the walk had been for nothing. He was going to throttle Fletcher. The man had intentionally steered him wrong. The ranch he'd gone to didn't offer horses; it was a cattle outfit. And a poor one at that. A waste of time and energy.

Something wasn't right. And the fact that Jude Bienville was in town made him all the more suspect.

Luke hurried to the café to get Eve.

He swung the door inward, the little bell above ringing. A man at the counter turned his head toward him, then resumed his lunch. Aside from him, the tables were empty.

Eve wasn't there.

He waited for a moment, wondering if she'd stepped out back. When she didn't show up, a coil of tension wound inside his body.

The door behind him fell against his arm as he quickly turned and made his way down the boardwalk in a run. Where could she have gone and why? He'd told her to wait for him. Something had happened. She wouldn't have just gotten up and left.

Or maybe she would have.

They hadn't made a pact, formed an alliance that would be kept at all costs. She had a free will and could do whatever she liked, and at any time. Maybe she liked to be rid of him. She'd gone out on her own.

Dammit.

He couldn't believe she'd do that.

The livery loomed ahead, the wide doors on bulky hinges kept ajar only slightly. When he'd left for the ranch, they'd been open. He didn't think much of them now as he pressed onward and came to the opening. Slipping into the yawning dim space, he immediately held back when he heard Jude talking. Trouble was, Jude saw him the same time.

Recognition wasn't instantaneous, but it came swift enough. "Well, I'll be a ring-tailed polecat, look who's here," Jude said with a dry chuckle. "This is my lucky day."

Then an angry shot of big fist came out and side-cuffed Luke on the jaw.

Reeling backward, he felt for the butt of his revolver through the shower of sparks heating his head and making his vision blurred-white. He came up with the Colt, only to hear the click of a gun already close to his ear.

"*Très bien.* I always knew I'd be faster on the draw than you, you goddamn roach."

"Luke!" Eve cried out his name, taking him by surprise.

Opening his eyes wide against the spear of pain shooting into his brain from Bienville's blow, he saw Eve standing in dismay by one of the posts, her wrists—

What in the hell? Her wrists were tied together in front of her.

"Don't go for the Colt, Devereaux, unless you want it to be the last move you make." Jude's warning commentary was clipped and precise.

Luke didn't move, but his cheekbone smarted like the devil and he could taste blood in his mouth. He spit on the ground, straightening to his full height with a stagger. Unsteady on his feet, he said, "You don't have an argument with her, Bienville. It's with me. Let her go."

Jude's laugh was laced with amusement. "I didn't even know you were in town until you walked in here."

Rape had never been one of Bienville's motives, but Luke couldn't take anything for granted. Gazing at Eve with her hat off-center and the collar of her dress tugged out of place, he could see she'd put up a fight. Bile rose in his throat at the thought of Bienville's meaty hands on her. "Why is she rope-tied?"

Movement in the livery, outside the open office door, drew Luke's attention. *Fletcher.* "Because of this," he offered, holding up a piece of paper too far for Luke to read.

Jude kept the gun at Luke's head when he replied, "There's a man at the Prickly Pear Hotel mighty interested in this little lady."

Flashing his gaze at Eve, he looked only long enough to see she'd inched her way closer toward the post where a shovel handle hung on a wooden peg. Fletcher stood under three feet away from her, the paper in his hand and a greedy smile on his lips.

Bienville eased back a fraction. "I aim to collect whatever she's worth. *You,*" he emphasized, "I have other plans for. Hot damn on a tin roof, but we prisoners dream about a day like this. You are dead, Devereaux. You are—"

Thwack!

The shovel blade had sliced through air and landed flat against the back of Fletcher's head, making the man fall to the ground unconscious. Luke had half-seconds to watch Eve sway back on her feet from the force of energy she'd put into the blow. The distraction was just enough for him to swing out at Jude, knock the gun from his hand and wrestle him down on the floor.

They rolled and locked hands and arms, each trying for a punch but unable to let the other go to do so. Fine pebbles sprayed, dirt caught in his eyes, and Luke fought the blurriness to see his opponent. Jerking and pushing and pulling, they ended up by the forge.

Jude kept reaching down his leg, grasping and dragging his hand but coming up empty.

Eve's hysterical screams were barely registering in Luke's head. A quick image of her skirt whirled past.

"Luke! He's got a knife in his boot!"

With a surge of strength, Luke brought Jude's hands up where he could see them, but it was Bienville who got off the first belt to his upper arm, driving his knuckles into Luke's taut flesh and muscles. The pain was deep and hot, but Jude, being off-balance from the violent effort, gave Luke an advantage. He pinned him under his heavy torso, knocked a left, then a right into Jude's jaw and finished him with an undercut.

Luke backed off a little, his breath rasping from his chest, his brow damp with sweat. Raising back on his arms, he looked down.

Jude Bienville lay stretched on his back—out cold.

The knuckles in Luke's tight fist throbbed and were raw; and he thought he might have busted a finger.

He struggled to stand. Eve's wrists were still tied, and he went to her and forced his eyes wide to clear his vision. With several quick jerks of the knots, he had her free.

She threw herself into his wide-open arms.

"Luke! I never was so glad to see anyone in all my life. That man, that horrible man, he tied me up and was going to take me to Cecil Woodworth and then— Oh, Luke. He hurt you. Your poor face."

Concerned less about his injuries and more about getting out of town, he moved her hand aside, his lungs still dragging air in and out from the fight. "We've got to get out of here."

"The only horses out there are those three nags." She leaned against a rafter post for support. Gulping, she added, "And that Ford. The car was by the fence, just behind a shed. I saw the fender."

"I'm going to tie and gag these two before they come around." Kneeling over Bienville, he finished, "You go out there and get that Ford started. We're taking it to El Paso."

19

Evelyn sat in the Ford touring car staring at a dial, a box of some kind with a knob on it, hand levers and foot pedals, in a panic of where and how to begin.

Though she had ridden in her fair share of automobiles, she had never started one before, much less driven one.

As soon as Luke had told her, she'd run out back and climbed into the car, stepping on the diamond-patterned running board and swinging the driver's door outward. The top was folded back and the hood straps dangled at the window-sides.

With her hands firmly gripping the steering wheel, the leather seat was springy beneath her, the feel of it familiar from the standpoint that she'd sat in passenger seats. Thompson had cared for the grand autos in Daddy's garage as if they were prized race horses. Once a week, he started them all up, given her a ride around the pasture, washed and groomed them with oils and polishes.

There was a big rubber bulb at her left—the horn. But what were the two side rods on the steering column? The lever and the three pedals on the floor were—brakes. Or no? She had to slow down and think carefully. She'd watched Thompson effortlessly put their cars into motion. She should be able to do this without ever having tried.

The back door to the livery slammed open, and Luke came running toward her. "Go! Go!"

Helplessly, she shook her head. "I . . . I can't. I—"

"You didn't start the car!" he shouted, realizing the motor wasn't running.

Gaining ground, he favored his right arm by holding onto it with his left. A bruise had begun to swell at his temple. His hair was ruffled and his black hat uneven on his head. He was without his traveling bag because she'd already thrown it in the backseat along with her satchel.

Impatiently, he commanded, "Prime the throttle!"

She had to shrug, her hands lifted.

"The one with the hard-rubber knob on the steering column!"

Evelyn put pressure on the rod and moved it.

Wincing when he let go of his arm, Luke bent in front of the hood and aligned his body with a cap that stuck out on the tank. He put muscle into cranking a handle. Up and down, he jerked his arm until the engine turned over with a few *pop-pops* and the vehicle began to vibrate.

"Move over," he ordered.

She slid across the seat and braced her hand on the window ledge. The touring car went into motion with a hard jerk as Luke manned the levers and pedals at the same time. He made a sharp left with the steering wheel to clear the shed, then turned away from the town—heading right back for Abilene.

Craning her neck to look behind her, Evelyn pointed out, "We're going in the wrong direction!"

"There's only one road in and out of Ysleta. I'm going to backtrack a quarter mile, then cut around and get on the road to El Paso. I hope like hell we don't get a flat tire before I can connect up with the road."

Cacti and desert plants grew alongside the rugged horse trail they were on. She was bounced and jarred in her seat, holding tightly to the front of the car and the door.

Luke's gaze was fixed steadily on the road, maneuvering them over the terrain and being careful not to drive directly into ruts. Briefly, he would glance at the dial box on what Thompson had referred to as the dashboard—she remembered that because she'd once heard him tell her father that he shouldn't rest his pipe on the dashboard anymore; he burned a mark on the Rolls-Royce.

The Ford's dash had a brass edge trim and an extended piece of wood wedged between the top of the dashboard and the windshield. The large rectangular-shaped glass cut the wind from hitting her directly in the face, but the air was still forceful enough that she had to hold onto her hat. She had no idea how to calculate speed or if the dashboard had a dial that even indicated it, but they were going at a pace a horse would in a steady run.

Not very far out of Ysleta, they could definitely be caught up to if Fletcher and the other man—

Bienville—were able to get free and come after them on those pitiful horses. If Luke could just push the automobile to give them a fifteen-minute jump, she'd feel better. The Ford would be difficult to catch up to, if indeed the duo looked to El Paso. They might very well follow the road to Rio Grande. How could they know which way she and Luke were headed? Which made her wonder if Cecil Woodworth had already covered the territory from Oiler to Ysleta and was continuing on to El Paso.

The car hummed and purred in good running condition in spite of the abuse of the trail. In no time, Luke connected with the road heading west. Not a soul traveled on it but them. Endless desert stretched ahead with only a single mountain thrusting upward.

With the wind constantly fluttering her hat brim, she removed it and set it on her lap. Luke shot her a short gaze, the dark color of his eyes resembling sharp pieces of gray rocks. She'd done something, rather, not done something and she knew that he'd want an explanation.

"Why couldn't you start this car?" he asked, his stern profile set in front of the mountain to the south. His hat was firmly in place, the ends of his hair moving in the breeze. Both arms held fast to the steering wheel, his biceps taut with strain. She could see the bruise at his temple turning bluish-black. "What about all those fancy Cadillacs and the new Pierce-Arrow? Your dad's the chauffeur."

Evelyn had never been taught how to operate an automobile, and even Thompson hadn't disobeyed that order from her mother, who thought women drivers were uncouth renegades. "You don't know the first thing about a Ford," he said.

Defensively, she pointed and said, "That's the dashboard. That's the horn." She redirected her hand. "You're holding onto the steering wheel."

"They don't mean anything if you don't know how to make them work. All this time, you led me to believe—"

"No, all this time, you believed what you wanted. I never said I could drive. And it doesn't really matter right now anyway. We got away."

"We aren't in the clear yet."

With a shaky hand, she touched her brow to ward off a sudden wave of dizziness. What exactly she'd done back in that livery was beginning to set in. She was amazed by her physical strength. "I've never hit another person in my life, but there I was with a shovel in my hand, and I . . . dear me." She shuddered, recollecting the brutality she'd enacted. "I struck him because he was trying to hurt you." She gasped, her eyes growing wide. "Do you think I killed him?"

"Hell, no. Bienville's got a hard head. He's fallen on it enough when he's been drunk."

Turning to Luke, she questioned, "How do you know him? What did he mean about prison?"

When Luke didn't reply, she began to toss out guesses. "He mentioned a yard and a hotbox. Even I know what one is. It's where they put criminals in prisons when they act up." Slowly swallowing, a notion sprang to life in her. "Are you an escaped convict?"

The Ford clunked into a shallow rut, throwing her

against the door. She righted herself, situating her hat on her lap once more. A hairpin slipped free under the constant beating of the wind at her hair.

"No, I'm not an escaped convict." A tick played at Luke's jaw. "I know Jude Bienville from New Orleans. He's a good-for-nothing larcenist."

Her throat grew dry once more. "Have you ever gone to jail with him?"

Luke gave a sudden burst of humorless laughter, as if forgetting to hold back. "I was the one who arrested him."

Arrested?

How could a civilian arrest someone? Unless he was . . .

You damn roach.

Roach.

The night she'd played cards with Luke, he'd said: *You've got flatfoot, long arm of the law, muldoon, bluecoat, and my least personal favorite—roach.*

They were all slang for one thing: Policeman.

Bienville had called Luke a policeman. How could that be so?

We prisoners dream about a day like this. Bienville was a former inmate with a vendetta against the man who'd arrested him.

Slowly, Evelyn turned to Luke. To study him. To see if there was any hint that she had missed before. Her mind raced as fast as the spinning tires. Clouds of confused dust began to clear; tiny pebbles of information were now beginning to make sense.

Evelyn stated bluntly, "You're a policeman."

Luke lowered his chin a fraction to ward off the setting sun's glare from the glossy blue hood and the chrome radiator cap. Bumping and jumping, the Ford's tires protested the uneven road. "I hope like hell there's a patch kit in back."

The terrain blurred past as Evelyn remained quiet. She couldn't take her eyes off Luke. Waiting. Watching.

He slanted her a heavy stare, one as long as he could afford without driving them into a ditch. "I swear, Eve, if you make me sorry I told you—"

"You have my word." And she meant it. No matter what he would say, she would keep it to herself.

With his profile firmly set, he admitted, "Yes. I'm a lieutenant in the Sixty-sixth Precinct in New Orleans."

While she had expected the answer, she had to catch her breath.

All this time, he made her think he was a thief. A criminal on the run from the law. Instead, he upheld the law. Why, then, had he been dressed as Mrs. Smythe, stowing away in her Pullman car with an assumed identity? What prevented him from telling her who he really was all along? Knowing he was a police officer would have been a lot more reassuring. Who was he chasing after? Why was he dodging and ducking the authorities?

"You led me to believe something else," she said above the rumble of the car as it sped over the desert floor.

"I could say the same about you, Evelyn."

Evelyn—not Eve—as if to remind her she hadn't been forthcoming as well.

The arid heat blew on her cheeks. While she knew

they could certainly talk about fabricated things from her life, it was his she was focused on right now. "Why are you running? What's your real story—Lieutenant Luke Devereaux? That is your last name, isn't it?"

Bienville had called it out and it just now connected for her.

"Yeah, it's Devereaux."

She remained quiet, and he took the cue to talk. It was as if he had to tell her about himself. "It's like I said, I'm looking for a guy who might be in New Mexico. He's a fellow officer—my former partner. He's involved with corruption and I don't know what else to make him lie the way he did about me. He's gotten into some bad politics and scandals. It's filtered through the department and even the city." Luke's fingers were tight around the steering wheel as he maneuvered the car out of a rolling tumbleweed's path.

"So you need to find your friend and then you'll be all right?"

"My life is up for grabs. There's no guarantee I'll find Henry. If I do, he's going to have to come over to my side." He gave her a fast glance. "If I can't get him to do that, things won't be looking real good for me. There's a warrant out for my arrest."

Her heart thudded. "For what?"

Without faltering, he supplied, "I'm wanted for the shooting deaths of two sergeants in my precinct."

"Y-You are?" She choked on a gasp filled with shock.

"I didn't do it." His voice was resonant and steadfast. "But I was there for the raid and I'm the one taking the fall for what happened. Henry knows why."

Disquiet ran through Evelyn's thoughts, but also a recognition that came from deep within her heart: Luke was telling the truth. She saw it in his expression and heard it in his voice.

"It's complicated, Eve. All I really know for sure is I'm innocent and I'm doing my damnedest to prove it."

"I believe you."

"I'm glad."

He grew silent for a long moment then said, "Jude Bienville doesn't have anything to do with my problems—but he knew something about you. What did he mean when he said he was going to collect what you're worth? Why did you leave the café? I thought you'd wait for me."

She felt an instant dampness to her palms. The pristine gloves she had bought in Dallas were soiled and stowed away in her satchel.

"I was going to, but I . . ."

To answer him with the whole truth would reveal more than she could bear to give up. Her reasons had nothing to do with doubting his trust. It had everything to do with her feelings for Luke.

She was afraid that if he knew who she really was, he wouldn't look at her the same way. That she'd lose him even though she knew what lay ahead for them by sundown. Different paths. Different lives. But when Luke said good-bye, she wanted him to say it to Eve Pierce. Eve, who wore the maid's uniform and jumped off a train with him—not Evelyn Thurgood-Baron.

For the first time in her life, a man viewed her as a woman, not as a commodity. She wasn't ready to give that up. To reveal the one thing about her that could change everything.

"I wanted to check on my horse." She couldn't look at him when she spoke. "I had a funny feeling about Fletcher. And I was right."

She didn't get into the fact she suspected Fletcher had her horse hidden for other reasons. He and Bienville must have teamed up to deliver her to the Prickly Pear. The two of them would have collected the reward money. Her true identity would have been uncovered and her freedom would have been over.

Luke didn't know it, but when he came into that livery and challenged Bienville and Fletcher, he'd saved her from going home.

"Bienville said there was a man at the hotel—Cecil Woodworth—who was interested in you." Pressing his teeth together, Luke tightly asked, "He was your fiancé, wasn't he?"

Fiancé—Cecil?

"Yes." Her gaze was trained on the gullies and Mount Franklin jutting skyward as they closed in on El Paso. "Cecil is my fiancé."

"He must want to marry you really bad to come looking for you."

"Yes . . . he does."

"Did you talk to him?"

"N-No," she shot back. "I don't want to see him."

"He wants to see you. He's obviously distributing notices across Texas."

"I know. Fletcher had one."

Lie upon lie was weighing on her shoulders, making it difficult to keep them all straight.

"So not only are we trying to lose Fletcher and Bienville," Luke went on, "we've got your fiancé knowing where you are now, too."

"That does seem to be the case," she said woodenly.

She squeezed her eyes closed, unable to watch the town as it sprung up ahead. Unable to acknowledge the adobe buildings that spread east and west as the road widened. She didn't want to go. She didn't want to—

A loud pop and hiss exploded, then an uneven *clump-clump* as the Ford came to a rickety stop beside the road.

Evelyn turned to Luke.

He turned to her.

Neither said anything. She sensed perhaps they were both wishing and wondering if things had been different, maybe . . . But maybe wasn't an option out in the desert where roads only went two ways:

Forward.

Backward.

"Blown tire," Luke finally said. "We'll walk the rest of the way."

20

Standing in front of Kline's Mexican & Indian Curio Company on El Paso Street wasn't how Luke thought he'd say good-bye to Eve. Automobiles drove past, choking the air with sooty exhaust. Wagons and buggies rolled over the streets of a city with hustle to it.

The grassy smell of sorghum hung like yeast in the air, with the odors from nearby chicken ranches blending into the mix of people, animals and machines. Telephone and telegraph lines soared overhead, strung on poles that suspended four lines.

The building he and Eve stood at had its doors facing the corner, and a steady clientele of tourists and townsfolk milled in and out while they talked about everything but what they were going to do.

They'd been avoiding the inevitable for a long time.

After leaving the Ford behind, it had taken twenty minutes to reach the main street. She seemed so slight in this fast-paced city. A place where she could disappear. He couldn't imagine letting her walk away, into the people who didn't know just how remarkable she was. But that was how things had to be.

From the start, this hadn't been a joint venture. Just a chance encounter that, over the miles, had turned . . . good.

Damn, but she was good.

Good for his soul. Good for his heart. Even now, it beat inside his chest at a rate that threatened his composure. To cause him to change his mind about Boyd and forget New Orleans. To not look back. To forget about his purpose and everything important to him.

"Do you suppose they sell gloves in that store?" she asked, her gaze averting his when she looked into the curio shop.

The ridiculousness of her question brought a half smile to his lips. From Abilene to here it had been hell, and she'd proved herself to him ten times over. She didn't have to dress in the fancy clothes and talk the fancy talk to be a woman he thought strongly of. He liked her wit; he loved her hair when it was down about her waist. He liked the feel of her in his arms; he loved the way she smelled. He liked the way she studied her cards when they played poker; he loved the sound of her voice first thing in the morning.

"I don't think so," he said, not really wanting to talk about ladies' gloves. He looked down at his boots, his travel bag slung over his shoulder. Her satchel was in her hand. Those delicate hands that he'd held. That had touched his cheek and roamed across his skin.

"Well . . ." She sighed, met his eyes, then bit on her lower lip.

"Well," he repeated, his gut churning in a dozen different knots.

A brightly painted, railless trolley rattled past. The sharp ring of its bell startled Eve, and she stepped back from the curb. Automatically, he took her hand and directed her beneath the awning of the curio shop.

He could feel the tattoo of her pulse in her wrist.

Luke slipped his hand into his shirt pocket and brought out nearly every dollar he had to his name. He'd had this money in his shirt since Ysleta, knowing the exact amount, and knowing he wasn't going to leave Eve without giving the folded bills to her. He saved a few bucks in his pants pocket to get by on.

"Here, I want you to take this." He pushed the money into her palm and squeezed her fingers around it. "You should buy a train ticket home."

"No." She quickly refused, trying to give the money back. "I won't do that. I'm not going home. I can't."

"Eve, I don't want to just leave you. I need to know you're going to be all right. That you're on your way back to your family."

"You don't have to worry about me. I'll be fine."

"I'd feel better knowing you were safely on a train."

"I'll be safely on a train. I'm going to California. And I don't need your money to get there."

Eve drew herself taller and held her head high. "I really appreciate the gesture. But it's not necessary." She tucked the money into the breast pocket of his shirt.

He stood there, unable to move. Wondering if she could see how his pulse beat at his neck. Wondering if she knew how much she had affected him in such a short amount of time.

"Well, then, this is it," she said, her voice shaky.

If she cried, he wouldn't be able to leave. Right now, he *needed* her to be strong. Like the Eve on the trail. The woman who sat tall in the saddle and talked to him about the flowers and what they all meant.

"Yeah," he said, his own voice thick and unsteady. "You take care of yourself, Eve."

"You, too," she quietly returned, her eyes growing moist. "I hope you find that man you're looking for."

"Yeah."

"So . . . then . . . g-good-bye, Luke."

That quiver in her words sent him. His heartbeat thundered with feelings he had no right to want to make her feel.

He reached out and took her by the arms and brought her to him for a full kiss on the lips. Her mouth was closed, her eyes open. He wanted her to give in. To kiss him like she meant it.

One last time.

He felt her go pliant in his grasp. Felt the resistance she tried to hold onto dwindle. Her fingers dug into his shirtsleeve, firmly and possessively. As if she would keep him there forever next to her.

There was no willpower. No holding back.

The kiss came in a rush, too intense and too fast, and she shuddered in response. But they had no privacy to languish in. Just seconds. Flashes to ingrain in their minds of where they had been. How they had come to stand on El Paso Street.

When he felt the moisture of her tears touch his cheek, they broke apart. Anguish roiled in his stomach as she quickly swept the back of her hand at the corners of her eyes. While she kept tears from falling, he pretended not to notice; and in truth, he needed that time to pull himself together.

"I have to leave," she murmured. Then thrust a tiny piece of paper at him and walked quickly down the street.

Luke let her go. He couldn't breathe. All he could do was watch the crown of her hat blend into the others moving over the sidewalk. A small hint of green calico from the sleeve of her dress, then nothing.

She was gone.

The pressure in his throat grew to an unbearable ache. He would have stayed still, entranced by the memory of her walking away in his mind if not for a man's voice intruding into his rattled thoughts.

"Excuse me, mister, can you tell me where the Mills Building is?"

The words barely registered, and when they did, he found himself looking into a stranger's face. "No." He had to clear his throat. "No, I can't."

The man moved on, and Luke remembered the paper in his hand. He unfolded the tiny note, and he studied the delicate loops and curls of the penmanship before the message settled into his soul.

I will never forget you.
Pansy

Pansy. The flower.

She'd told him what they meant from one of her many discussions on the language of flowers.

Remember me.

Evelyn sat in one of the booths at the El Paso Telephone Exchange. Voices carried through the room as telephones rang and people spoke into the receivers. The cubicle was cramped and the walls were only half the normal size of the building's walls. Three sides of oak paneling closeted her, and directly in front, a Kellogg wood wall telephone.

She'd paid for five minutes connection time and was waiting for one of the operators to ring her. She'd given explicit orders not to divulge what station she was calling from.

At a short counter across from her, five women wore matching black skirts with kimono-sleeved white shirtwaists, and gold cording in bows at their collars. They had heavy ear sets over their heads, the black dials closing them off from all the conversations in the large exchange. Stopwatches were in front of each of their switchboards as they pulled out and plugged in wires.

Blinking against the hot moisture filling her eyes and blurring her vision, she wiped the tears that slipped down her cheek. She sniffled and tried to gather her fragile wits before the phone would ring. Fresh tears took the place of the ones she smoothed away with her fingertips.

Stop it, Evelyn.

She'd made it down that sidewalk without looking

back, without running back. She couldn't fall apart now.

Don't think. Don't think about him.

Sniffling, she rummaged through the meager items in her satchel to look for a handkerchief. Of course, she had none. No gloves either. She pulled out Conchita's Mexican blouse and used it as a hankie.

Two passersby gave her curious gazes and exchanged glances with one another; she turned her back from the couple while making a valiant effort to bring her emotions under control.

The three clipped rings of the telephone's two brass bells startled her, and she took in deep gulps of air to steady her nerves. The voice on the other end had the ability to plaster her feet to the floor, yet she didn't feel the same cloying trepidation she once had when confronting him.

Evelyn laid the blouse on her lap and picked up the receiver. She leaned toward the faceplate cup while raising the earpiece to her ear.

A woman's businesslike voice said, "Western Electric. Operator speaking."

"Ah, yes," Evelyn responded.

"Your party is on the line, ma'am."

Static greeted her as the connection became true.

The operator said, "Oiler-4, go ahead."

A man cleared his throat and dread inched its way up her spine.

The switchboard buzz dimmed.

She swallowed, then ventured, "Daddy?"

"Evelyn?" Her father's voice boomed in a barreling growl through her eardrum. "Is that you?"

"Yes, it's me."

The relief she'd hoped to hear in his tone was nearly nonexistent. "What in the hell is going on? Where are you?"

"It's not important."

"What do you mean? What were you thinking by disappearing? Are you out of your mind? Is there a kidnapper holding you against your will?"

Undaunted, she uttered one word. "No."

"You mean to tell me you left of your own accord? Nobody busted into the house and forced you to go with them?"

"No."

"Then Flora was right. I practically grilled the hide off that maid and she finally gave in and told me that you *wanted* to head off on some train in Beaumont."

The fact that he didn't ask if she was all right crushed her spirits.

"I had to leave, Daddy." She adjusted the earpiece and shifted positions on the round stool, tucking her feet beneath her. "You were going to make me marry Guy Hadley."

Momentary static merged through the connection.

"William Hadley is fit to be tied. He said if you don't come to your senses, the deal between you and his son is off."

"That's a relief."

"A relief? Is that what you call it? This is an important deal. I had an arrangement with Hadley but I'm not keeping up to my end of it because my daughter is missing." He was in full tirade now. "Just where are you?"

She didn't reply.

"Evelyn! Goddammit, you tell me where you are and I'll have Cecil Woodworth come fetch you home. He's as far out as West Texas trying to find you. You tell me where you are and I'll tell him where to go. Then he'll put you on the first damn train back to Oiler and you can stop all this nonsense."

"No." The tears she had cried were over. She was dry-eyed and actually feeling a slight bit stronger. Resolve made her shoulders go back with determination not to buckle under. "I'm not coming home. I still have too much to see and too much to do."

"See? Do?" *Puff-puff-puff.* She could hear him angrily smoking on his pipe. "What are you talking about?"

Drawing in a breath, she said, "I'm experiencing all that I've been missing."

"Experiencing? You have plenty to experience here. Your mother is beside herself."

"She needn't be."

"She hasn't been able to attend a social function without her lady friends asking after you, wondering why you weren't with her. She told them you were visiting her sister in Atlanta. But a pretense like that can only go so far."

Evelyn grew light-headed, feeling unwell; warm and flushed. Her disappearance was nothing but an inconvenience to be fibbed about.

She was glad she wasn't like either of them. Self-indulgent in their whims, caring only what others thought, and spending money for show. It was questionable to Evelyn why she hadn't turned out like them. What had made her so different? In hindsight, she thought perhaps it was Grandfather Jimmy. He'd always had common sense and the strength of an old oak. He'd called her parents a pair of barnyard chickens dressed like peacocks.

"Tell Mother I'm sorry. But she'll have to keep informing the ladies I'm in Atlanta."

"Stop taxing my patience, Evelyn. Where are you?"

"No place special."

"Vanderhoff said you were on a train headed toward Dallas. That you jumped, for God's sake, with some woman! You could have been killed." That statement was the first he'd uttered about her safety. He added in a bristle, "And by the way, Vanderhoff was good enough to return your valise to me with the money you stole from my safe."

"I was going to pay you back."

She would have much rather had his understanding than his staunch desire to see her back under his control, if only for a short while before Guy Hadley took over.

"Evelyn, I'm warning you. If you do not tell me where you are, I will cut you off. There won't be a dowry. And when I'm dead, you won't get a penny of my estate."

"Daddy, I don't want to think about you dying." And she meant it. For all his flaws, she didn't wish him gone. Just . . . softened. What would it take to make him see her side?

"Where should I send Woodworth? Are you in Dallas?"

The fact that he wouldn't come get her himself burdened her already heavy heart. She fought off the unwelcome tears that came to her eyes. She knew better than to get emotional. She'd expected the telephone call to go like this, so why was she letting it close around her lungs and squeeze the air from her?

"You won't last without cash. Evelyn, you can't support yourself. You have no money. You know nothing about working."

"I do, too!" she said loudly. This was not like her at all. She tried to be complacent where he was concerned. To be the daughter he wanted. But no more. It hadn't done her any good in the past and she was a new Evelyn now. "I can sing and that's how I made some money."

"Good God! You were up on a tavern stage again?"

"Yes."

"If word of that leaks out to the papers, we'll be laughingstocks—"

"Operator," the woman's voice intruded. "Thirty seconds."

Then a click came as she departed the line.

The operator's intrusion changed the tone of her father's voice to one that held more patience, and guarded urgency. "Tell me where to ring you back so we aren't cut short."

She remained quiet.

"Evelyn, dear." The endearment had been spoken to her in such a way when she'd been a child. And she had believed its sweet caress, just as she'd believed in Santa Claus. "Your mother and I love you very much and we want you to come home."

He had the ability to twist things in a way to make her surrender. She had, so many times throughout her life. Memories flooded her at once as she pressed her forehead against the telephone box. There had been many happy moments in Oiler. It wasn't as if she hated it or her parents. She just wanted things to be different. Arguing was a pattern between them. Daddy's lecture, her mother's deportment reminders, with Evelyn voicing her opinion then having it completely disregarded. This time, a reconciliation would have to come on her terms.

"If I do," she said, "will you insist on this marriage to Guy?"

"Now, we'll talk about that when you get here."

"No, you'd have to promise me. Give me your word."

"Evelyn, you're being difficult. You know what the merger means to me. You have to—"

"Just as I thought."

A buzz and click. Then, "Operator. Five seconds."

"Evelyn—where are you?" her father shouted.

Staring at the threads in the sleeve of her Mexican blouse, she ran a fingertip over the red and gold, letting the seconds slip away. Then, a final *click*, as the telephone was disconnected.

To the dead tone in her ear, she lowered the receiver and hung it up.

Luke felt like going into a bar and drinking himself into a stupor. But he didn't. Because he somehow knew that Eve would be disappointed in him if he did.

He had to force himself into action. Force himself to refuel his mind with purpose and will himself to forget . . . for now . . .

Before Luke got on the evening train to New Mexico, he decided to find out if Henry had come through El Paso. This meant risking being identified as a man with a warrant.

The layout of the town was large enough that he could blend in without causing attention; however, going to places to ask after Henry would set himself apart. But the way Luke saw it, he had no choice.

There were a lot of rail lines leaving town and he couldn't afford to get on the wrong one and lose time. While his hunch had led him this far, with a confirmation in Midland that Henry Boyd was in Texas, any number of things could have put Henry on a different course. There were no guarantees he was headed to New Mexico to see family, although it still made the most sense.

The fact that Henry was sick gave Luke a solid lead. *Talk to the doctors.* Boyd could have needed to seek medical attention once more.

There were four doctors in El Paso, all listed on the town registry. Luke began at one end of town and worked his way across it. Three separate times, he walked out of an office with no information. And thankfully, no questions about him in return. The fourth office had a shingle hanging above the door: Otis Clark, M.D.

The windowshade on the glass door was drawn and the interior lights dim, but Luke knocked.

A moment later, a man opened the door; he wore a handlebar mustache so stiff with wax, it wouldn't have budged a curl in a windstorm.

"Are you Doctor Clark?" Luke asked, the tone of his voice falling into a flat accent.

"I am."

Luke stepped around him and let himself inside.

The doctor closed the door and put on a pair of spectacles. "What's the problem?"

"I'm looking for a man you might have treated in the last week. He's about your height, has a full head of red hair and a light complexion with some freckling on his arms. He's got a stomach condition that might have been giving him trouble."

Dr. Clark nodded. "I know who you're taking about."

Luke felt a powerful sense of relief flood through his tense body. "Have you seen him recently? Maybe today?"

"No."

"When did you last see him?"

"I couldn't say for sure unless I read my notes." Dr. Clark went toward his wooden filing cabinet, but didn't open a drawer. Instead, he gave Luke a cursory examination. "You don't look like you're related. I took an oath that prevents me from telling you anything about this case."

Luke couldn't let a technicality stand in his way. "I'm a friend. I need to find him. It's a matter of extreme importance."

Sitting behind his desk, the doctor knit his fingers together. "Friends usually know each other's business."

"I know that he's getting sicker. This past year, he tried every stomach tonic there is and none of them helped. He's got a lot of nervous tension."

"He was nervous, but that's not why he's sick."

Luke pulled out a chair and sat across from the doctor. "Look, I won't tell anyone we spoke. I can respect your oath but sometimes a situation calls for breaking the rules. This is one of them."

When the doctor made no move, Luke laid his hands flat on the desktop. "All right, let's do this. Let me lay out what I think happened and you tell me if I'm right or wrong. I'm thinking he saw you, you gave him some medicine, then he headed up to Silver City."

After a drawn out silence, Dr. Clark replied, "You're partially right. I gave him something."

"But he wasn't going to Silver City?"

"He mentioned it, but I advised him not to. I told him he needed to get help that I couldn't give him."

Hope filled Luke. "Do you know where he went?"

"He took my advice."

"You sent him someplace? Around here?"

"No."

Breath caught in his lungs as Luke wordlessly stared at the doctor.

Dr. Clark sorted through several papers on his desk, singled one out and studied it. The reluctance he'd displayed dissipated for reasons Luke wouldn't question. "This morning I received a telegram from the Santa Barbara Clinic for Illness."

Luke leaned forward. "Santa Barbara? Texas?"

"California."

"Henry's in California?"

"The physicians there want me to forward all the findings of my exam so they can compare it with their own. I'm sure they know far more about a case such as this than I."

From the heaviness in the doctor's somber tone, quick and disturbing thoughts held Luke still. "He's going to be all right, isn't it? He just has an ulcer."

Removing his glasses, Dr. Clark rubbed his eyes. "I'm sorry to tell you this, but your friend's dying of cancer."

Cancer. The word hung heavily in the center of the room.

"It's in his stomach," the doctor elaborated, "and from what I could tell, the tumor has been growing for the past few months. The rate of his deterioration is moving quickly. He's lucky to have lived this long."

Luke pushed himself to his feet, raked his hand through his hair and gazed at the doctor with disbelief. "Are you sure?"

"To the best of my knowledge. That's why I sent him to a place that can help make him comfortable for his last days."

Last days.

The urgency that coursed through Luke's blood was swift and hot. "How much time does he have left?"

"I couldn't give you a particular day. The clinic doctors are specialists in that area. But given the amount of blood your friend was losing, and the size of the tumor in his belly, not long."

Luke caught the train just as its powerful engines were pulling the cars from the depot. He had to grip the outside handle to bring himself aboard.

Please let her be here.

Entering the moving car, Luke walked down the

aisle looking for Eve. When he'd bought his ticket to California a moment ago, there had only been one outbound train scheduled for this evening. It was headed for Los Angeles. Although he and Eve had never talked about exactly where she'd go, he hoped like hell she was on this train.

But he came to the end of the car and she wasn't there. So he stepped onto the platform and made his way into the next one.

It can't be too late.

This car was empty, too, leaving him feeling just as empty inside.

He went to the next. And the next.

But then, sitting in the last seat on the right-hand side of the aisle, he saw her. He could actually feel the breath leaving his lungs in a hard exhale that made him hold onto the chair in front of him.

With long strides, he went toward her and sat.

She looked up, startled.

"Change of plans," he said. "I'll take you to your California ocean."

21

"But I thought . . ." Evelyn's question trailed. Her pulse was spinning and her senses reeled in different directions. She had to conquer her reaction to his unexpected presence or else she'd throw herself into his arms.

"I thought I was going to New Mexico, too." Luke settled beside her, his thigh pressed next to hers. "But I found out Henry's gone to Santa Barbara."

Her mind was still trying to adjust to the fact that Luke was sitting next to her while the train's wheels clacked over iron rails as the locomotive picked up speed.

Luke is really here!

"How do you know?" she asked in a voice that was barely composed; she was in a state of disbelief.

"In Midland, I found out Henry was sick. So in El Paso, I checked with doctors before I went to Silver City on the off chance one of them saw Henry. A doc did treat him. He sent him to a special clinic in Santa

Barbara because Henry is sick with cancer. Dying from it."

Evelyn didn't understand all the ramifications, but she knew it wasn't what Luke had wanted to hear. "I'm so very sorry."

"Yeah, me too." He sounded tired and drained. "We were friends once. I don't know what the hell happened. Everything is mixed up, and I was so damn hoping I'd find Henry and he could tell me what went wrong. But it might be too late now."

"Maybe not. You don't know for sure. The doctor could be wrong."

"Henry's been sick for a while. I always thought it was the stress of the beat. The way the department had started to fall apart." He removed his hat and ran his hand through his hair. "I've thought about it over and over and I still can't figure out why Henry got involved."

"Involved with what?" Evelyn's heart lurched from both sadness over Luke's dilemma and excitement that they were together. For a while longer, there would be no good-bye. Selfishly, she wanted to make the most of every minute, of every second. "Tell me about it. Tell me about New Orleans, and being a policeman and where you live."

Luke gazed into her upturned face, touched her chin with his fingers and smiled. The bruise on his temple was swollen and looked painful. She resisted the urge to gently brush her fingertips across it. "I'll tell you, Eve. I'll tell you everything. I want to."

For a long while, Luke told her about his life in New Orleans. He had three brothers, all policemen just like him. And a mother whom they all adored. His father had passed away, which she knew.

Luke told her stories about when he was little and how they had gone on family picnics and fishing trips—his mother, too. She enjoyed the outdoors and was proud that her sons had gone on to fill her husband's footsteps.

He lived in a townhouse in the Garden District. It was white and had a verandah with flower boxes at the lower-floor windows—something he didn't maintain. But he did spend a lot of time in his garage with his Roadster. The automobile was something he'd worked hard for with long hours and savings.

The corruption in the Sixty-sixth Precinct was complicated and Evelyn didn't quite follow it all. There seemed to be a great scandal and it trickled to all corners of the city. The shootings were an escalation in the downfall of the force; Luke was convinced the raid had been plotted from the beginning by a captain and one of the other lieutenants. The two sergeants who were killed apparently had something on their superiors and had been about to blow the whistle. Ultimately, Henry Boyd had been a witness against him and that's why there was a warrant out for Luke's arrest.

Luke felt Henry was his best hope of having his name cleared by the new police commissioner—who had taken a strong stance against the bad seeds since coming into power.

Evelyn let Luke talk until his voice grew low and hoarse. She sensed he'd needed to unburden his heart, and she was glad she was the one he'd picked to listen.

When he'd grown quiet for a long moment, lost in thoughts, she laid a hand over his. She didn't say anything. She simply let him know she cared.

His fingers meshed with hers, and they held hands.

Evelyn felt safe with this man beside her. He put his arm around her and tucked her next to him; she rested her cheek on his shoulder.

"If you hadn't been on this train," he said, and she felt his voice in his chest, "I don't know what I would have done."

"You would have gone on. You have to prove your innocence."

"There's nothing stopping me from going straight to your Pacific Ocean and never turning back. I could take on a new identity, start over."

"I think you'd always regret that. You have family at home who loves you. Who's worried about you. You don't know how lucky you are, Luke. I wish I had that, too."

A mix of hope and fear held her still. Then slowly, she said, "Luke, that man in Ysleta—Cecil Woodworth—he's not my fiancé. He's a detective from the Woodworth Detective Agency."

She ventured a quick gauge of his reaction to her disclosure. His head was tilted toward her, waiting for clarification.

"My father isn't a chauffeur."

"I kind of figured that by now."

"He's a prominent businessman." She closed her eyes for a moment to collect her thoughts. "He's very wealthy, and he wants me to marry the son of one of his associates. Guy Hadley." She groaned. "I think he's a weasel and a namby-pamby. And I wouldn't care if he came to me on bended knees with undying devotion. I wouldn't marry him. I couldn't live with a man I didn't love."

Luke let her continue, absently stroking the sensitive side of her neck with his thumb.

"Cecil is supposed to find me and bring me in. By now, he knows I was in Ysleta. I telephoned my father from El Paso on the off chance he wouldn't make me go through with the engagement. Word hasn't gotten to Daddy yet I was right under Cecil's nose, but when it does, his blood pressure is going to boil over."

"He can't be that bad," Luke offered. "He's your dad."

"He can. And he is. That's why I stole his bourbon flask and ended up wandering out of the Imperial Hotel."

Luke's chin tilted, and he looked at her. "You did what?"

She told him about the stifling social circle she felt trapped in. Growing up in a house where she wasn't allowed to leave without a chaperon. About her trip to Beaumont with the Ladies Society of Texas. That led to her telling him about her days at Miss Hunnewell's Boarding School and her expulsion for reading racy poetry. Luke grinned at that story.

It seemed she talked forever, relating details and pieces of her life. But she omitted one thing. Her real name. She reasoned it didn't matter what it was right at this moment. She had admitted she was from a well-to-do Texas family. That was a step in the right direction.

Spent from conversation, she fought against sleep, not wanting Luke to see she was beyond the point of exhaustion. But when it became hard for her eyes to remain open, he brought her closer.

"Go to sleep, Eve."

"I'll be all right."

"I'm tired, too."

The rattle and motion of the train lulled her to a near-complete relaxed state. In the drowsy haze that began to envelop her, Luke's voice broke into her fading conscious thoughts.

"Evelyn." He spoke her name in a caress. "Have you given any thought about where you're getting off in California?"

She let out a long, audible breath. "I was hoping . . . with you."

They traveled for four days, and at four-thirty on the afternoon of July the Fourth, the Southern Pacific railroad cars screeched to an unplanned halt in San Buenaventura, California. It had been raining for the better part of the day, and when they stopped, a conductor came through the car and told them all they were going to have to disembark. A wire from Santa Paula had been sent to the San Buenaventura depot. A flash flood had been reported in the barrancas near Canyon Falls and the tracks to Santa Barbara were covered with mud.

There would be a delay until morning.

Luke stepped down from the car, helping Eve by bracing her elbow; he looked around him. They were in a small coastal town where the air smelled of salt, and the breeze would have been warmer if not for the rain. It lent a little chill to the wind.

He couldn't see the water, but gulls sailed high overhead, squawking and dipping on the air currents.

Eve stretched her back and gazed skyward, a few raindrops falling on her face. The weather was breaking up in the west, and farther out above the horizon, a glimpse of the sun could be seen.

"It's wonderful," she said with a smile.

In Los Angeles, they'd switched trains and boarded the San Francisco Union Pacific and taken the northern coastal route. While she'd caught pieces of the coastal shores that bordered the tracks, this was the first opportunity they'd had to stop and take a look.

The radiance on her cheeks was stunning as her golden curls teased her cheeks. Her lips were lush and pink, and her eyes bright.

He would have liked to stand there forever and watch her, but he was unable to let one significant thought out of his head—

He was close to Henry Boyd.

So close, Luke should have been moving quickly. Directly into action to get a horse or hire an automobile—anything, to take him up to Santa Barbara. Immediately. If a train couldn't get through, something else could, or at least he could try. The clock was ticking. Time wasn't on his side.

But as Luke gazed at Eve, and heard her laughter as her shoes sank into a wet patch of sand, he felt lost. Lost from his objectives, putting what he had to do second. Because he knew this was her moment. She would see her ocean.

And, God help him—Henry Boyd be damned. Luke didn't want to miss Eve experiencing it.

His reaction was very telling about how deeply his feelings ran for her.

"Eve, we should get out of the rain," he said at length, his voice not as sure as he would have liked. "Let's find someplace dry."

"We can. But after I go to the shore." She gave him a wide smile and held out her hand to him. "Will you come with me?"

A war of emotions collided inside him. He hesitated, torn. Then tried to imagine what it would be like to go on without her right now.

"Yes," he replied, as a cloud parted and the sun shone down on them.

Evelyn explored the sand and ice plants with pink flowers that grew in long clusters. The clouds had broken up and a hint of warmth touched the breeze. Foot-tall grasses danced. Palm trees soared, their fronds wispy and wavering.

She heard, before she saw, the rolling waves as they crashed upon the shore. The sun sizzled downward as the day waned over the horizon.

Luke held her hand as they walked over the dunes to see the ocean.

Evelyn's first glimpse of the Pacific Ocean was breathtaking. Seagulls swooped low over the white foam that fanned up the shore, then slipped back into the tide. Deeper into the ocean, the water became a resplendent shade of blue. Like the sapphire earrings she had in a velvet-lined case in her bedroom back in

Oiler. She'd never fully appreciated their brilliance
until now, as she compared the sea to their glittering
color. Sandpipers on skinny legs darted over the wet
sand, then took flight.

There was no one else around. The other passengers had gone on to one of the hotels or restaurants.

She and Luke went closer to the water and encountered soft sand that made it harder to walk. She
paused, using Luke's shoulder for balance as she
undid the buckles on her shoes. Her feet were
instantly chilled. But walking without her shoes felt
wickedly delightful. She dangled them in her fingers
as she debated whether or not to take off her stockings.

"Go ahead," Luke said with a half smile.

"All right."

Each stocking came off and she stuffed them into
the toes of her shoes. The wet sand felt icy cold
beneath her feet. She marveled in the way the ocean
rose upward, then swallowed itself back into the rip-
pling waves.

There really was no vast difference between this
ocean and the one in Corpus Christi—except for one.
She'd found this one by her own means and by her
own desire.

Filled with pleasure, she hiked her skirt and ran
alongside the rolling surf ahead of her. Wind kissed
her cheeks and she raised her face skyward to watch a
pair of gulls sparring before they sailed away.

Luke caught up with her, standing higher on the
shore. He looked so handsome, so incredibly wonderful. From the harsh sun, his shirt had paled in color to

turn a soft blue shade; his tan seemed richer in contrast. The black locks of his hair were untamed at his collar. He gave her an intimate smile, one which she returned just as easily.

He let her get her feet wet as long as she wanted, and after a while, she sank down on the sand and watched the sun begin to set. He sat at her side and they entwined their fingers and quietly observed the show.

When the sky grew dusky, and she never thought she'd live a happier moment in her life, Luke asked, "Are you ready to go?"

"Hmm," she dreamily replied.

They made their way to one of the hotels built on the waterfront.

The Pierpont Inn was supported by sturdy pilings that could stand up to the surf crashing beneath it. Bicycles leaned next to the entrance, available for customers to ride along the beach. Matilija poppy plants well over six feet tall were woven through an iron archway. Their centers were puffballs of golden pollen; the circumference of the flowers themselves were as wide and round as small dinner plates. The white petals were crepe-paper thin. At the double-open lobby doors, wrought-iron potted plant holders held blushing red geraniums. Off the lobby was a restaurant decorated in mission style.

A short while later, they were settled into a patio room that overlooked the beach. The double-glass French doors were thrown open to the view; rain puddles were scattered about the terrace.

Yellow hibiscus flowers were painted around the

perimeter of the room, halfway up the walls. Below, maple paneling. The bed had a spread of equal color and design as the painted flowers. A willow bark rocking chair was by the bedside, a reading lamp above it.

They'd taken shower baths and were dressed for dinner. Luke surprised her by having her Mexican blouse and skirt freshened and pressed. He wore a clean shirt and denim trousers and waited for her to finish pinning her hair so they could go to dinner. As soon as she was ready, she stepped out of the tiny lavatory hoping for his approval. Luke stepped back and gave her a gaze that brought tingles across her skin. They linked arms and went to eat.

Seated at a corner table, Luke ordered for both of them from the menu. When she protested the expense, he told her that tonight there were no limits—just the two of them, and he intended to make the most of it. To make her as happy as he could.

They dined on white plates bordered with pink peonies that had been painstakingly painted around the rim. They ate lobster tails in a cream sauce, bacon crumbled in green beans, hot tortillas, local fruits—strawberries that were sweeter than cake, and lemon custard. It was the best meal Evelyn had ever eaten because Luke sat across the table from her to share it.

Afterward, they strolled on the beach, hand in hand, gazing at the full moon. There was an opaque ring around it. The rain was returning. Before they reached the inn, it began to fall in soft, warm droplets.

When they dashed through the lobby, Evelyn's

eggshell-thin blouse was damp. Her skirt was wet around the ankles. His shirt was soaked through. Rain beaded on their eyelashes and lips.

Once in their room, she went to the patio to look outside. Milky light from the moon illuminated the beach and the sprawling gardens of blooming blue and orange birds of paradise.

A warmth filled Evelyn, as did a kind of peace.

Facing Luke, she found him sitting in one of the wing chairs behind her, his shirt off. Wall sconces were lit above him, casting him in a mellow light. She gave him a sideways glance, smiling as he brought the towel to his head and vigorously rubbed his hair to near-dryness.

He rose and came up behind her to put his arms around her waist. He nuzzled the side of her neck and kissed her behind the ear.

"Did you have a nice time?" he asked.

"The best . . . oh, Luke . . . it was wonderful. Everything."

"Good." His lips were close to her ear, his breath a warm and evoking tingle across her skin.

White moonbeams reflecting off the ocean danced across the walls. She leaned into Luke, tilting her neck. His mouth traced a caressing path to the crook of her neck and shoulder.

"I've missed this," she breathed with a hitch in her voice.

Long days on a train had left no moment for kisses, stolen touches or embraces.

"Me, too." He pulled the pins from her hair, took a curl and wrapped it around his finger. "I've missed lying beside you at night, talking to you and hearing your voice when I go to sleep."

She turned to him and rested her head on his shoulder. His naked skin was perfectly smooth and taut beneath her cheek. Sculpted muscles flexed and rippled beneath her as he settled her into his arms. Her body molded perfectly to his. Luke's lean strength comforted her. His arms, his embrace, felt right. This was the best evening she had ever had. She didn't want it to be over with one of them taking the bed, the other the rocker. She wanted to move things further . . . to have intimate memories for the scrapbook in her heart.

Luke took her hands and knit her slender fingers through his. She ran her thumbs over his knuckles; the skin was taught and rough from the miles on the road. She tilted her face to his.

"Eve," he uttered her name with passion-darkened eyes. The touch of his mouth to hers released her to abandonment. The torrent of desire for him leaped to life. She could feel his uneven breathing against her crushed breasts, the heat of his thigh next to her hip. She needed this. She needed him.

They kissed, long and exploring. Her heart thumped and ached for him at the same time. She wanted Luke more than she could ever imagine. That strange want in her body when he kissed her was real, needing to be fulfilled.

The strong hardness of his lips against her aroused a hunger in her. She fit herself more tightly to him. Their fingers unlinked to give their hands the freedom to explore. Blood coursed through her veins like a reawakened river; a reminder of that night in the Red Banana. Only now, anticipation mingled with her excitement. Cupping his face in her hands, Evelyn kissed him with everything in her heart, all she felt.

The kiss held a lifetime of romance she had never known, and feared she would never know again. This was shameless. But she didn't care. She felt no guilt. In this, their own special place, nobody judged. Or came to conclusions about names and social positions.

Luke trailed his fingers down her shoulder to slowly lower the sleeve of her blouse. He dipped his head to kiss her bare skin, causing her to shiver in delight. Then his mouth came back to hers, gently and warm, while his hand continued to explore. He cupped the curve of her breast, evoking sparks of desire to erupt through her. As he traced her taut nipple through the thin, damp fabric, the kiss changed. Nibbling her lower lip, he inched the blouse from her shoulders and it loosely bunched at her waist.

His mouth was persuasive and hot, raising her impatience. Each new kiss made her long for Luke more. Her hands skimmed over the marble smoothness of his skin, the tightness of muscle across his back. He was magnificently made. She ran her palms down his side, over the contours of his torso; then raised her fingertips to his chest and the sprinkling of hair. Sculpted to perfection, she brought him closer as he deepened their kiss.

He moved in, his thighs pressing hard into hers while he caressed the heavy fullness of her breast. A wave of shock went through her. She should have been embarrassed, but she wasn't. Everything she felt was magnified; her emotions, her desires and her love.

Luke silently brought her to the bed and lay down, bringing her with him by holding her hands. She rested on top of him, her breasts crushed into his chest. They kissed, the passionate tempo of their mouths taking her to a new place as she felt the velvet slickness of his tongue sweep through her. He traced her, sucked and kissed. The combination of sensations were divine ecstasy.

His hands slid across her back, feeling her bare skin. She wanted to be free of her clothing. Everything. All of it. And be naked for him. She had no reservations; only wanting.

Luke rolled onto his side taking her with him. They faced one another, stroking and caressing. His finger traced a circular pattern over the outline of her taut nipple. It heightened her pleasure to a degree that it felt like sweet torture. She could hardly breathe.

Moonlight from the night sky spilled over the bed in a hazy shadow as Luke asked, "Eve, are you sure?"

The crashing surf below drowned the ragged gasps from Evelyn's lips, but she could hear the thunder of her heartbeat.

"Yes. I'm sure. So very sure."

His hand rose to touch her cheek. "Eve," Luke's rough voice broke into the dark. "I love you."

Unbidden tears heated her eyes. She sensed they weren't spoken in the heat of the moment, but honest and sincere.

"I can't help it. I couldn't stop even if you told me to." He kissed her, softly and gently.

He cupped the back of her head, sank his fingers into her hair and brought her down to him for a searing kiss.

She felt as if her body was on fire. Their clothes were rapidly shed and his hot mouth consumed the hard bead of her nipple. She clung to him, crying out. This was bliss. Pure and simple.

The length of him rested between her legs and she parted them with an instinctive need as he rolled her onto her back. He'd aroused her senses and awakened her sensuality. The pleasure she felt was explosive and she felt it down to her toes. She wrapped her legs around his as he slipped inside her. There was a brief moment of pain, of uncertainty. But it ebbed as quickly as it had come. The friction of his body against her caused her to moan in a low voice.

Her arms locked around Luke's hips in response to his movements. He thrust deeply, then pulled back, then once more in a rhythm that she matched. They were one, moving together and reaching a higher degree of surrender. Once there, she shook from the shudders that gripped her. A satisfaction she had never known claimed every fiber of her; her heart filled with wonder. And love. A love so profound and so deep, she trembled.

"I love you, Luke . . ." she sighed into the crook of his shoulder as he lowered himself into the fold of her arms.

"Eve . . ." His gasps touched her ear, his breath choppy. "I love you so much that I never want to let you go."

22

Luke packed his travel bag as quietly as he could, gazing at the woman sleeping in the bed. Eve's hair was fanned out on the pillow, her lips parted. He still felt them against his mouth, warm and sweet. Her scent was on his skin, the memory of last night forever etched in his mind.

He loved her.

He'd made love to her.

Throughout the night, he'd held and cherished her. Slowly. Ardently. Never in his life had he experienced such complete satisfaction as he had with Eve. His heart swelled with feelings he never thought he'd know. He'd given himself over, surrendering completely. Wanting Eve to take his heart, to give hers in return. And she had. Hearing her say it had been a welcoming to his soul, and knowing he had to leave in the morning had pushed him to make every second count.

He didn't know what lay ahead in Santa Barbara, but it was time he found out.

He had to go.

Dawn barely streaked through the room and flickered through the doors of the patio. He strode to the bed and watched Eve. She looked so peaceful; so at ease. Her face was lightly tanned, her eyelashes long and shadowing the swell of her cheeks. She breathed tranquilly. Slowly. Probably the best night's sleep she'd had since they'd jumped the train outside of Dallas.

Luke sat next to her and stroked her hair. "Eve . . ."

She stirred and sighed, her eyes still closed.

"Eve . . . I've got to leave."

On that, her lashes fluttered open. "Luke?"

"Yeah, honey." He tucked a curl behind her ear. "I'm leaving for Santa Barbara. I checked with the depot when you were sleeping—the tracks aren't cleared yet so I'm going to get a horse and ride up."

She pushed the covers aside and sat. She was naked and the sight of her bare breasts made him ache. "I'll go with you."

He grazed his knuckles across the top swell of her breast, then laid a hand on her shoulder. "No. I've thought about it. I'm not sure what's waiting in Santa Barbara. Sockeye might have set a trap—gotten to Henry first. It sounds crazy, but I can't leave anything up for chance. I haven't been able to reach Jayce so I don't know what's happening back home. The last thing I'm going to do is risk having you hurt."

"But I can take care of myself. I helped you with Bienville."

"Bienville is a pebble on your beach next to

Sockeye." His hand trailed down her arm. "No, Eve. You stay here. I'm leaving some money on the bureau so you can stay in the room. I'll come back."

"Promise?" As soon as she asked the question, she covered her face with her hands.

"I'm sorry. I shouldn't ask you to, but I . . ." She gazed at him. "Luke, be careful. I love you so much."

He kissed her sleep-soft lips, lingering over her mouth and wishing he could lay with her and hold her tight. Lifting his head, he said, "I love you, too."

He rose from the bed and slung his travel bag over his shoulder. "Eve, I promise."

Her eyes filled with tears. "I'll be waiting."

The first thing Luke noticed were the smells. Sickness. Medicines. The odor of chloroform mingled in with cleaning solutions. The tartness of lemons that were squeezed to scrub the floors with thick-bristled brushes. The Santa Barbara Clinic for Illness had a stark interior. Walls were painted sage green and the corridors were wide enough to wheel patients on their rolling beds.

Luke walked across a tiled floor, the sound of his boots ringing out low and slow. His chest felt tight, like he couldn't breathe. Like he had to get out of here. But he couldn't. Because when he'd come and asked if a man by the name of Henry Boyd was staying here, he'd been met with the answer he'd come so many miles to hear—

Yes.

Henry Boyd had checked himself in and was in Ward D. It was only when Luke took the corridor that

he understood what it meant as a patient in the hallway gazed at him with the look of death in his eyes.
Ward D equaled the Death Ward.

Everything in Luke knotted, his fingers made fists.
He tried to control his labored breathing as he listened
to his heartbeat pound in his ears. When he came to
the last door on the left, he stopped. Swallowing, he
opened it and let himself inside.

Sunshine didn't make its way into the room. It was
dim and the stuffy air that greeted him had him backing up a step. The acrid medicine smell nearly burned
his nostrils.

He took shallow pulls of air into his lungs, then
proceeded forward once more.

Visible from behind a thin green curtain was the
foot of the bed and the outline of a man's feet and legs.
Quietly, Luke moved the curtain and stared at the
patient whose state of deterioration immediately sent
hot shock waves through his body.

This man wasn't Lieutenant Henry Boyd. He
couldn't be Henry. His skin was gray and pale. The red
hair that had often gotten him the nickname "Rusty"
was dull and lifeless. His breathing was labored, his
closed eyes were sunken and his mouth was pinched
thin. The swell at his abdomen had not been there
when Luke had last seen him.

Backing away, Luke hit a table and instruments rattled.

The man in the bed slowly opened his eyes. Their
color was green and if the eyes were the window to
the soul, then this man had to be Henry. For in that
flash of time, everything that had ever been between

him and Henry was uttered in those depths of green. Times spent on the beat, sitting at their desks or drinking beers at the local pub. Laughter and amusement over department pranks and a joy of watching new recruits commit to the Sixty-sixth.

For that brief encounter, Henry was his old self and Luke forgave him.

He held back the choke that ached to be released from his burning chest and came forward to stand above his old friend.

"Henry . . ." Luke managed.

"Dev," Henry said in a weak sigh. "I knew you'd find me. You're a good flatfoot."

Luke ran his fingers across his jaw, emotions pulling him in different directions. "Christ Almighty, Henry. Do you hurt?"

He attempted to shake his head. "Morphine."

"Can they fix you up? Is there any hope?"

"Hope died that night Cook and Bashioum were shot."

Spying a chair, Luke drew it up to the bed and sat beside Henry. There were too many questions; he feared hitting Henry with all of them at once. It took great patience to lay things out slowly, but as soon as he began to talk, it was hard to hold back the frustrated anger that had driven him so far. "What happened? Did Sockeye put you up to it? My life—hell, I've got a warrant out for my arrest. It's killing my mother. My family."

"I know . . . sorry . . . Luke." He licked his dry lips.

Bracing his arms on the sides of the bed, Luke leaned closer. "Why? If you needed money, I could have loaned you some. You didn't have to go on the take. We could have talked. Knocked back some suds down at Daniel's Pub and figured something out."

"Sorry I did this to you," he said again. "I'm a coward. I took the easy way. I wanted the money. I didn't n-need it for anything but my own greed."

"You were never greedy, Henry. Not in all the years I worked with you. You were a good policeman."

"I made a devil's pact with Paul and Sockeye. They told me I'd go down with them. I had to say you did it. You killed Sergeant Cook and Bashioum. But it was Paul. He shot them. I watched—oh dear Lord in heaven, help me. I watched him do it and I didn't stop him."

Luke brought himself closer to Henry when he asked, "Did Bashioum and Cook know who was behind the corruption?"

"Yessssss." Henry coughed, dry and hacking. "They told me what they knew and I told it to the captain. When I was doing it . . . taking the bribes, it didn't occur to me I was destroying lives."

Luke listened, his every muscle stretched taut.

"We victimized them . . . and the families who loved them. Down at the warehouse by the P-Pontchartrain Club . . . it happened a lot down there. I was supposed to be chasing criminals . . . and I became one." On a shallow gulp of air, he wheezed, "I crossed the line. I'm sorry . . . I'm sorry."

Straightening, Luke felt numb. "I accept your apology, Henry." But that didn't mean he could go against Captain James "Sockeye" Mullet and Detective Paul

Regale with a dying man's confession. He needed hard evidence to show to the commissioner. Big Pat Ellroy wouldn't take his word for it.

"Do you have anything concrete, Henry?"

Henry tried to sit up, but was too weak to lift his head more than a few inches from the pillow. "It's in a vault. At the bank across the street."

Luke's pulse surged with a steady rhythm. "What do you have?"

"Photographs. I knew I was in too deep. I started taking them. I've got Sockeye and Paul at the docks with city officials. And other people they don't want anyone to know they know. The guy who runs the Bayou Quarter mob."

"That's good, Henry. What else?"

"Documents. Files from the precinct. One of the books. I took them for my own protection. I think they were going to kill me, Dev." He attempted a snort of laughter but only gasped. "They don't have to bother. This cancer is doing it for them. I won't be around much longer. The docs say I'm bad off." His bony arms rose; shaking hands fumbled to pull down the loose collar of his clinic gown. "H-Help me, Dev. Get the key."

Luke stood over Henry and helped as Henry pulled out a long necklace with a key secured through it.

"I made a nurse do it for me. So nobody could take it. I got instructions to send you the key when I d-die." There was a pause, a falter; a voice choked with pain. "But now there's no need. It's yours. You go home, Dev. Put the bastards away."

*   *   *

Four days had passed with no word from Luke.

Evelyn fought off the loneliness with walks on the beach and teaching herself to ride a bicycle. The manager of the hotel had allowed her free use of an old one that was rusted from salt air and in no condition to rent out to the hotel guests.

There were moments when she felt a suffocating desolation. An icy fear that Luke wasn't coming back. That she'd never see him again.

But he'd promised.

It was that promise that kept her going each day. Waking and keeping her spirits lifted. And every so often, looking at the road across the street for the man who could set her heartbeat racing.

On this particular afternoon, she'd ridden down the boardwalk not too far from the hotel. Her green calico skirt had gotten caught in the gears, and she sat beside the overturned bicycle trying to free herself. She was having a hard time getting the fabric out without tearing it. As she gently worked, her emotions began to get the best of her and she felt tears welling in her eyes.

The breeze touched her face. She knocked an annoying stray curl from her temple, trying to keep her mind on what she was doing. If she'd been paying more attention, her foot wouldn't have slipped off the pedal.

Oh, Luke.

Her hands stilled, and she gazed down the beach. There were moments when her misery was so acute, she ached.

She missed him terribly.

You said you'd come back.

What if something had happened to him? He'd worried that there could be a trap. If there had and he'd been— No. She wouldn't think like that. She couldn't.

Lowering her head, she assessed the damage once more. She could see a series of tiny holes in the calico that refused to give. It felt as if her heart had tiny holes in it as well.

In a fit of frustration, she pulled and tore herself free.

The last shreds of control failed her. She began to cry.

"Don't worry, Eve, I'll buy you a new dress."

The sound of the voice shot her chin up. Luke stood not far from her. A shallow sob rose in her throat, and she pushed herself to standing. She nearly tripped over the piece of skirt she'd ripped as she ran to him and threw herself into his arms.

"Luke! Oh, Luke! You came back."

He held her tightly against him, his mouth brushing next to her ear. "I told you I would."

They shared a kiss filled with love and longing, a gladness to at last be reunited. There would be time later to answer questions, for now, it was the two of them, mouths clinging together. The seagulls flew and cried overhead as the surf crashed around them.

"Henry wasn't in any pain at the end," Luke said as he held Eve. They were in the Pierpont Inn hotel room, lying naked beneath the smooth sheets. "The doctors gave him enough morphine that I don't think he felt much of anything at all. But he knew I was there."

"You were kind to stay with him," Eve said, the palm of her hand resting on his chest.

Nestled in the crook of his arm, her warm breasts crushed against him. They'd just made love. Slowly. Sweetly.

"I owed him."

Though Henry had been the one to jeopardize Luke's life in the first place, ultimately Henry would be the one to save him.

Luke had gone to the bank and opened the depository box where Henry had said all the evidence would be. Everything was in place. The photographs were the most incriminating. Nobody could dispute who the men were in the pictures with their hands out for the payola. Now all Luke had to do was hand over the documentation to the commissioner and petition to have all the charges against him dropped.

Luke planned on showing up in New Orleans and going straightaway to Pat Ellroy's house and turning himself in. He looked forward to going home and putting the pieces of his life together. He wanted Eve to come with him.

He tilted her chin so he could look her. Her eyes were like heaven; he could stare into them forever. He suddenly felt quite anxious. She had, after all, mentioned she'd had men ask her before and she had obviously declined.

Luke brushed a curl from her cheek. "Have you ever considered living in New Orleans?"

"I would live anywhere just so long as I could be near you."

Her words warmed him. They were what he'd needed, hoped, to hear. "I'm going back. You know I have to."

"Of course."

"I can beat this thing with Henry's information. Afterward, I'll be the best damn policeman the Sixty-sixth has ever had. I'm not giving up on the precinct."

"I don't think you should, Luke."

"It may not be easy, but police work is all I know. I love it. And I love you." He kissed her fully on the mouth. Quietly, tenderly, he asked, "I want you to come with me. Eve, will you marry me?"

He held his breath while waiting for her reply; she didn't keep him long. "Yes, Luke. I'll marry you. You and only you."

"Eve." He held her close. "I love you so much." Everything inside him felt a bottomless peace and contentment. It was a new beginning for the both of them.

"You've made me so happy," she murmured against his ear. "I'll be proud to be your wife."

He spoke quietly. "You have to know—I don't want a cent from you. We'll live on the money I earn."

"That sounds wonderful." An amused twinkle came into her eyes and gave him pause.

For a long moment, he measured her with his gaze. "Just how 'wealthy' is your family?"

"Very wealthy."

"Like how wealthy?"

She sighed. "My name is Evelyn Thurgood-Baron and I'm the heiress to the Baron Oil fortune."

Luke nearly choked; his heartbeat kicked into double-time. "Baron Oil? *Baron Oil?* You're the Baron Oil heiress?"

Wide-eyed, she nodded.

"Everyone knows who Seymour Baron is. He's so famous, what he does on the stock exchange and who he closes a deal with makes our newspapers in New Orleans. Your name might as well be Rockefeller."

"I think my mother's related . . ."

His eyebrows shot up.

"Oh . . . Luke, none of that matters. I'm your Eve. The maid you found in your compartment on the train."

There was no question. She was his Eve and always would be. Her title didn't change a thing about the way he felt about her.

"If you're that Eve, then do I have to be Mrs. Smythe again?" he teased, stroking her cheek.

The jolt of her thigh against his hip as she slid over him made his body instantly respond. "Not a chance. I want all of Luke Devereaux."

He brought his mouth up to hers and kissed her. Against her lips, he whispered, "You have me, Eve."

And he intended to spend all night showing her just how much.

A salty breeze ruffled the curtains, bringing with it the sound of the ocean. The sensual woman in his arms was soft and warm. And she loved him.

He counted himself the luckiest man in the world.

The tips of her breasts grazed his chest as her hair fell in a honey-blond cloud around them.

"When I left Oiler," Eve said softly, "I knew there

were things I wanted to experience that I never would have had the chance to do if I'd stayed home. But it was you who showed me what I've been missing. It wasn't an ocean or an adventure across Texas or sneaking a sample of bourbon. It's been falling in love."

Epilogue

The New Orleans police scandal trials lasted over two weeks, and in the end, twenty-three officers were found guilty of misconduct. Captain James Mullet and Detective Paul Regale were convicted of the murders of Sergeants Cook and Bashioum and sentenced to life in prison at the State of Louisiana correctional facilities—the yard that Jude Bienville knew too well.

During the proceedings, evidence aside from Henry Boyd's stacked up in Luke's favor. The defense destroyed the credibility of the prosecution's main eyewitnesses to the Pontchartrain Club shootings. Members of the Sixty-sixth who feared their necks were about to be slipped into nooses, came forward and ratted on their counterparts in the hopes of receiving lighter punishments.

The *Daily Picayune* reported that the scandal that rocked the city was now over, but the backlash from indictments wouldn't be easily overlooked. It would take effort to reorganize the departments, but that had already begun to happen. And newly appointed Captain Luke Devereaux was determined to get the job done.

On a late August evening, Luke walked home after work. The humid air hung low and thick in the sky. Sweat beaded on his forehead. His coat had been too warm, so he'd removed it and walked the rest of the way in his shirt and vest, his cuffs rolled to his elbows. He carried a large paper bag and the aromas wafting from it made his mouth water.

He hadn't driven the Roadster to the department since returning home. He found that reconnecting with the people on the streets served his job much better.

"Cap'n Devereaux, sir," the florist said as Luke passed by. "Nice night to be walking home."

"It is, Mr. Gladstone. I'll take a bouquet of mums and carnations."

"Very good, sir." The florist went to work and put together a mix of red chrysanthemums and white carnations. "On the house, Cap'n—for bringing the city back to its citizens."

"The judge and Commissioner Ellroy did that, Mr. Gladstone." Tucking the bouquet into his bag, Luke counted out the correct amount with a tip.

"Thank you." Mr. Gladstone nodded his appreciation. "Good to see you again, sir."

Luke moved on and encountered the butcher on the south side of the street. "Evenin', Captain," Mr. Hunsinger said.

"Mr. Hunsinger," Luke returned.

"I'll see you tomorrow."

"I imagine you will. And I hope one day to get my wife in the store."

"Delightful woman, Captain. She looks in the window a lot, but seems a bit unsure about the chickens I've got hanging."

Luke chuckled, thinking back to the night he cut and boiled a hen and Eve had been put off by the cooking method.

The tall magnolia branches on his block momentarily shaded the view of his home. But then he saw the townhouse with its wraparound verandah and the wrought-iron gate. It was a welcoming sight because of the woman inside waiting for him.

The muscles in Luke's body relaxed and the heat didn't seem so bad.

Luke opened the latch on the gate. He took the steps, pausing briefly to appreciate the window boxes overflowing with abundant flowers. Eve had planted a bunch of stuff—all the varieties had a special meaning.

Once he reached the screen door, he opened it and entered the home. In the vestibule, he didn't smell supper cooking. He never did. He hung his police cap and coat on the hat tree.

Evelyn came racing down the stairs. She wore a simple white dress and an apron with flowers on it. Her steps were light and her cheeks flushed to a rosy hue.

She about knocked him over to give him a hug. "You're home! Wait until you see what I planted in the garden. The most wonderful rosebushes. Yellow. But not too yellow. More like lemon chiffon. Why, I . . ."

He kissed her cheek, then mouth. "You can show me later."

"Hmm. All right . . ."

They kissed for a moment, then Luke remembered the chrysanthemum and carnation bouquet. He gave it to her, and she kissed him once more with delight. "Luke, you spoil me."

"I wouldn't have it any other way."

She went into the kitchen and he followed her.

The stove was bare and cold.

"The flowers will be fresh this weekend when your family comes over for barbeque," she said, putting them in a vase and setting them in the middle of the table. "We haven't seen your youngest brother since the trial and I'm so looking forward to talking with Jayce's wife. She's a wealth of domestic information."

Their wedding had been a quiet affair in the local parish church. His mother and brothers and their wives had been in attendance as well as some friends. Eve's parents hadn't come to the ceremony. In fact, Seymour Baron had refused to take the call that he'd placed while he and Eve were in Dallas on their way home. The man had spoken briefly to Eve, and while she hadn't said so, he knew she was devastated by her father's dismissal.

Since then, Luke had written a letter to Mr. Baron and explained how much Eve meant to him, and that he didn't want anything but to see his wife happy and not hurt. Their family rift over her failure to marry Guy Hadley was unfounded. It was better to accept an honest, hard-working son-in-law than to lose a daughter. Luke had yet to hear back from Seymour, but he had received word from Oiler today.

Eve turned to Luke. "Did you get my cans?"

He hadn't made a single complaint about Eve's cooking. Ever since she learned how to use the can opener, she'd been as proud as could be she could open anything packed in tin. Most every night, a hot meal was on the table for him, compliments of Heinz or Borden's. And while he appreciated her efforts, tonight not even his stomach of steel could face another plate of corned beef.

"Not today," he replied.

"Something smells good," she said, curiously reaching inside the bag. Rather than coming up with cans of hash, creamed corn and sliced fruits, she discovered his surprise. Foot long beef sandwiches with gravy, slaw and fresh beignets. "Oh! You dear, dear man! Real food."

Then guilty, she blushed.

Luke pulled the bow on her apron. "Honey, you get the plates and we'll sit out on the upstairs terrace." Taking her into his arms, he gave her a sweet peck on the lips. "I've got another surprise for you."

Gazing into his eyes, she replied, "And I have one for you."

A short time later, they finished their dinner on the patio table. They looked beyond the rooftops of Garden District homes to the taller buildings of the city. The hum of traffic and noises from Canal Street could be heard, and the occasional horn from boats on the river.

Luke had retrieved the letter from his coat pocket and now handed it to Eve. She took it and read the name across the front of the envelope.

"A letter from my mother." Her chin lifted. "Addressed to you."

"I wrote to your father, Eve. I have to tell you, I took him down a few pegs."

"You did? What did he say? Oh my . . ." She looked at the letter once more.

Gently, Luke prodded. "Read it."

Eve lifted the seal and scanned the words inside. When her eyes met his they glistened with unshed tears. "Mother said she misses me. Very much. And she wants to come to see me." Her lips parted in a sigh of disbelief. "That you made my father angry with your letter, and he said you had a lot of nerve. But he likes men with nerve. Mother says it's hard for her to understand me but she's trying. And it will take some time to bring Daddy around. She's asking if I can be patient."

Putting her hand over her heart, the letter still in her grasp, Eve said, "I can't believe it." She leaned forward and touched her lips to his. "Thank you, Luke. For everything."

She held him, her cheek next to his chest. Then she pulled back and gave him a loving smile. "Now it's my turn. I have a surprise for you."

Eve rose from the table and rummaged inside the bureau drawer. She returned and held something behind her back. Grinning, she presented him with a book.

He read the title aloud. "*Mrs. Paulette Hornsby's Culinary Kitchen Advice.*"

"And that's not all." Eve reached for the cover. "Open the inside."

He did so and found an enrollment receipt.

"Starting next week, I'm taking classes to learn how to cook," she said with enthusiasm. "I'm going to be able to fix you the biggest chicken from the butcher's window. Our first lesson is how to ignite a stove."

Luke laughed and closed the book. Setting it on the table, he took his wife into his arms. "That'll be great, sweetheart. In the meantime, there are other things you can ignite."

Then his mouth covered hers in a searing kiss that simmered with heat and passion.

Dear Readers:

Writing *The Runaway Heiress* was great fun and I hope you enjoyed the romance of Luke Devereaux and Evelyn Thurgood-Baron.

While the town of Oiler was made up, the other Texas cities in this book are factual and depicted the way they would have appeared when Luke and Eve passed through them. Beaumont's train depot was located on Calder Avenue. The Metropolitan Bar and Buffet where Evelyn ate a hamburger was in Dallas, as well as the Neiman-Marcus department store. Sweetwater was known for its waterworks at this time, but also cattle. And Midland had recently suffered from a fire prior to my characters' arrival. Ysleta, while small, existed outside of El Paso.

As for New Orleans, a corruption scandal within the police department in 1911 is purely my own fabrication. The Bayou Quarter doesn't exist except on the pages of this novel; the Sixty-sixth Precinct is also my invention.

Telephone wires across the states were increasingly becoming a common sight, and the El Paso Telephone Exchange is my interpretation of a telephone office. And while wristwatches for men were slow to have acceptance in 1911, by 1914 World War I necessitated a fumble-free way to read the time, thus dwindling the manufacture of pocket watches. Automobiles built by a variety of makers were also increasing in popularity; the steps to get Jude Bienville's stolen Ford to start were accurate.

My heartfelt thanks for giving me the opportunity to take you to another time and place for a short while. I love to hear from my readers. You may visit my Website at http://www.stefannholm.com or write to my post office box at:

Stef Ann Holm
P.O. Box 1206
Meridian, ID 83680-1206